"Don't touch me."

Her eyes were pure ice.

John pressed her against the wall. "There was a time you couldn't get enough of me touching you."

"Right up until you helped an agent try to kill me."

It took every ounce of his self-control not to force her to look at him. "You believe him over me. After everything we were together."

Alicia drew a ragged breath. Then he saw it—the passion in her eyes. It was the same torment that was tearing him up. She was no longer the refined femme fatale, but a real woman. His woman.

He touched her cheek with his hand, expecting her to demand he remove it. Instead, her eyes closed on another tremulous breath. "I hate you."

"I know."

He cradled her cheek in his palm. Pulse pounding, he ignored all the reasons he shouldn't be doing what he was about to, then leaned down and pressed a kiss to her closed mouth.

Dear Reader,

I must confess: every time I write a book, I fall in love with the hero. And sometimes, when the hero and heroine are perfect soul mates, I feel a little guilty about crushing on him, as though that feeling betrays my friendship with the heroine. Isn't that silly? Maybe not, because if you, as a reader, crush on the hero and think about the heroine as a friend, that means I'm doing my job as a storyteller. Trust me—you are definitely in danger of falling hard for John Witter in *Hot on the Hunt.*

When I started writing this story, I affectionately nicknamed John "Underdog Alpha." He first appeared in *Tempted into Danger* as the funny friend, a wisecracking sniper with an affinity for Michael Jackson songs. But, typically, the funny friend never gets the girl, does he? In *Hot on the Hunt,* I tackled the question: How does a man like that reboot his life after he's lost everything, including his homeland and the woman he loves?

John is an underdog in every way—underestimated, living under the radar and written off as a has-been. But from the ash of his former life emerges an alpha warrior...and I guarantee you'll approve of John's transformation. You might even feel a tad bit guilty for crushing on Alicia's man, just as I did. Happy reading!

Melissa

HOT ON THE HUNT

Melissa Cutler

◆ **HARLEQUIN**® ROMANTIC SUSPENSE

Recycling programs
for this product may
not exist in your area.

ISBN-13: 978-0-373-27879-4

HOT ON THE HUNT

www.Harlequin.com

Printed in U.S.A.

Books by Melissa Cutler

Harlequin Romantic Suspense

*ICE: Black Ops Defenders
§The Coltons of Wyoming

Other titles by this author
available in ebook format.

MELISSA CUTLER

is a flip-flop-wearing Southern California native living with her husband, two rambunctious kids and two suspicious cats in beautiful San Diego. She divides her time between her dual passions for writing sexy, small-town contemporary romances and edge-of-your-seat romantic suspense. Find out more about Melissa and her books at www.melissacutler.net, or drop her a line at cutlermail@yahoo.com.

To Eric—you are my everything

Chapter 1

There was no one on this island of partying rich kids and vagabonds who cared about the washed-up sniper taking practice shots at the buoy eleven hundred meters offshore. Most mornings, John hit his target without fail. Not today. The wind was all wrong, which should have been John's first clue that his exile in the Virgin Islands had gotten too comfortable. One shift of the wind and he didn't instinctually adjust.

It was about time. He'd been waiting to exercise this particular mental muscle. The one that guarded against complacency—the false sense of confidence in himself, in his environment and in the people surrounding him—which had been the root cause of the implosion of his former life.

The problem with confidence was that it led to trust. And trust led to assumptions like there's no way a blood brother who he went to war with would betray him. Or that loving a woman with every cell of his being would earn her loyalty, if nothing else. Dangerously naive assumptions like those were why John Witter—former Green Beret sniper, former ICE black ops agent, former somebody—had spent the past twenty months waiting for complacency to set in so he could kick his own ass back into fighting shape.

It was a far cry from a do-over, but earning the status of persona non grata with the U.S. government and its world allies didn't leave him a whole lot of viable options.

He lifted away from the rifle and peered through his scope at the buoy swaying in the waves and wind. He should have this shot. He'd adjusted for elevation given the tide, he'd lain in the exact same position he always did, with only a plain cotton T-shirt between his shoulder and the rifle butt, with a wad of gum sandwiched between his left-side molars. All the lame superstitions and habits he'd long ago forgiven himself for. Every sniper he'd trained with seemed to have them, or even nuttier ones than John, as symbols of control and consistency.

Ah. That was the problem, right there. *All the things he always did.* Control and consistency—the most dangerous illusions of a complacent mind.

He spit the gum into the sand, then shifted from his belly into an awkward hunching seated position. Then he did the most uncomfortable, distracting thing possible—he thought about Alicia. He thought about her the second to last time they were together, about her lying on her stomach and the path of water left by the ice cube he'd trailed along her spine—one of the many memories of her that hurt in a physical, permanent way.

He could still hear the hiss of protest she'd given when the ice cube had first touched her skin, followed by a giggle that had quickly turned into a purr. He'd loved the sounds she'd made in bed. Sweet, vulnerable, girlie sounds that were totally incongruous to the Alicia the rest of the world knew—the soldier, the computer genius, the femme fatale. His secret Alicia. His Phoenix.

At the next knife of pain to his heart, he steadied his gaze through the mounted scope. He thought about the wind and the rate of the incoming tide. He studied the buoy's pattern of movement, then set his finger on the trigger. Breathe in—Alicia's hair fanning over her smiling cheek. Breathe out—her hand finding his and holding tight. A squeeze of the trigger. The buoy bell gonged with the hit.

He loaded another round and repeated the process, twice as fast this time. *Gong.* Maybe that was why he wasn't entirely sure, at first, that he'd heard the chirp of the alarm from his computer alert system. He stood and shook out his legs, then dusted the sand from his shirt.

The computer chimed again. Sometimes it was easy to forget that life in the real world had gone on without him. He went weeks now without tuning in to world news or checking his email accounts. A long time ago, he stopped caring about war or what his old friends were up to. But guarding himself, resisting complacency, meant keeping tabs on the two people who'd destroyed him. The email alert meant that Logan McCaffrey, his one friend left in the Department of Homeland Security's Immigration and

Customs Enforcement—better known as ICE—was contacting him with news about either Alicia or Rory.

Maybe Rory had been moved to a new wing of the prison. Or Alicia had decided to rejoin ICE. Most likely, the news was something benign, but still beneficial for John to be aware of. Someday, he planned to reenter the world and it'd be good to know exactly where his enemies were and what they were up to.

He propped his rifle against the wall just inside the cabin door, then unloaded the spare ammo from his pocket to the shelf next to it. From the fridge, he grabbed a bottle of cola, then crossed the wooden floorboards to the communication console he'd set up on the far side of the room. An email window had popped up.

John dipped his head to read it without sitting.

Rory escaped at 0700 hours. Alicia is missing.

He paused with his hand around the cola's twist-off bottle cap and read the message again. Stunned into numbness, he drew a slow, lung-filling breath through his nose, set the unopened bottle down and braced his hands on the table. Then he read the message one more time.

On this last reading, two thoughts burst through his shock. One, Alicia wasn't missing. People with her particular skill set never went missing; rather, they chose not to be visible anymore. And two, Rory was a dead man—unless John got to him first.

Not that John cared if Rory died, but he was the only man who knew the truth about John's innocence. John had made peace with the reality that he'd never have the chance to press Rory into coming clean about the lies he'd gone on record with about John, locked away as he was in the ultramax prison—the one that didn't officially exist—inside Fort Buchanan, the U.S. airbase on Puerto Rico.

Seven hundred hours was only thirty minutes ago and Puerto Rico was only one hundred and twenty miles northwest. How far could Rory have gotten? Fort Buchanan was solid, security-wise. A man imprisoned there didn't simply hide in a laundry cart and steal away under everyone's noses. With the full press of the U.S. military, ICE and whatever other federal agencies the government sent looking for him, it wasn't likely that Rory had gotten very far at all.

What if John got to him first, before the government or Alicia did? The idea sent a thrill coursing through him. This might be John's one chance to clear his name. It was the opportunity he never knew he'd been waiting for. Talk about a shock out of complacency.

He looked northwest across the Caribbean, the vibrant blue sea that had acted as his buffer against reality since Rory, John's closest friend and sniper partner for a decade, self-destructed and tried to take John down with him.

Like being startled awake after a long, deep sleep, John's heart beat loud and fast, pumping adrenaline-laced blood through his body. He pivoted and grabbed a hammer from his tool chest. Normally, he pried off the boards from the wall behind his sitting area, but the clock was ticking, so he wound back and smashed the planks to get at the metal locker.

Into a black canvas bag, he stuffed all the gear, cash

and weaponry he could fit, reserving a brick of C4 explosives for his immediate use. He set the C4 on the table next to his computer. Whatever happened with Rory, whatever came next, John wouldn't be back to this place. Not that he had anything to hide, necessarily, but it was bad form in the black ops world to leave a trail.

He unwound the cable from the C4 to the door, then grabbed the key to his boat and the plastic package of a new, untraceable cell phone, slung the bag and his rifle over his shoulder and stuffed the extra ammo in his jeans pocket. He took one last look around, then stepped into the morning sunshine. Trailing the C4 cable behind him, he followed the path downhill toward the water until he was far enough away to be safe from the blast. He'd wait to call Logan for more details once he was on the water.

No time for ceremony, he flipped the switch to initiate the reaction, then set the detonator box on the ground and broke into a jog to his boat as an explosion ripped through the air behind him.

It was a good sound—loud and angry and full of force. Like John. It was a sound that said, "Goodbye, exile. Hello, last chance."

Ninety percent of murders were committed by men. The Department of Justice statistic made sense to Alicia. Most men she knew weren't exactly creative thinkers. Of the 10 percent of murders committed by women, Alicia bet the vast majority of them were crimes of passion against boyfriends or husbands. Again, not a surprise.

Alicia, for one, had debated long and hard about

whether she'd kill her ex-lover. She still wasn't sure she'd made the right call to focus her revenge solely on Rory and leave John unharmed. After all, what kind of world was it when a man conspired to kill one of the most lethal women on the planet and lived to tell about it? Even now, twenty months later, his betrayal burned like acid in her heart.

Swallowing back the hurt, she adjusted the gun hidden in the concealed holder between her breasts and fixed her eyes on the nasty trail of water and sewage trickling from the drainage pipe through the sand and into the surf. Disgusting. This was one section of beach St. Thomas wasn't going to put on its tourism brochures.

She'd been here for two days, putting the final pieces of her plan in place. Everything was going according to script, except that she hadn't anticipated that every step closer she took toward executing her plan evoked a fresh surge of memory—about the ICE black ops team she'd been part of and about the day her teammate Rory tried to kill her. About John.

Annoyed that her thoughts had slipped so easily to him again, she stared past the sewage to the pristine water of St. Thomas Harbor and counted the cruise liners. Three had pulled into the harbor so far today, unleashing thousands of tourists onto the four-by-thirteen-mile island. The ferry from Puerto Rico had landed on this less-scenic end of the harbor an hour earlier, along with an attempted murderer stowaway in a crate of cheap Puerto Rican rum bound for one of the waterfront hotels that fed into this drain pipe. Unless he did something stupid and impetuous, Rory would be emerging from the pipe any minute.

Alicia was ready for him. Even if she weren't a virtual ghost, the Department of Justice didn't keep homicide statistics about women like her, who'd devoted more than a year to plotting cold-blooded revenge, not against a lover, but the man who'd shot her and left her for dead.

The idea of coming face-to-face with Rory for the first time since that fateful day made her anxious. Not scared or intimidated, per se, but filled with disquiet over the memory of what it had felt like to be weak. To hand her power over to a man.

Never again. Killing Rory was the first step in rebuilding her reputation, but it was about so much more than an encore. It was the start of a new career. A fresh beginning. A plan not undertaken to help her make a debut splash as a black ops mercenary, but to blow the water out of the pond. Or out of the Caribbean Sea, as it were.

Any minute now, a dangerous criminal would be released into the world. Lucky for the masses, Alicia would be there waiting with the kill shot.

Laughter and a child's squeal forced her attention away from her duty. Three children were frolicking in the water nearby, amid the concrete storm wall and shallow beach. Her heart sank. This was not the place for them, nor the time. If Rory showed up now...

The children were a motley bunch, with rags for clothes and dirty faces, wild hair. Every one of them thin and undernourished. Perhaps their parents worked in the hotels' kitchens or factories pushing so-called "island handicrafts" on tourists. Alicia's least favorite part of living in the shadows was that the poor lived there, too. Not because she was a snob, but because nothing made her heart ache like children in the kind of desperate poverty she'd seen the world over. It never got easier to accept.

She hated even needing to shoo these children away. Adults probably shooed them away all the time, treating them no better than stray dogs. She'd watched it happen too many times to count. And who was she to interrupt their fun? She was the intruder in their happy day, the morally corrupt American about to commit an act of violence in their community—in public, in broad daylight.

Fishing money out of her pocket, quarters and dollars, she walked their way, waving it to show them she meant no harm. They skipped to her, hands out, smiling eagerly. She filled their hands with the money and they thanked her in Spanish. She pointed up the road toward the cruise terminals where the food vendors were, telling them in their language to go buy sweets and food for their family. One of them hugged her.

With a glance at the drain pipe, she hugged back, trying not to be impatient. Finally, they hurried off, chattering about what they'd buy and how to divide the money. Alicia was free to turn her attention back to the pipe. The only thing worse than children witnessing what she was about to do was her being caught off guard or Rory slipping by while she was distracted.

She heard a splash before she saw a swish of movement in the shadows. She gripped her gun and pulled it from between her breasts. It was about time, too— the silencer was digging into her middle. She flattened against the storm surge wall adjacent to the pipe, her finger on the trigger.

Rory's arm appeared first, then his face and body.

He high-stepped through the water in relative silence, dressed in tourist clothes—a Hawaiian shirt, cargo shorts and sandals. That was a surprise. She hoped whoever he stole the clothes from was still alive, but there was nothing she could do about it now.

She had a clear shot and could've pulled the trigger already, but the cruel streak in her wanted to make sure he knew who was ending his life.

She pivoted away from the wall, gun first. "Hello, Rory."

He froze in midstride, then turned in her direction. "So it was you. I thought that might be the case, but I had to give it my best try, anyway." His expression was stoic, like a man resigned to his fate.

She walked closer, until she stood at the entrance to the pipe. "I was counting on that. Though I would've preferred it if you'd been a bit more surprised, perhaps begged me to live."

He sneered. "And I'd really like a steak dinner before I die, but we don't always get what we want, do we?"

She aimed at his heart, her own heart pounding madly. It was supposed to feel better than this. She'd counted on it being a relief to her broken spirit to have achieved revenge, but it was harder than she'd expected. Conjuring the way she'd felt when their positions had been reversed, when he'd stood before her—her teammate, her lover's best friend—and looked her in the eye as he pulled the trigger of his Kimber 45.

Yeah, Rory Alderman deserved this. He knew it; she knew it. Karma knew it.

At the slight movement of her finger on the trigger, a shot broke the stillness from somewhere to her left.

It ricocheted off the lip of the pipe. Alicia ducked back and flattened against the pipe's interior wall. Rory took off along the beach.

Another shot rang out, but whoever was shooting at her had terrible aim not to be able to hit her or Rory while she'd been stationary, so she decided it was safe enough to keep moving.

With a fortifying breath, she shot out of the pipe at a sprint. She wasn't about to let her reputation and her one chance at revenge slip from her grasp while she cowered in a sewer pipe. She'd unleashed a vicious murderer into the world, and, so help her, she wasn't going to stop until she'd snuffed him out.

Chapter 2

Rory had only a small lead on Alicia, but he was moving fast. Alicia's boots churned up the sand in hot pursuit, leaping like Rory had over the boulders that marked the beginning of a jetty, then up and over the concrete partition and onto the street. Rory disappeared into a wholesale hammock warehouse.

Alicia shoved her gun back in her shirt for easy access without causing a panic among civilians and looked over her shoulder, hoping to catch sight of the shooter who'd ruined her one good chance at vengeance. She was still going to catch up with Rory, still going to kill him, but now it wasn't so pretty and clean.

Seeing nothing out of the ordinary, she flung herself through the door and sprinted after her quarry, ignoring the shouting workers and dodging hammock displays as she followed Rory back to the work area. Rory flailed as he ran, knocking weaving looms and empty wood spools behind him, barring her path.

A year and a half ago, right after she was shot, she'd gotten winded climbing stairs and had needed to re-teach her body how to move like a black market operative needed to. Her need for revenge against Rory and the pain of John's betrayal kept the fire of her determination lit until she wasn't merely as physically capable as she had been before, but better. She kept up handily, bursting out of a rear exit into a narrow alley.

The same pack of children she'd thrown money at stood near the entrance of the alley, nibbling sweet buns. Rory pushed past them, knocking one over. Alicia didn't have time to console them or explain. She jumped over the fallen child and into the street, running as hard and fast as her legs could go.

Another shot rang out from somewhere to Alicia's right. The mystery shooter. She'd go after him next, but first, Rory. She kept her focus trained on the back of Rory's head, at the buzz cut that made his bald spot look like a bull's-eye. All she needed was a straight-away free of pedestrians and cars and she could take the shot. But it was rush-hour traffic on Veterans Drive, the road that ran along the harbor, and traffic was crawling. As long as he kept weaving a path among the cars and bicycles, she was helpless to do anything but follow.

The mystery shooter wasn't as concerned with collateral damage to bystanders as she was, as evidenced by the crack of another gunshot. This time, the bullet grazed Rory's thigh. He stumbled right, bullied past a line of wooden barrels and half fell into a seafood processing plant.

Alicia gave chase. Stunned workers whined their protest and waved fillet knifes and rubber gloves at her. One speared a massive butcher knife in her direction, scolding rather than threatening. She followed the trail of blood drops out the other side of the warehouse. Something flew through the air at her. She ducked back into the warehouse, slamming the door as something knocked against it. She opened it again. A fillet knife was stuck in the other side. With a growl of frustration, she continued following the blood trail out of the alley. Rory must not have been wounded too badly because he was on a bicycle and had taken off across Veterans Drive again.

He jumped the curb onto the pedestrian and bicycle path that curved around the harbor toward the cruise ship terminals. The path immediately around him was empty. This was her chance. She ground to a halt and drew her gun. Before she could pull the trigger, a bang sounded from behind her. Rory's bike collapsed. He fell out of sight, off the edge of the path and into the harbor.

Cursing at the stranger who was really becoming a thorn in her side, she set her hand on the partition, preparing to jump. The whine of a motorcycle's engine caught her attention. She turned to see a man on a motorcycle, his face obscured by the visor of his helmet, his bike picking up speed as it wove through traffic in approach of the partition between the street and the foot path.

"Oh, hell, no," was all she could mutter.

The mystery shooter. He was young, judging by his fit, muscled body barely concealed by a snug blue T-shirt and worn jeans. He held an HK45 pistol against the right grip of the bike and didn't seem to be paying Alicia and her Glock any mind.

Why he was interfering with her operation remained to be seen. Was he helping Rory escape or trying to kill him? Until now, Alicia hadn't considered the possibility that she wasn't the only person in the world hell-bent on extracting lethal justice from Rory, but now it seemed a naive way of thinking.

Then again, it didn't matter how many people wanted Rory Alderman dead. Alicia was going to be the one who pulled the trigger, and the only sure way to guarantee that was to neutralize the mystery operative before he mucked up her operation any more.

She vaulted over the partition and dropped onto the pathway, affording the felled bike a nominal glance. Rory was nowhere to be seen. Using the partition as cover, she steadied her Glock. The motorcycle was coming at her on her right. She took aim at the front tire, and that's when he finally took notice of her. Swerving left, he brought his gun up and squeezed off a round in her direction. She ducked and felt the force of the bullet hitting the partition.

Ready to give it a second try, she peered over the lip of the partition at the same time she registered that the bike motor's whine had risen an octave, the sound of it gaining speed. She watched it jump the partition and land on the walkway in front of her. Whoever he was, this man was a professional. A damn good one. Probably, the shots he was taking didn't hit Rory or Alicia by design, for reasons she had yet to figure out. He could be any one of dozens of black market operatives she knew of, or perhaps someone new to the scene. He afforded her a passing glance over his shoulder, then took off on the pathway.

She stood, ready to shoot him in the back, but he was too skilled to give her an adequate target, moving the bike in unpredictable dips and swerves. A solid hundred meters in front of them, Rory had reappeared, slogging along in soaked clothes and barefoot toward the nearest dock—the one advertising parasailing adventures in which a tourist is harnessed to a parachute that's then pulled along in the air behind a speedboat.

Alicia cursed and took off running, pushing herself beyond the pain of her now burning quads, knowing he was going for that speedboat. It was the only one on the dock that looked remotely functional, much less built to go fast.

A sunburned, schlubby tourist was presently being strapped into a parachute harness by a local man who was giving a safety talk judging by his gestures. When he saw Rory, he directed his gestures to him, protesting Rory's presence, most likely. Rory shoved him in the water. The tourist screamed and frantically tried to unstrap himself as Rory leaped onto the boat his harness was tethered to.

The mystery shooter sped around the turn onto the dock, but not fast enough. With a rev of the engine, Rory took off in the boat, the parasailer floating into the sky behind him, screaming his fool head off. Not that Alicia blamed him. She would've been screaming for help, too.

Alicia ran for the dock. There were other boats nearby. Not as fast, but what choice did she have other than to give chase? Rory angled the boat toward the mouth of the harbor, then left the throttle up and moved to the back of the boat with what looked like a fillet knife in his hand. He worked to untie the rope and before the boat had gotten too far, the tourist went floating back, up into the sky in his parachute a solid ten meters before the chute buckled and he free-fell into the water.

Alicia turned onto the dock as the motorcyclist swung off the bike and ran to the edge of the dock. He dropped the bag that had been slung over his back and withdrew a Remington XM2010 sniper rifle. The prototype model. The same limited-edition prototype Alicia and the rest of her black ops team had been gifted with three years earlier.

Her breath caught in her throat. Of its own volition, her body went still. She should be making a break for one of the other boats in the harbor, stealing it and racing after Rory, but she couldn't move, couldn't think beyond the one thought repeating in her head. *No. It couldn't be him.*

He lay flat on his belly against the dock, the rifle butt against his shoulder, its stabilizing legs extended to the floor. He ripped off his helmet, revealing tousled, dark blond hair. *No.*

Her gaze roved over his body. That strong, broad back, narrow waist, perfect backside. Just as she remembered it. His eye was glued to the scope. He pulled the trigger. The rifle quivered as the boom ripped through the harbor. Rory ducked. The speedboat faltered, its glass windshield shattering.

"Damn it," he muttered, dropping his head.

His voice sent shivers over her skin. How could it be, after so many months, that he still had that effect on her?

He'd appeared out of nowhere and, whether he meant to or not, he'd helped Rory escape. And yet, she couldn't get her mouth to close. She couldn't catch her breath or convince her body to move. She couldn't even find the will to tell him off for ruining everything. Again.

Bringing the rifle with him, he pushed into a squat then stood. The jeans hung low on his hips but snug around his quads. She'd forgotten this part—the perfection of him—and she hadn't even gathered the courage to look at his face yet.

Rory's boat was a blip on the horizon now, headed south in a direct path to St. Croix. She afforded the boat only a glance because she couldn't, for the life of her, stop staring at the man before her, absorbing his nearness and heat, the raw power radiating from his every cell.

She could feel him watching her and forced her gaze to meet his smoky-blue eyes.

They were angry, colder than she'd ever seen them. He might have the body of the man she'd once called her lover, but she could see it in his face that he was a changed person. Harder, humorless. She wanted to slap him for what he'd done to her, slap him because she'd almost shot him in the back just now and she would've never forgiven herself for it. Most of all, though, she wanted to throw her arms around him and hang on forever. Like a fool in love.

"John," she croaked.

"In the flesh."

A tingle swept over her body. In the flesh was right. But it didn't matter how powerful her unexpected shock of awareness of him was, because Alicia re-

fused to yield her power to a man, especially one who'd
betrayed her. It didn't matter how he made her feel in
the innermost, darkest places of her heart; she knew
better now. His sudden appearance might've stripped
her bare, but so what? The only defense against the
pervading sense of vulnerability she always felt in his
presence was to get mad.

She stomped over the dock toward him, not that he
seemed to notice while he ran a check of the Remington for unspent ammo, so she got right up in his face.
"You helped him escape."

He huffed and shook his head as though she'd told a
joke that was in poor taste. "Is that it, huh? You think
that's what this Remington's for—to help him escape?"
He turned away and shoved the rifle in his bag, then
took his HK45 out of the back of his pants.

The ache of longing in hearing that growl of a voice
that had haunted her dreams for twenty long months
was so powerful that she hardly knew what to think
anymore. She forced her anger back up to the surface.
"Of course you helped him escape. You're the Robin
to his Batman. Always the sidekick, never the alpha.
You're not capable of being the alpha dog. Never were."

As far as insults went, she knew that one had to
hurt, especially to an elite soldier like John. It was an
old nerve of his, one she'd learned when they were lovers. She felt like a sore loser exploiting the intimate
details of their time together—God knew she had as
many secret flaws and faults as he did—but she was
desperate to regain the power she'd lost in his presence.

And maybe, if she were being honest with herself,
she was a bit desperate to see if she could spark a fire

in his eyes again. Anything but the ice-cold steel that they were now.

Rather than show fire, though, his eyes got colder. He ran his tongue over his lower lip, then gave her body a dispassionate once-over. Jaw tight and eyes frosty, he swaggered the few steps to her and leaned his face in. She held her breath, held perfectly still, as his lips brushed her temple, then grazed her hair. "You won't believe what I'm capable of, Phoenix."

She wanted to touch him so badly the need ached inside her like a hollow, brittle thing. She balled her hands into fists. *Show me,* she almost said. "I'm not Phoenix anymore. At least not to you."

He backed his face up. Rubbing his jaw, he nodded. "I'm going to get to him first, you know."

"I can't let you do that."

"I can't let you stop me," he countered.

With any other person, if she wanted to stop him, she'd shoot him in the leg or wrestle him to the ground, then bind his hands and legs. With John, she could get away with neither. He had his gun in hand already and, besides, he was a faster shot than she. To top that off, he knew all her close-combat moves, which eliminated the element of surprise—her only advantage when trying to physically dominate a man nearly twice her size.

Back to basics. The police were going to descend on the harbor at any moment, the U.S. military, too, as they searched for Rory. She swiveled, gun extended, and shot out the tires of the motorcycle. At least now he couldn't speed past her to steal the next fastest boat in the harbor.

He raised his brows, bemused but unimpressed. Then he lifted his gun and aimed past her, to the street beyond the boardwalk. With a casual squeeze of the trigger that belied the complicated nature of the shot, he took out the front windshield of her rental car at least a hundred meters away. Guess he'd seen her drive up earlier. That meant he'd seen her interaction with those kids, too. The realization brought a sudden flush of heat to her cheeks. Not cool.

He flicked a lock of her hair off her shoulder. "Are you going to shoot me next? Because I'm not really keen on reciprocating that one."

She flipped the rest of her hair behind her and gave him her best scowl. "I've been shot enough to last a lifetime, thank you very much."

The allusion to her injury at Rory's hand hung in the air between them. John's jaw went stiff and the ice in his eyes seemed to spread to the rest of his body. The peal of police sirens cut through the tension.

John stared out over the water. Alicia followed his gaze. Rory had shot straight out of the bay and was heading south toward St. Croix. John hitched his canvas bag higher on his shoulder and walked past her. "Those sirens are my cue to beat it. See ya around, Phoenix."

"He's mine to kill, John."

He didn't even bother turning around to answer. "Maybe so, but I have other plans for him." He gave her a little salute before breaking into a run to the right, moving southwest along the boardwalk.

Alicia shook some clarity into herself, shoved away the overwhelming flood of emotions John had evoked and concealed her gun. Then she took off left in search of something—anything—that would get her to St.

Croix faster than either of the two men who'd wrecked her life for the second time in as many years.

Well. That was something else. This day certainly wasn't turning out like John had thought it would when he'd woken up that morning. True, he'd been looking to shake himself out of complacency, and being in Alicia's orbit certainly rocked him off his axis.

He roared through the Caribbean on the boat he'd docked not too far away from the one Rory had stolen, the speedboat that was now visible through his binoculars, as he fought to recover from the confrontation with Alicia.

He hadn't been prepared for the toxic cocktail of relief that she looked to be thriving, at least physically, after her injury mixed with a fresh shock of fury at how she'd dismissed him as a corrupt agent without ever hearing him out about what had happened that day. Beyond the fury from his memories, she'd known exactly how to hurt him.

Always the sidekick. How dare she slap him in the face with one of the deep, secret parts of himself he'd shared with her after they'd made love. It wasn't even a valid argument. Green Beret snipers always worked in pairs, with each able to perform both jobs of spotter and shooter with deadly, world-class accuracy. Just because John had been the spotter more times than not didn't mean he was any less skilled than Rory. And she couldn't be talking about their stint on ICE's black ops team. A team could only have one leader, and that hadn't been Alicia, either, so he wasn't sure how she got off separating her experience in black ops with his.

And there he went, arguing the point as if he was

trying to convince himself. He smacked his forehead, royally pissed at his stupid, middle-child insecurities rearing their ugly heads. While the lingering, unjustified sensation of being *less than* compared to the rest of the team had taken a turn for the justified after the entire crew assumed the worst of him on the turn of a dime, exile had forced him to rely only on himself. He was stronger, faster and more lethal than he ever had been in the group or as Rory's sniper partner.

He pushed the throttle to the max, careening into the open ocean until St. Thomas was nothing but a shadow behind him. St. Croix was forty miles south, not too much of a stretch on the Caribbean's relatively calm waters. This was a well-traveled boat route for ferries and locals, and despite it being hurricane season with one such predicted storm a day or two away, he spotted cruise ships, luxury yachts and even the occasional water skiers and kayakers.

After thirty minutes of travel, he no longer needed binoculars to keep tabs on Rory's location. In another twenty minutes, the nose of John's boat raced alongside the back of his, and in no time flat, they were careening neck and neck toward the green hills rising on St. Croix in the distance.

Time to step up his efforts. Bracing for impact, he slammed the side of his boat into Rory's. The blow knocked Rory's boat off course, but didn't slow him down. John had to crank the wheel to stay even with him. He couldn't see how it was possible to damage Rory's boat enough to stop it without doing the same to his. He needed a new strategy.

When they were neck and neck again, John climbed onto the captain's chair. With a hand on the windshield for balance, he crouched with one foot on the chair and the other on the rail. He maneuvered the boat so close to Rory's that the hulls knocked, then he pushed off, throwing himself over the edge.

Chapter 3

While John was airborne, Rory noticed what he was doing and jerked the wheel left. John's hands closed over the metal bar atop the rail, but he didn't make it on board. His body slammed against the side of the hull and the pull of the water on his legs nearly sucked him under, the boat was moving so fast.

His hands slipped on the wet metal. With the wake and the water pressure, he slid along the rail to the rear corner of the boat.

The next thing he knew, Rory was over him, stomping on his right hand with his bare foot as the boat sped on. John tried to swing his leg up to catch on the bottom rung of the ladder, but Rory's assault was too much. John lost his grip with his right hand and swung out, perilously close to the nearest of the two motors.

With a shaky, smarting right hand, John moved his

grip to a lower rung on the ladder so Rory couldn't stomp on him anymore, then reached for his gun. The trouble was, Rory had started prying off the ladder with a metal gaffe. John barely had time to grab the frayed end of the parasailing rope dangling off the back before the ladder separated from the boat and flew backward. Blinking sea spray from his eyes, John wrapped the rope around his wrist and tried to line up a nonfatal shot of Rory with his gun while Rory grabbed the fillet knife and sawed at the rope.

A loud bleat shocked them both. Rory whipped his head around to see a large luxury liner bearing down on them, still far enough away for Rory to change course. He lunged for the wheel and John seized his chance to climb aboard. Replacing his gun in its holster, he rallied his grip and core strength to hoist himself hand over hand until, with a growl of effort, he fell to the floor of the boat. Rory cranked the wheel right, out of the yacht's trajectory, and set the course toward St. Croix once more.

John wiped the back of his hand across his face, as if it wasn't as soaked through as the rest of him. "Rory, you bastard. Stop the boat."

Rory turned and faced him, but he left the boat racing over the water at an impossible speed. "Not a chance. What the hell are you doing in the islands?"

He bore an angry flesh wound on his thigh where John had grazed him with a bullet, but it had clotted and he didn't seem any worse for wear.

John, on the other hand, felt as if he'd been locked in a washing machine during the spin cycle. He rolled his shoulders and flexed his hand. "I had it on good authority that Alicia was going to kill you."

Rory let out a wheezy laugh. "And you thought you'd beat her to it? Nah, I bet you two are working together, am I right? You always were her lovesick whipping boy."

Okay, wow. Rory knew about John and Alicia's affair. That changed things. Intimate relationships between members of an ops team weren't exactly endorsed by ICE or their team leader, and he and Alicia had worked hard to be discreet. But somehow Rory had figured it out, which meant that John needed to rethink what Rory's motives were for shooting Alicia and broadcasting for all the world that John was his accomplice. Was it to twist the proverbial knife he'd stabbed John with? Why else would Rory shoot John's lover? Even after all this time, it didn't make any sense.

Looking into the face of the man John had once considered his brother, John felt his blood start to boil. Whatever Rory's motivation, he'd tried to kill Alicia. Whatever muck he'd made of John's life, he tried to kill the woman John loved. Another flex of his right hand told him all he needed to know—none of his bones were broken and he was in top shape to brawl.

He flew at Rory and landed a satisfying blow to his gut with a left hook chaser that knocked Rory into the steering wheel. Rory pushed off with a fist meant for John's cheek, but the boat zigged right.

John gave Rory a shove, sending him stumbling toward the rear of the boat. "You don't get to talk about Alicia like that. You don't deserve—" He swallowed back his next words. Rory might know they were lovers, but no way would John give him even an inkling of how very much he'd cared about her.

Rory bounced back swinging, this time catching

John with a blow to the chin. He absorbed the pain and grabbed Rory's neck, yanking his torso down to John's waiting knee. Damn, it felt cathartic, this fight. Letting Rory experience a fraction of the pain Alicia must have felt at Rory's hand.

John tried to back up a step, but Rory locked his arms around his middle and pedaled forward, pushing John to the steering console. His midback hit hard against the rim of the console, knocking the wind out of him. Any moment, U.S. authorities were going to descend on them. It was inevitable. Rory was a violent offender and a traitor. They knew he'd escaped, and John, Alicia and Rory had made enough of a commotion on St. Thomas that officials were going to pick up their trail in no time flat.

He needed to get Rory subdued and take control of the boat, stat. But Rory had a whole lot of fight left in him. He let fly with a fast hook, but John blocked with his elbow and sent his fist into Rory's wounded thigh. The blare of a warning horn sounded from off the bow and John played the sucker by looking. A massive barge snaked by their boat with only feet to spare. While John was distracted, Rory caught him with an uppercut that made contact with John's jaw. He staggered back and wasn't sure, for a split second, if only he was pitching sideways or if the whole boat was.

By the time he decided the boat was jumping a wake at a dangerous angle, he was toppling overboard. He flailed his arms as he careened toward the water, but didn't come in contact with anything but air. He plunged into the water.

He came up spluttering and gasping for breath. The speedboat was moving fast toward St. Croix and overhead, a helicopter hovered. His first thought was that the navy or police had found him, but after blinking water from his eyes he took a closer look. It was a private chopper and Alicia was in the passenger seat. She leaned over the edge of the open passenger doorway, her hair waving wildly in the wind created by the rotors.

"You okay?" she called.

He had to admire her wit, hiring an aerial tour pilot for a private island hopping escort. That was a smart move.

"Yeah." Sort of. The only damage was to his pride, and that wound stung like an SOB.

Alicia turned her body and looked back toward St. Thomas. In her hand, John glimpsed a flash of metal. Her gun. Which meant she hadn't exactly *hired* the pilot to take her to St. Croix. She'd used force, digging herself even deeper into a criminal hole. Desperate times, desperate measures and all that jazz. The question was, why had she put herself in such a desperate position? It'd been a miracle that she'd survived the gunshot wound Rory had inflicted on her, so why was she squandering her second chance at life with vengeance? It didn't add up.

"The navy's coming," she called.

Not unexpected, but he still needed to get away before U.S. authorities found him. They'd already accused him of being Rory's accomplice after Rory's initial arrest, but though one criminal's claims alone hadn't been enough proof of John's guilt to charge him with a crime, finding him there and Rory gone might be the corroborating evidence the Feds had been waiting for to put John away for life.

He hated to ask for help, not from her. Anyone but Alicia. She already thought him as less of a man. *The sidekick. Never the alpha.* Damn it all to hell. "Throw down a rope."

Her attention swung to Rory's boat. Even from that distance, he could see it in her eyes, the disdain for John, her desperation to get to Rory. Unbelievable. She was going to leave him there in the middle of the ocean, tens of miles from shore or the nearest boat.

Anger at her and Rory and the entire rotten farce that had become his life made him snap. He smacked the water, shouting, "Don't do it, Phoenix."

Ignoring him, she nudged the pilot's shoulder. He couldn't hear her for the thunder of the rotors, but he watched her mouth the word *go*.

Just like that, she was gone.

The Caribbean Sea had never felt so vast. John tipped his chin up and looked at the clouds. His boat was miles away, the U.S. Navy was bound to catch up with him and try to pin him with orchestrating Rory's escape, and he'd had no choice but to beg Alicia not to abandon him. Triple ouch.

Most of the time, he relished being the perpetual underdog. His whole life he'd been a scrapper, but he'd used it to his advantage. In warfare and black ops combat, it was rarely a bad thing to be underestimated by the enemy. But sometimes, clawing for a seat at the table sucked. Today, it sucked.

His only hope of getting through the next hour without becoming shark bait or getting arrested was to get the attention of one of the yachts or sea kayakers passing by. Treading water, he turned in a slow circle, assessing his options. The navy was maybe only five or ten minutes back. In the distance, a modest luxury yacht cruised his way, coming from St. Croix, blasting reggae music and with sunbathing, barely clothed women adorning its deck.

One thing John loved about his HK45 was that water didn't jam it up. He raised the gun overhead and squeezed off a round to get their attention, hoping they'd process the sound as an emergency flare gun instead of a lethal weapon, then tucked the gun out of view and waved his arms high, saying a silent prayer that the boaters were feeling charitable.

"You know how you can guarantee I won't kill you?"

The pilot's eyes were wide with terror and bugging out of his beet-red face as he gave a spastic shake of his head.

The real answer was *Because I would never kill a civilian—ever.* But honesty like that wasn't exactly an A-1 coercion technique. Alicia burrowed the muzzle of her gun deeper into his neck. Her finger wasn't anywhere near the trigger, but it didn't need to be. The metal on his skin was convincing enough that she meant business.

"Because you're going to hover over that field, no funny business, and I'm going to jump out. And then you don't ever have to see me again. Sound like a plan?"

He nodded, right on cue. Holding the helicopter pilot by gunpoint hadn't been her first choice, but money hadn't worked as a bribe and she couldn't take the chance of Rory making it to St. Croix—or, worse, disappearing—before she got a read on him.

She hadn't wanted to abandon John in the water, either, but what choice did she have? She'd unleashed a vicious criminal and now it was her duty to stop him at the sacrifice of everything else. Not only her duty to herself, but to the planet. Wasn't that a disquieting thought? In the twenty months since she'd been shot, she'd barely thought of anyone but herself. That's the way rehab and physical therapy worked. If you weren't thinking about yourself 24/7, thinking about healing and regaining your strength until it was almost an obsession, then you weren't doing it right.

She jiggled her gun against the pilot's skin. "But if you try to be a hero or do something stupid, the deal's off and I shoot. Got it?"

Another nod.

"Take it down as far as you can without landing." She didn't need marks left from the chopper's landing skids. Her footprints would be evidence enough of her presence on the island. With any luck, the pilot would return to St. Thomas and shake off his flight under duress. Maybe he wouldn't even call the police. Yeah, right.

Jumping out of a helicopter into a soggy field in the middle of St. Croix's wilderness wasn't ideal, but the airport was on the west side of the island—miles from any one of the harbors Rory was almost certain to have chosen as a landing point on the east side and way too central a location for her to disembark at. After a sweep of the coastline, she'd spotted Rory's speedboat drifting in the calm waters near a secluded high-end resort, with Rory nowhere to be seen.

If she'd been in his position, she would've done the very same thing because the resort's remote location tucked into the lush green tropics of the northeast shore meant fewer witnesses had noticed him drive up and jump out. Plus, the resort sported a whole parking lot full of cars ripe for the stealing.

Contrary to St. Thomas's *Let's-help-the-tourists-spend-their-money-fast!* vibe, this was a sleepy island of wealthy, older vacationers who liked their tennis games at the club in the morning and their naps in their beach hammocks in the afternoon, thank you very much. An escaped convict couldn't hide here long—at least, that's what Alicia was counting on.

Unfortunately, that meant she couldn't hide out here long, either, so it was a good thing that she didn't plan to. The idea was to locate Rory, execute him and vanish before the vacationers had woken from their naps. The closest, best place to make a clean break with the helicopter and its frightened pilot was a field two kilometers from the resort.

She poked the pilot in the neck with her gun once more for good measure. "Hold it steady now." She yanked his radio wire from its socket and tossed it out the door opening, then his earphones. No sense giving him a chance to call the police the moment she jumped, even if she'd never said directly why she needed him to get her to St. Croix or what she planned to do while there.

She tucked two one-hundred-dollar bills in his shirt pocket to cover replacing the equipment she'd destroyed, secured the computer bag she'd retrieved from her rental car across her shoulders, then walked to the edge of the doorway. He'd done a great job getting low. She had maybe a two-meter jump. No problem.

On the ground, she ran out from under the helicopter's shadow and sought cover beneath the tree canopy. She watched the helicopter rise and head off, not back toward St. Thomas, but in the direction of the St. Croix airport. Just terrific. With the navy on its way to the island, she had ten, maybe fifteen minutes to vanish before the U.S. authorities he was most likely on his way to notify descended on the resort.

Cursing at the messiness of it all and how screwed up her vengeance plan had gotten, she made a break for the hotel. What she really needed was a quiet place to log on to her computer. Maybe that was less glamorous than stealing a car and scouring every inch of the island, but Alicia could cover a lot more ground that way, so to speak.

She could tap into the local police phone line and radio and let the police and civilians do the grunt work. If what she'd seen on St. Thomas as the helicopter lifted off was any indication, St. Croix's main town of Christiansted would be crawling with police and soldiers, too, so the less visible she was, the better.

In the resort's parking lot, she scanned for a sign of Rory or any indication that he'd been through. She didn't expect a top-rate operative like him to leave a trail, and he didn't surprise her with one. She jimmied open the door of a rusty, early 1990s model American-made sedan—the kind that only took the touch of a screwdriver to the engine's solenoid starter to jump-start and so were, statistically, the favorite choice of auto thieves the world over—that probably belonged to one of the resort's employees.

With another look around, she pulled the driver's door closed, but it caught on something and bounced back open. Her gaze shot sideways to see a man's black boot propped on the bottom of the door frame.

Squelching a gasp, she pulled her gun and twisted to aim at him, but the man was faster. Cold metal of a gun muzzle jabbed at her neck. Didn't karma have an ironic sense of humor?

"Not the best idea, Phoenix."

There were only a handful of men in the world who called her that, and none of them owned that smug, smooth voice. She followed the boot in the doorway up past a pair of black cargo pants, black leather belt and gray T-shirt concealing a lean, fit build to the smirking face of a man who looked a few years older than her thirty-two. It was going to take some effort and strategy to best him and escape, but she had no doubt that she would.

Her first strategic move was to bide her time and wait for an opening. Blanking her expression, she released her gun into her lap and raised her hands in a show of surrender. "What do you want?"

He cocked his head and looked sideways with mocking amusement. "You and I haven't had the pleasure of meeting yet. Do you know who I am?"

A navy SEAL, she'd bet, given his clothes and high and tight haircut—and, if the gleam in his eye was any indication, one with a mean streak. "Should I care?"

His lips twitched into a smile. "I think you're going to want to remember my name. ICE Special Agent Logan McCaffrey."

ICE. That was not the agency she expected to catch up with her first. How did they get to the islands so fast? And why target her? She would've thought that if she had any remaining allies in the government, they would be the men and women she'd worked with for twelve years. She guessed loyalty and an exemplary service record didn't count for much after she'd broken their most notorious corrupt agent out of prison.

The name Logan McCaffrey didn't ring a bell, but then again, she'd been out of the loop for a year and a half. As if she'd ever paid much attention to the loop the first place. Their black ops crew had operated largely as a solitary unit, their identities classified, which had kept them isolated from the politics and flow of employees within the government bureaucracy that paid their salaries.

McCaffrey tightened a hand around her upper arm. "That was quite a show you put on with Rory Alderman."

To test his strength, she tried to jerk her arm out of his grip, but he clamped his hand harder around her. Okay, then, he was as strong as he looked and with reflexes to match. The faster she separated his gun from his possession, the better her odds of success. She lowered her gaze to her lap, where her gun lay. So close, yet she'd never be able to wield it before he reacted.

"It wasn't supposed to be a show." It was supposed to be quiet and fast, elegant even. Not the spectacle it'd turned into, thanks to John.

"Nevertheless, I've been waiting for you to make that move for a long time. Alicia Troy, it's my pleasure to place you under arrest."

Chapter 4

John didn't have time to worry about Alicia, especially with his fate hanging in such limbo. He had enough to think about with hunting down Rory and dodging the military and coast guard vessels that swarmed the water surrounding St. Croix as he considered where and how to sneak ashore.

He'd hitched a ride back to his boat from the yacht owner who'd heard his gunshot, and though his clothes were almost dry and his bag of guns and money had been right where he'd left it on the floor of the boat, it had been a pride-swallowing, tough slog of an hour.

With military and federal forces descending on the island and the dark, threatening clouds of Hurricane Hannah forming in the distant horizon, John doubted Rory would linger there long. There were only a few ways one could get on and off St. Croix, and John had no doubt the airport and main port in Christiansted Harbor were already on lockdown.

The next closest island was over a hundred nautical miles away. Since there was no way Rory would chance returning to St. Thomas, he would have to hire a private charter or steal a private helicopter, plane or a boat large enough to handle the choppy open waters. Even then, the coast guard and military would have satellites and radars to keep tabs on the water and airspace surrounding the island.

As far as John was concerned, he was in the best position to find Rory, not only because of his intimate knowledge of both St. Croix and the man who was his former best friend, but because he was in the ironic position of being the forgotten one, the ghost operative. There wasn't anyone in the world who cared enough about John's movement to pay attention to where he was or what he was doing.

The only person who even knew John was an interested party in what happened to Rory and Alicia was his ICE buddy Logan, and even if Logan thought he might go after Rory, he had no idea how close John had been living to the unfolding events or how quickly he was capable of responding. With any luck, he would slip onto the island undetected, nab Rory, extract a confession from him, then turn him over to ICE before Hannah's wind speed hit fifty knots.

John's plan not to think about Alicia was easier said than done, though. Because the moment the luxury estates and resorts dotting the green hills of St. Croix's coast got near enough that he could make out balconies and artfully arranged palm trees in courtyards, all he could think was that she was out there, too. The same 134 miles that trapped Rory with scores of federal agents and U.S. troops also trapped her.

Had she already found and killed Rory? He hadn't forgotten her hesitation back on St. Thomas to do just that, and he wasn't sure what to make of it. On their black ops team, there was no getting around necessary violence when their duty to defend their country demanded it, which occasionally meant making a kill. Alicia's conviction to do what was right for her country and her lethal grace were two of the things he loved about her. Perhaps, now that duty to country had been stripped from her job description, her moral compass had changed. *Unless...*

Unless what if she'd lost her touch? Post-traumatic stress disorder was common in victims of violence. Either that or there was some reason, deep down inside her, why she wanted Rory alive. Regardless of why Alicia had done what she did, it was time to set his musings aside and admit the very real danger that she wouldn't have the chance to try to kill Rory again because she'd be apprehended by authorities here on St. Croix, if she hadn't already.

The idea made his chest tight, which pissed him off. She'd abandoned him in middle of the Caribbean Sea, of all the damn things. She hadn't even seen fit to throw down a floatation device. So what if the authorities got her? He had no business caring what her fate was anymore. If she got caught, then his path to Rory would be clearer. Try as he might, he just couldn't sell himself on that argument, though. Despite everything, she was the woman he'd once loved. Despite everything, there as a part of him that cared about her still.

He wove a path along the north side of the island,

away from busy Christiansted Harbor. With the binoculars he kept in the boat's console, he scanned the coast, but he couldn't keep his thoughts from returning to Alicia.

It had always been that way between them—he cared too much and she acted as if she barely afforded him a thought. She'd made him fight for a spot in her bed. Made him demand it. At the time, in the middle of it all, he'd liked being the one calling the shots in their relationship. Fighting for what he wanted was his comfort zone. As with everything else in his life— his career, his family—with her he'd let his stubborn streak act as a battering ram, breaking through her self-protective walls. He'd not only loved Alicia, body and soul, but he'd loved the challenge of her, too.

He saw no sign of Rory's boat at Salt River Bay, which had been his first hunch. Intimately familiar with almost all the docks, piers, bars and hotels on St. Croix because St. Croix had been the first haven he landed on after his life fell apart, he pressed north, where the shoreline evolved into looming green cliffs untouched by civilization and edged with shallow, yellow sand beaches. It was unlikely that Rory had ditched the boat and swam ashore—which would've been hell on his gunshot wound—so he'd either tied off at one of the few docks on this end of the island or he'd gone to the island's south side.

Sure enough, bobbing in the water alongside kayaks and dinghies tied to the small private dock jutting from the Grand Ammaly Bay Resort, he spotted the boat Rory had stolen.

That cleared up where Rory's touchdown point had been, but John knew better than to take the bait. Even if the boat hadn't been left in plain sight as a decoy and was a bona fide signal of Rory's trail, Rory wouldn't have lingered at the Grand Ammaly for long. Most likely, he'd gone shopping for unattended purses and wallets at the resort's restaurants and lounges, then stolen a car. John's best bet was that Rory's next move involved treating his gunshot wound.

He also bet that Alicia had started her hunt for Rory at the resort. She didn't have many weaknesses as an operative, but she was a computer genius, first and foremost, and had the accompanying literal, statistical logic to go along with that gift. John had witnessed it enough back when they were teammates. It was the same mind-set that made her an expert at computer technology, but it would only hurt her in the Caribbean, where scarcely anything followed the rules of American-bred literal logic.

The question now was, after Rory ditched the speedboat and gathered funds, where would he go to tend his wound? Compounding the issue was that Rory didn't need someone else to administer first aid. Green Berets were trained to take care of themselves and each other. It was a critical skill to have when operating behind enemy lines, as they often had on their missions. Once, in Afghanistan, John had sustained a nasty slice to his side while training Afghan soldiers in hand-to-hand combat techniques and Rory had administered ten stitches in the kitchen of an abandoned, bombed-out house.

All Rory would need was first-aid supplies and a secluded, clean place to patch himself up. On the sleepy, vacation paradise of St. Croix, there was definitely no shortage of secluded hideaways. Good thing John knew Eugene Flyer, bar owner and island informant extraordinaire.

He cranked the wheel of his boat in the opposite direction of the resort, toward Eugene's bar, but something stopped him from taking the throttle out of neutral. *Alicia.*

What if she'd caught up with Rory before he'd had time to flee the resort? What if she was on the verge of killing him? John was so near, he had to check. The idea of seeing Alicia again made his heart pound. He wished he knew how to sever the grip she had on his heart, but the best he could do for now was try to ignore it.

But as he spun the wheel back toward the resort and pushed the throttle, he couldn't stop the rush of memories of the woman he'd loved and lost. It was a bitter pill to swallow to realize that even with everything on the line and his future hanging in the balance, Alicia's face, her voice, remained stubbornly in the forefront of his mind—forever there, yet forever out of reach.

Alicia followed McCaffrey's hand as he snatched her gun and tucked it in his pants pocket. Arrest, huh? So he didn't have the green light to kill her. Good to know. Part of her was spitting nails that her mission had gone so royally FUBAR, but another part of her had to give thanks for that small favor. At least she was alive. She sat still, forcing him to make the next play.

He took hold of her left arm again and repositioned his gun against her neck.

"Right hand on top of your head, right now."

She complied, biding her time. Next, he'd probably

order her out of the car. One could hope he'd do something so stupid, anyway.

"Real slowly now, you're going to get out of the car. One wrong move and I shoot. Don't think for a second that I don't understand how dangerous you are."

If he'd truly understood how dangerous she was, he would've cuffed her hands to the steering wheel, then climbed in the backseat and ordered her to play hostage taxi driver.

She unfolded one booted leg to the ground, then the other. Predictably, he tugged her arm to force her to stand. Harnessing the momentum in his tug, she pushed off the ground with her left leg, kicking out with her right.

Her boot slammed into his gut as she grabbed the wrist of his gun hand. She banged his wrist against the door frame as she kicked his legs out from under him. With an *oof,* he fell forward into her lap like she'd hoped he would, his grip on her arm loosening. She jerked her arm free of him, and before he had time to gather his wits, she kneed him in the head, then grabbed the wrist of his gun hand.

They grappled for command of the gun. She nearly lost the battle when he grabbed her hair and yanked. The pain of it made her stomach ache, and the lack of air made her light-headed, but she fought through it, banging his gun hand against the door frame over and over until it fell from his hand, either onto the ground or the car floor, she couldn't tell. Time for part two of her plan.

Her hands shot out, groping the steering column until her fingers closed around what she'd been after.

The gear shifter. She wrenched it down but didn't have enough force behind the movement to snap it off.

She threw herself backward, arching her hips and creating a slight window to get her knees up. Her boots hit his legs, though she couldn't guess how high up. Gasping and grunting, she kicked against him, but his hold on her was too firm. Before she could stop him, he pulled her from the car. She put all her effort into one last tug on the gear shifter as they moved. She was about to give up and come up with a new plan when it snapped off.

There was no time to waste. As soon as she was out of the car, she got her legs under her and swung the jagged-edged shiv toward his neck. She felt it snag on skin. He hissed through his teeth and grabbed for her arm. No way was she going to let that happen. Instead, she used his power against him and as his arm whooshed past her, she countered with a block, just as she'd learned as a student of Krav Maga, the discipline of Israeli martial arts her father practiced and had taught her, his only daughter, from the time she could walk.

The memory and discipline of her training settled into her bones, eclipsing the need for conscious planning. They merged, becoming one fluid series of spins, kicks, jabs and blocks. McCaffrey gave as good as he defended himself, employing a dangerous combination of lightness and power that spoke of a background in mixed martial arts. For every lock and strike she issued, he countered with a punch or kick, but she was able to finally create a pocket of space to swing the shiv out. She brought it down hard and stabbed him square in the thigh.

Grunting in pain, he stumbled back, gripping his bleeding leg.

She turned her attention to finding her fallen gun. She didn't see it on the ground, so it had to be somewhere near the driver's seat. She'd nearly reached the car when Logan grabbed hold of her waist. She was no match for his strength. He twisted her elbow behind her, then body slammed her face-first into the side of the car near the rear wheel. Painfully.

He pulled her back, then slammed her into the car a second time. His gun found her neck again. "Give me a reason to squeeze the trigger."

Her mouth went dry. There was more than patriotic duty or irritation that she'd temporarily bested him behind those words, which had dripped with hate, anger. But why? She'd never seen him before, so what could he have against her on a personal level?

Besides the shiv she still held in the hand he'd twisted behind her, she had a hell of an arsenal strapped to her body under her clothes, none of which she could use at the moment. So she waited and tried to ignore the piercing pain in her twisted arm. *Patience, patience...*

"Got her," he said low, as though speaking into a phone or earpiece. He rattled off their coordinates.

She gazed down the side of her leg, checking out his stance, calculating how much room she'd need to create so she could slip sideways enough to take control of his gun arm. His right knee had her leg pinned against the car. The shiv had been removed from his leg and, though the pants were torn and bloody, the blood wasn't spreading or dripping. She must not have caught him all that deep.

She was contemplating her options to get him to loosen his hold when she spied an edge of black peeking out from beneath the cuff of her pants.

Her ankle holster.

"Roger that," Logan said, his tone indicating he was still on the phone. She glanced over her shoulder as he pocketed the phone.

He narrowed his eyes at her, so she made a show of glancing at her ankle, as if she was considering making a play for the gun. He took the bait, following her line of sight.

"Loaded down with firepower, hmm? I'd expect nothing less. I bet you want me to squat down and get it, make it nice and easy for you to kick me in the face from that position, right?"

"A girl can dream."

His gun scraped over her shoulder, then her back as he repositioned it between her ribs, aimed at her heart. "How about you get it, nice and slow, then drop it on the ground. I'll stay here with my finger on the trigger."

This guy was good. Too good. For the first time, a flutter of nerves started inside her. This was going to be harder than she thought, especially with no crew backing her up. John's image flickered in her mind. Guess it was too much to ask for him to surprise her with a well-timed ambush.

No.

This was what she wanted—to work alone. She didn't want to be rescued, especially by the man she'd once dreamed of spending the rest of her life with. Even now, the thought of him made her chest ache. It was stupid, pining for a man who'd conspired to kill her. But even as she thought the words, they felt hollow. Did she really believe him capable of that? The same nagging doubt she'd fought for twenty months to ignore came creeping back into her consciousness.

No. She didn't have time for doubts and heartache, not with Rory on the loose and herself in a battle of wits with a highly trained ICE agent.

She shoved her wayward thoughts aside and gave an exaggerated squirm. "You'll have to let go of my arm for me to get that gun."

His hand slid to her wrist, loosening the twist, but he didn't release her. With his mouth near her ear, he whispered, "If you try anything clever, I have no qualms about hurting you."

She didn't doubt it, given the way he'd threatened to pull the trigger of his gun earlier. "You must have some qualms or you wouldn't have said that. In fact, I think you're pretty damn offensive. You would have never said that to a man. Don't be such a sexist pig."

He let out a sardonic chuckle. "I couldn't give a damn that you're a woman. Truth is, you're a worthy adversary, and I would've loved to have you on my team. It breaks my heart a little to have witnessed your fall from grace."

There were so many questions that sprang to her mind from that comment that she didn't know where to start. His team? She'd already figured out that he was no run-of-the-mill ICE field agent. He had the sophisticated moves and toughness of a black ops agent, which begged the question, once again, of why she'd never heard of him before today.

At a slow, deliberate pace, she bent and stretched her right hand down toward her gun. "What's your real job with ICE?"

He tsked. "I'm sure you've already guessed the answer to that. You want me to tell you, anyway?"

She tugged her pant leg up, then ever so tediously unbuttoned the strap holding her backup nine millimeter in place. "Why don't you go ahead and spell it out for me what you're doing here and why you had a front row seat to my so-called fall from grace?"

"Did you think the need for a black ops crew disintegrated when you and your team did?"

Honestly, she hadn't given much thought to ICE since they forced her to go on disability leave. Just thinking the term made her temper catch fire and gave her a fresh surge of adrenaline.

Closing her eyes, she visualized the position of his gun-holding arm, his stance and his height and breadth, calculating exactly how she'd need to move and strike to gain the upper hand. Then she dropped the gun between her legs, the barrel propped against the top of her right foot.

"What's your plan with that move? Are you going to kick it up and grab it from midair?"

"Something like that."

"It'd almost be worth letting you try that, but how about instead you shuffle it behind you."

"I would, but I can't move."

He lifted his knee away from where he had her leg pinned, so she slid the gun back just as he'd asked, biding her time. She gave a start as she felt his hands on the bare skin of her waist where her shirt had pulled up from her pants. He must have spotted the belt she'd strapped to her ribs under her shirt. She remained doubled over and let him look.

"I wasn't going to strip-search you, but you're not

giving me a lot of choice." He used his gun to push her shirt higher, revealing her concealed carry-gear belt. "You're like a one-woman army, here. Grenades, ammo, flash bangs, multi-tool. And I'm sure there's more in here somewhere."

He felt along her bra, then gave a humph as he reached the hilt of the knife she'd sewn into it. His touch was clinical, free of any sexual undertones, but she still had to ignore the sensation of being violated. "Ingenious. Makes me wish I was more creative with my concealed carry."

"Yeah, well, I don't look as good as you do in cargo pants." She pushed off her left leg and stood, twisting into the hand that still held her wrist to pin it behind her and bringing his face into strike range. She elbowed him in the nose, then ducked under his gun-holding arm and twisted again, locking out and twisting the arm of the hand that held her wrist until he had no choice except to release her.

Before he could spin to face her, she kicked him with all her might, then reached under her shirt and ripped her knife from its sheath in her bra as she dropped to her knees near his head. She held the knife to his throat.

Wearing an expression of respect, he touched the clotting blood on his thigh from where she'd stabbed him. His eyes were watering, his nose bloody. He reached with unsteady hands into his pocket for her gun and she let him get it clear of the fabric before she elbowed him in the gut, then plucked it from his hand and aimed it at him with her left hand.

"Should I shoot you or slice your neck open?"

"Nicely played. There's just one little problem."

She registered the sound of a vehicle at the same time he raised his head and looked past her. A van done up like a resort's airport shuttle, but with darkly tinted windows, screeched to a stop not two meters away. She supposed the shuttle look was as much camouflage on a tropical island as the type of run-down A-Team knockoff van she and her black ops crew had driven in the Third World countries they often found themselves in.

The side door of the van swung open to reveal two ripped, fit men holding automatic rifles, both aimed at her. Driving the van, and with a handgun aimed at Alicia, was an equally fit young woman.

"Alicia Troy, meet your replacements." The glee in McCaffrey's voice made her want to punch him in the face all over again.

Damn it all.

"Drop the gun and get your hands in the air," Logan said, the smug smoothness returning to his voice. "We're done dancing."

Out of ideas, she complied, setting the knife and gun on the ground.

While she processed the turn of events, Logan scooted from beneath her, gathered her discarded weapons and stood. He returned to the car she'd planned to steal and retrieved her computer bag from the passenger seat. "We'll need this as evidence."

And, boy, would they find it on that computer. Her gut twisted.

"I see you weighing your options, but the only one that'll keep you alive is to get your hands in the air. We're the best of the best and I wouldn't underestimate us if I were you."

"If you're the best, it's only because my team's out of the picture."

Logan and his crew all chuckled. Logan shook his head. "Nearly two years ago, you and your merry band of misfits nearly destroyed a billion-dollar, international operation, and Rory Alderman sold national secrets to the highest bidder. If you ask me, it's a miracle ICE decided to give their black ops experiment another try."

Given all the guns pointed at her and that she was outnumbered four to one, her best option—her only option, really—was to do as he said, at least for the time being. For the first time in her life, she raised her arms in a show of surrender.

Chapter 5

Through the painted iron bars of the Ammaly Bay Resort's pool enclosure, John watched resort security take statements from a couple who had apparently been robbed of all their belongings during the water volleyball tournament less than an hour earlier. So John's hunch had been right. Rory had used the resort as an ATM to fund his disappearance.

The question still was, had Alicia caught up to him before he was able to slip away?

Cutting a wide berth around the pool, he walked the winding path through the hotel grounds, then through the lobby. After Rory gathered funds, the next logical step would be to steal a car. With that in mind, John headed into the parking lot, but what he saw had him cursing and ducking for cover behind the nearest parked car.

Alicia. But she wasn't alone.

He watched as she climbed into a white hotel shuttle van along with at least four others.

He raised up slightly as the van cruised past him. He didn't recognize either the woman behind the wheel or the man in the passenger seat, but they both looked calm, yet vigilant. Something was definitely not right about the situation, but he couldn't put his finger on it.

Then his eyes widened and his stomach dropped. Something akin to a boiling sensation started in his chest. Sitting right beside Alicia in the middle row of the van was Logan effing McCaffrey—the man John had thought was his only friend left in ICE. Guess they weren't such great friends, after all.

No wonder Alicia had been so cavalier about breaking the law by hijacking that helicopter. No wonder she hadn't shot to kill Rory. It wasn't that she'd lost her touch; it was that she had something going on with ICE that John didn't understand.

No, check that, he did. There was no two ways about it. He knew exactly what had happened. "Mother of God, Logan and Alicia set me up."

He watched the van roll out of the parking lot headed north, toward Frederiksted, then jimmied the door of an old hatchback. The once-silver paint had turned gray, and the engine strained before it caught, but it blended in with most of the other vehicles on the island, which was John's only requirement.

His palms sweating against the steering wheel and his throat tight and sore as though from screaming, John waited until the van was a good distance away before pulling onto the road behind it. It was a slow crawl along the two-lane coastal road to Frederiksted.

He hung back as far as he could while still maintaining a visual on the van, biding his time to strike as his anger gathered force.

They'd played him a fool—Logan, Alicia, ICE. Everyone. In his mind, he could see the email from Logan that morning. *Alicia is missing.*

Oh, they played him good. He huffed out an exhale, fighting to get a grip. The van drove slow and steady over the straight stretch of the highway toward the heart of Frederiksted, with John following at a distance.

John had spent a lot of time in Frederiksted, the second largest town on the island, yet far and away more charming, with its rustic buildings, Dutch history and killer beaches. He used to love the place, but this was the spot where he'd realized, a year or so ago, that his complacency had finally consumed him and he'd lost his taste for life.

It'd happened on a moonlit rooftop deck across the street from the pier, with a beautiful woman in his arms and four shots of rum in his veins. She'd trailed kisses over his chest, her hands exploring lower, and he remembered looking up at the moon and thinking, *I feel nothing.* Not drunk, not desire, not even anger at Alicia or Rory. Nothing.

It'd been enough to scare rationality back into him. That was the night he left St. Croix and sequestered himself with his weapons and computer on a barely inhabited island east of St. Thomas. That was the night he'd started training again—when he'd started preparing for this, his first and most critical mission back in the game.

And all the while, through his pain and rebirth,

Alicia and Logan had been plotting something, preparing to use him.

Instead of stewing on why it seemed to be his lot in life to be a patsy, he should be asking himself what Logan and Alicia were trying to accomplish with Rory's escape and John's pursuit of him. It didn't make sense. Logan was the ICE recruiter who'd brought John and Rory over from Army Special Forces and had facilitated their training. He didn't work cases, so what was he doing in the field?

Come to think of it, maybe an even better question than that was why would Alicia help ICE in the first place? She'd quit the agency more than a year ago, and as far as John could glean at the time, not on the best of terms after they'd put her on disability.

All John knew was that he was sick and tired of being jerked around and played for a fool. That was going to end right the hell now. Seething inside, he gunned the engine and swerved right, ripping around one corner, then another, onto a side street that ran parallel to the coastal highway on which the van continued to travel. With a whining protest, the hatchback complied. Keeping one eye on the road and his foot pushing the gas pedal to the floor, he reached into his bag and brought out his rifle.

At a corner where the van was set to pass by as it headed in the direction of the airport, he screeched to a halt in the middle of the road, threw the car into Park and ran up an exterior set of stairs to a rooftop deck, rifle in hand. This plan might ruin his getaway car, but John couldn't worry about that now. There were plenty of other cars on the island to steal.

No more than a minute after he flattened to a shooting position, the van came into view.

His index finger slipped to the trigger. Compared to hitting a buoy, this was going to be a piece of cake. Taking aim, he squeezed the trigger and held it down until the two front tires were shredded.

The van's brakes smoked as it jerked into a spinout. John then took aim at the windshield and squeezed off a single round that hit right in the corner as the van turned. The windshield beaded into thousands of white balls of glass, but the plastic safety film covering the glass kept the windshield erect, though no one could possibly see through it.

Someone in the van fired a shot out of an open window, then another, but John ignored the danger. It was a little hard to squeeze off an accurate shot from a vehicle spinning out of control. He stood, ready to spring. The van slammed into the side of the building adjacent to the one John stood on, nearly taking out the beams holding the second-story balcony up. The airbags exploded as it shuddered to a stop.

John climbed onto the corner of the ledge and jumped, rifle in one hand and his HK45 in the other. His boots slammed hard onto the hood of the van, but all the fury and adrenaline pounding through him kept pain the furthest from his mind. He kicked the windshield. This time, the glass did shatter, raining down over the airbags.

He fired shots into the bags, deflating them in seconds, then kicked the female driver and the man in the front passenger seat both in the faces as he took a seat in the empty windshield frame and had a look inside at the handful of operatives aiming guns at him, looking ready to act should he give them the slightest opening.

He didn't recognize anyone except Logan and Alicia, but the other three had the physiques and postures of highly trained special agents. Their firearms were top rate and high-powered. Too bad for them because John had an automatic military-grade M4 rifle and an HK45 semiautomatic aimed right back at them—and every person there knew that in the time it would take to get one good shot in him, he could level them all to the ground.

Boots still on the driver's and passenger's necks, he locked his knees, pinning them to their seats. Then he plucked their guns from their hands and threw them over his shoulder. Call it a product of growing up in the South, but he hated using physical force against women—seriously hated it—but it'd been Logan who'd retrained John after the army that in black ops, nothing mattered except getting the job done, including an opponent's gender.

Alicia had confirmed Logan's words for him more than once that it was insulting to women in the field to be treated differently. So he did what he had to without flinching, when he had to, but he didn't have to like using force against the female driver right now.

There were two guns still aimed at him—Logan's and the one held by the man in the very back of the van. John focused one gun on each man, even though there was no way he'd take a chance of hitting Alicia by firing at Logan.

Alicia's expression was cold, blank. He let his gaze flicker over her before it landed on Logan. He swallowed, caging the impulse to beat that shadow of a smile off his former friend's face.

"Alicia and Logan, you make quite a pair." He swallowed, correcting the emotion in his tone, replacing it with steel. "I want answers. And I want them now."

"Thriller, that was quite an entrance. I wish I could say it's a shock to see you here," Logan said, using John's old code name and a slick tone that made John want to bare his teeth. "Because I was in the room when your superiors gave you explicit instructions to stay out of ICE business and off U.S. soil. Here you are violating both directives."

"And yet, you knew exactly what would happen when you contacted me this morning." And he was downright pissed at himself for being so gullible. Guess he had further to go than he thought toward rebuilding himself as a warrior.

"Predictability always was a weakness of yours."

"No, not predictability. Loyalty. That's why I'm here." The woman in the driver's seat looked as if she might be making plans to counterattack. He unlocked his knee and kicked the underside of her chin hard enough to serve as a warning. "And I'll tell you, Logan, Alicia, it's the damnedest thing because two years ago, I never would have classified my loyalty to my fellow soldiers and teammates—the people in the world I should trust most—as a weakness."

He met the gaze of the man in the way back of the van, the one with the flat Polynesian nose and the Kimber 9mm trained on him. "That's ironic, right? Because when I was a soldier, they drilled it into our heads over and over again that loyalty was everything."

The man's eyes narrowed. John winked at him, just

to be contrary, before returning his focus to Logan. "This is a good-looking crew you've compiled. I guess your superiors have you working in the field now?"

"Wait…you two know each other?" Alicia said.

The question gave John pause. If she'd really teamed up with Logan, she would have known that. Unless she was playing dumb.

He didn't take his eyes off Logan when he answered her. "Logan recruited me for ICE from the army."

"I trained you, too. Don't forget that part of the story."

John shifted the aim of his rifle to Logan's face. "Then how is it that there are five of you and only one of me, and yet we find ourselves in this position? This must be one of those times where the student surpasses the teacher."

"I wouldn't bet on it." At the first movement of Logan's gun, John engaged the muscles of his trigger finger, but didn't take the motion any farther. Instead, he schooled his features against the bolt of panic that hit him as the butt of Logan's gun found Alicia's throat. "Where are my manners? I owe you my thanks for leading us to Alicia. She was our target all along and I knew you'd be the one to help us neutralize her."

Steady, man. Loyalty is your weakness, remember?

Odds were that this was just another ploy to manipulate him. Keeping his focus on Logan's trigger finger, he noted in his periphery that Alicia's hands were behind her back. A bruise was forming on her cheek and he saw abrasions on her neck. Her shirt was dotted with debris, as if she'd been flung on the ground. In fact, the more he studied her, the more beat up he realized she was.

So much for his theory about her and Logan teaming up against him. Alicia wasn't here of her own free will and clearly someone, probably Logan, had roughed her up pretty good. And that made John want to do some killing in a bad, bad way.

Steady...

"What about Rory?" he asked. "How does he factor into this grand plan of yours?"

"Don't you worry about him. There are only two ways off this island—by boat or air. The airports are on lockdown and the island is surrounded by navy, ICE, the U.S. Marshals Service, FBI—you name it, they're here and all trying to be the ones to take Rory down first. He won't be leaving this place alive. Bringing Alicia into custody was my crew's one and only mission."

"I'll help you find Rory," Alicia said. "Think of how it'll boost your careers if you find him first. I can track him better than anyone."

"Why would you help us capture him? You're the one who broke him out of prison."

"You have no proof."

"Don't I?"

Alicia swallowed, which looked as if it took effort given how hard Logan had his gun jammed against her neck. Bastard.

While Logan and Alicia kept up a back-and-forth about proof and being set up, John assessed his options. The van was shot to hell, its tires and windshield destroyed. At some point they were all going to have to get out of the vehicle because this stalemate they were in couldn't go on indefinitely. John knew they'd try to get out of sight before the authorities showed up. Sure,

Logan and his crew were law enforcement officials, but there wasn't a black ops agent alive who wanted a bunch of uniforms slowing them down or mucking up their operation.

The question John needed to answer in the next thirty seconds or so was how did he get Logan and his crew out of the van, their threat neutralized without killing them, and all while maintaining his position of power? Problems, problems…

"What about me?" he asked, interrupting Logan's snide response to something Alicia had said.

Logan huffed. "What about you? You're free to walk away. And I suggest you do so before I change my mind."

In other words, Logan thought he was harmless. How insulting. Did he not notice John had disabled their van and was holding them all at gunpoint?

"You haven't left yet."

"Keen observation."

"Don't get ideas about saving your lady love here. Consider this a lesson in who not to give your loyalty to…because it sure isn't this one. If your positions were reversed, would she save you?"

Not in a million years. She'd already deserted him in the middle of the ocean. He probably could've forgiven her for that, except for the minor detail that she still clung to the belief that John was a traitor to his country and helped plot her murder.

The hard truth was that John's most strategic move would be to walk away, leaving Alicia in Logan's custody. Since Logan and the rest of the Feds didn't perceive John as a threat, and with Alicia out of commission, John could hunt down his quarry unencumbered. He had no doubt he could find Rory faster than any of them. The truth was, Alicia being captured and ICE's underestimation of John's abilities worked in his favor in every possible way…except for John's conscience.

Alicia's life was on the line here. The thought of her languishing in a prison cell for the rest of her life made John's heart race with panic. No matter what disgraces she thought him guilty of, her opinions didn't change who John was, with his weakness for loyalty and all.

Rory's accusations had stripped him of his reputation, his career and the woman he loved, but no one could take away John's integrity. All he was now was the soldier and man he and his Maker knew him to be. And a soldier didn't walk away from a teammate in trouble, just like a man didn't walk away when his woman needed him—even though he wasn't her man anymore and his days as a soldier were nothing but a fading memory.

Besides, John had never been a big fan of taking the easy way out.

He took his finger off the triggers of his guns and held them up, aimed in the air, like he was surrendering. Really, though, it was a great ruse to get the guns over the top of the van's roof and out of sight. "All right. Here I go. One question—are you going to shoot me in the back while I walk away?"

"You're not worth the bullet."

"Gee, thanks."

"You're welcome."

Alicia hadn't reacted to the news that John was walking away. Not that he'd expected her to—she was too much of a professional. Keeping his expression passive and his eyes on Logan, he squeezed the trigger of his rifle, spraying the teetering balcony post with shots until it gave way and collapsed onto the passenger side of the van with a loud crack.

John dived off the van, out of the way, just before impact.

The force of the falling balcony tipped the van onto its side in a clatter of metal parts and broken glass. It hit the ground hard, dust billowing all around.

John scrambled to his feet and leaped onto the side of the van, to the broken window.

Alicia was grappling with Logan and the woman from the front seat. He'd get to them in a sec, but his first order of business was taking out the man in the back of van. He was partially covered by a fallen beam but still had command of his gun and was shooting wildly. John smashed the butt of his gun into the man's face.

He stopped shooting and his eyes rolled back before he crumpled, passed out.

John grabbed the man's gun and tossed it out the window, then transferred his own gun to his left hand, seized Logan by the shirt with his right and hauled him up.

Logan came up swinging and clipped John in the jaw. "What happened to walking away?"

John returned the favor. The impact of his fist on Logan's cheek felt good. Like when he'd let his fists do the talking with Rory on the speedboat. "Did you really think I could?"

He ducked out of the way of Logan's next hit, then slammed his shoulder into Logan's chest and punched him in the gut, knocking him off the side of the van into the ground.

The woman from the front seat had crawled to the back. She and Alicia were going at it in a messy, opportunistic fight, both clearly prevented from making use of their close-combat training given the tight confines of the vehicle.

John jumped up onto the van's side and got the barrel of his gun right in the woman's face. "Yeah, you can go ahead and get your hands off Alicia now."

Shooting daggers at him with her expression, she opened her hands and backed off.

John kept the gun on the operative as he offered Alicia a hand up. "Let's go. I'm getting you out of here."

She had the wherewithal to look offended. "I can take care of myself."

"Really? Is that what was going on here—you taking care of yourself?"

"I was biding my time. I don't want to owe you."

John nearly got a cramp in his eyeballs from rolling them so hard. "Phoenix, you already owed me. This doesn't change anything."

Ignoring his hand, she pushed past him onto the side, now the top, of the van.

"John, look out!"

He wrenched his gaze up in time to see Logan coming at him. Logan grabbed him and pulled him off the van. With another lunge, Logan sent them careening over the side of the road, down a grassy ridge. John kept a grip on the other man's shirt as they tumbled.

They landed near the base of a giant metal silo located out back of the rum distillery that was St. Croix's claim to fame. John shoved him off and scrambled back. Panting, snarling, they faced each other down.

"You're ready for round two?" John asked.

Logan swiped at a spot of blood in the corner of his lips. "Do you really think you can best me? I trained you."

He holstered his gun, then withdrew his knife. "You keep saying that like you think I haven't picked up a single new move since then."

Logan sprang forward with a roundhouse kick aimed at his knife-holding hand that John easily side-stepped.

"And I guess you forgot that in training me, you taught me all your moves."

Logan regained his footing, then reached into a pocket on his cargo pants and brought out a massive, steel sawback bowie knife. "You say that like you think I taught you all my moves."

For the first time, John noticed the dried blood on Logan's pants and on his neck. *Good job, Phoenix.* "I thought you were my ally, but you used me."

"Try not to sound so hurt. It's unbecoming."

They circled each other, breathing hard. John had no idea what Alicia was up to or where she'd gone—for all he knew, she'd taken off in the car he'd stolen—but he didn't have time to worry about that at the moment.

"Why go after her? She was one of ICE's best operatives."

"You don't think ICE keeps track of its highly classified operatives once they've left the agency? Spare me your selective ignorance. You know how the system works. Since Alicia was shot, she hasn't been mentally sound. She's a loose cannon loaded with national secrets and lethal skills, which was why I was assigned to keep tabs on her. It was only a matter of time before she broke bad. She proved that today with Alderman's escape."

"And you thought I was the perfect tool to get to her?"

"I knew you'd lead us right to her. Which you did."

And here he'd thought he'd gotten beyond complacency and assumptions about the people in his life. How had he been so naive? He let his anger at himself and his anger at Logan fuse inside him. Adrenaline and power pumping through his veins and right into the hand that held his knife, he rushed Logan, growling as he cut through the air with the blade.

Logan counterattacked. They came together again in a clash of blades and perilously close misses. Logan proved himself the more experienced hand-to-hand fighter of the two, but what John lacked in sparring practice, he made up for in sheer grit and reflexes that were far superior to his opponent's.

Logan slammed him into the side of the distillery wall, then threw his knife. John ducked, then aimed his knife at the bloody hole on Logan's pants and lunged.

Together, they crashed through a door on the side of the distillery. He'd fallen into a warehouse loaded floor to ceiling with rows and rows of wooden barrels sitting on shelves. There weren't any employees in sight, which wasn't surprising being that it was Sunday.

Satisfied that he wasn't going to be attacked from some new foe, he whirled around to face Logan, holding the knife in front of his body. He turned in time to see Logan lunging at him.

With a primal growl, Logan hooked his arm, slicing the air with his knife. Rather than clash blades, John dived sideways, putting all his momentum into a rolling tumble that crashed him into the nearest row of barrels. The shelves teetered and the barrels sitting on it jiggled, but none fell on his head, which was all he really cared about at the moment.

He leaped to his feet, but Logan didn't let him get far. He came at John again, brandishing his blade. John met him halfway. Their knives clanked against each other, buying John time to get his other arm involved. He clamped his left hand around Logan's right wrist, holding his knife away as he threw his weight forward, sending Logan's back into the shelves behind him.

This time, the shelving unit teetered, then crashed. They fell into the mess of leaking rum and splintered wood, John still holding Logan's wrist.

This wasn't going to work. He wasn't crazy about the idea of killing a government operative, despite Logan's betrayal, and he was wasting time he should be spending in search of Rory. Add to that the irritating truth that Alicia had deserted him again, this time with John's stolen car and his bag of money and weapons, and the inevitability that the police were going to show up any minute, if they weren't waiting outside to arrest him already, and John felt confident in concluding that he needed to get the hell out of Frederiksted and regroup.

What he needed was a new plan to take Logan down in a temporary way, then get on with the business of capturing Rory. He dropped his knife and socked Logan hard in the jaw, disorienting him long enough that he was able to push off with his leg and roll them over, pinning Logan to the ground.

"Give it up, Logan. I'm going to best you in every battle. Just like I did when you were so-called training me."

"Freeze!" shouted a voice in the distance.

John raised his attention. Through the broken door, up high on the hill he and Logan had slid down were two of Logan's teammates, racing toward them with their guns trained on John, though he knew they'd never shoot until Logan was out of the way.

"So much for your training," Logan said with a sneer. "You're forgetting about the first and most important rule I taught you—always have backup." Logan spoke in that smooth voice that made John want to punch him again. In fact, that wasn't such a bad idea. He wound back and slugged him in the jaw just for the pleasure of watching his eyes cross in pain.

Logan was right, though. He was about to be outnumbered and outgunned—which meant he was right back in his comfort zone as an underdog. No problem.

He kneed Logan in his family jewels to slow him down, then leaped to his feet and zigzagged through the aisles and into a second room, this one housing enormous vats as tall as a one-story house.

He took a side trip up a set of metal stairs to a catwalk over the vats of fermenting sugarcane to give himself the benefit of a superior position, then squeezed off a handful of rounds at Logan's legs as he took the catwalk stairs three at a time in pursuit.

John got his gun up and took a few more shots at the two black ops commandos bursting into the room. One of the bullets must have hit the fermenting liquid in one of the vats behind Logan because it exploded in a whoosh of flames and energy that knocked John off his feet. His leg lolled over the side, dangling over the bubbling vat below. He let go of his gun and gripped the opposite edge of the metal walk, stopping his momentum before he fell any farther off the edge.

"Are you crazy?" Logan spat. John raised his head to see most of Logan's body dangling off the walk as he pulled himself up using the safety railing. If John weren't so determined to avoid killing Logan, all he would've needed to do was squeeze off a single round to the vat below him and *boom!* Bu-bye, frenemy.

Since he wasn't keen on adding murder to his growing list of crimes, he chose to turn and run. There was no shame in taking the path of least resistance in black ops, not when it avoided further violence. At the top of the catwalk stairs on the opposite side of the building, he squeezed off a couple purposefully wide shots to slow Logan's momentum, then flew down the stairs.

"At this rate you're going to blow us up, along with this entire building," Logan shouted.

Great idea.

He pivoted in place, assessing his options. Logan's teammates had joined him on the catwalk, leaving the aisle wide-open for John to dart back into the barrel room. As predicted, Logan and his men followed. John held his breath against the alcohol fumes, knocking barrels over and shooting holes in others as he ran through the room. Brown liquid splashed down and pooled on the floor.

As soon as he reached the threshold door leading to the gift shop, he turned. Logan and his men were standing a few feet behind the closest spilled rum, their guns out and ready and a trail of rum streaking from the puddle to their feet as though they'd overshot the rum before realizing that John's intention was to set the room on fire.

John ducked behind the metal gift shop counter and took an incendiary grenade out of his bag. He crouched, ready to bolt, then peered around the side. One of the men shot at him, dimpling the metal counter. Nice try.

He held the grenade out so it was visible to Logan and his men, making it real clear that he was about to throw it and they'd best be on their way before it detonated. He shouted, "Fire in the hole!"

"Don't do it, John."

Like he was in the business of taking advice from the people who were trying to kill him. He glanced around the corner of the counter again, zeroed in on a spot right in the middle of the room, pulled the pin and tossed it.

Chapter 6

Logan shouted for his men to run. Goodness knew that's what John was doing. The rum distillery's gift shop door was locked and chained closed, so he unloaded the rest of his magazine onto the glass, then shouldered his way out as the barrel room exploded into a belch of flame and violent energy that threw him to the concrete ground.

With a shake of his head to clear it, he jumped up and sprinted past the front gate of the distillery, his head on a swivel looking for Logan's crew or the cops. Above the ringing in his ears from the roar of flame and explosives emerged the sound of sirens wailing in approach. He pushed himself faster, eyeing a car repair garage two blocks away.

At his first glimpse of a car bumper, he threw himself into a thicket of vines and shrubs on the side of the road. Another look, though, and he realized it was the stolen hatchback, with Alicia at the wheel. He gaped at the car in shock and wonder…and a heaping dose of relief.

She screeched to a stop in the middle of the road. "Get in," she called through the open passenger's window.

She didn't have to ask twice. Before he'd gotten the door closed, the tires squealed as she stomped on the gas pedal. He didn't inhale a full breath until the rum distillery was out of sight and she'd slowed to a respectable speed that wouldn't draw attention.

He couldn't figure out how to ask what he was most curious about without sounding offensive, but he decided to ask her, anyway. "Why did you help me? You could have taken off."

She sent him a sidelong glance and fiddled with the Glock in her lap. "I already told you. I don't want to owe you."

That was amusing. What world did she live in where she thought this one act of reasonableness repaid him for all the crimes she'd accused him of, as well as abandoning him in the middle of the ocean? "And you think we're even now?"

"To my way of thinking."

He glanced over his shoulder to the backseat. At least his bag was there where he'd left it. Even still… "I believe we've proven that your way of thinking isn't getting you very far."

She rubbed her lips together and concentrated on the road, her brows furrowed as if she was contemplating the best retort. With a twitch of her head to get her hair out of her face, she looked at him again, frowning this time. "Touché."

Wow. A concession without a fight? He stemmed the urge to point it out. "Turn right at the next intersection. Time to pay a visit to a friend of mine." And see if his old buddy Eugene had any leads for John regarding Rory. He also figured that The Salty Parrot, Eugene's bar, was a good place to part ways with Alicia because it was off the radar enough that he was reasonably sure she wouldn't be ambushed by the Feds, the military or the police as soon as he left.

"Is that really the best idea? Shouldn't we stay mobile?"

He wasn't sure where the *we* came in, because Alicia had made it crystal clear that when she found Rory, she was going to kill him. Being that Rory getting killed was exactly the opposite of what John needed to have happen, any kind of *we* was out of the question.

"Did you have a lead on Rory before Logan caught up with you?" he asked.

Her gaze scanned the horizon, like talking about Rory might conjure him from the thick foliage carpeting the hills they drove through. "You expect me to trust you now? How do I know you weren't trying to help Rory escape on St. Thomas?"

Really, after he risked his neck to rescue her from Logan, this is what she came back with? "On my honor, Phoenix. I'm not your enemy."

"And here I thought you and Rory had proven your concept of honor was more about honor among thieves."

He almost commanded her to stop the car and get out. This close. Because honor was all John had left and he didn't take it lightly. He also wasn't a huge fan of insinuations that he was a traitor and attempted murderer. He was sensitive like that. "If you're still convinced I'm guilty of helping Rory try to kill you, then why are you in this car with me? Why did you come get me at the rum distillery? Why did you think you owed me in the first place if I'm such a villain?"

Her complexion went pink. "You saved me from McCaffrey. I saved you from McCaffrey. Now we're even. End of story."

End of story was right. As soon as they got to The Salty Parrot, it was time for them to go their separate ways again.

A tense silence settled in the car. Not just because she'd insulted his honor or the hard truth that they were now wanted criminals being pursued by the Feds, but because this was the first time he'd been in close confines with her since the night before Alicia was shot during the RioBank operation that Rory had sabotaged.

He aimed his face toward the open window and tried not to think about her. He tried not to think about that last night together, though he'd replayed it in his head almost daily ever since.

He directed her in a roundabout way past the airport that didn't involve any major thoroughfares, and finally drew a full breath once they'd passed Christiansted and were only a mile or so away from Teague Bay—a favorite mooring location for live-aboard boaters who called the ocean their backyard and spent their lives island hopping as the mood suited them. It was a tight-knit community of which John wasn't a member, but his time in the army had taught him that the number one rule of intel gathering was to make friends with the people who were the eyes and ears of a locale. Such as Eugene.

Knowing that his time alone with Alicia Troy was almost over, and against his better judgment, he turned his head ever so slightly and took a long, careful look at her from his periphery.

Her body was as strong and lithe as ever, her face and hair still the most beautiful he'd ever seen. What had she done with her life since her rehabilitation was complete? What had she given up to seek her revenge—a new boyfriend, a house, a job? All he knew from Logan's updates was that she'd quit ICE when they'd put her on disability and that she was back in Phoenix, where she'd grown up, and living a quiet civilian life there.

Bitterness contorted his mouth. Of course, since all that information had come from Logan it was probably a lie. Suppressing the desire to ask her about her life, he directed her to cruise past the entrance to Eugene's bar.

"The Salty Parrot?" She didn't sound impressed.

"They have excellent rum."

The Salty Parrot, in all its kitschy pirate-themed glory, sat toward the mouth of the bay and looked in the direction of Christiansted. Instead of a door, the bar boasted an automatic garage door exactly like those used in home garages. Eugene said it was the bar's secret weapon to stay standing during hurricanes, which were an unenviable fact of life in the islands. It was fully retracted today, allowing a loud, merry ribbon of ragtime jazz that Eugene listened to when the bar was free of patrons to flow freely over the water.

"How do you know the bar owner won't give us up to the police?"

"I told you, he's a friend of mine. And even if he weren't my friend, there's an unspoken rule in the islands that says he won't. Restaurant and shop owners don't bring heat down on their establishments because it scares away the tourists. And tourists are what keep the flow of cash going in the Caribbean. So, no, Eugene wouldn't tell."

After confirming that the place was quiet, with no authorities lurking nearby, they parked the car in a crowded apartment carport several long blocks away, then crept in alert silence to The Salty Parrot's rear entrance.

Before Alicia could open the bar's back door, John put himself in her path. "Had you met Logan McCaffrey before today?"

A nasty-looking bruise on her left arm in the shape of a handprint caught his eye. Anger boiling inside him all over again at Logan's betrayal and mistreatment of Alicia, he curled his hand into a fist before he could indulge in the urge to touch her.

"No. Never heard of him," she said.

John wasn't surprised. She'd been recruited for the CIA straight out of high school and from there had been recruited to join the ICE black ops unit John and Rory had joined several years later, which had been formed by the Department of Homeland Security after 9/11 to look out for U.S. interests in the global theater. They wanted a black ops team to handle the finesse, under-the-radar jobs. It was a worthy line of work, and John had been honored to be a part of it.

He was a true patriot—he wouldn't have risked his life over and over again for it otherwise—but for him, the military and ICE had been more about brotherhood with his fellow soldiers, with Rory in particular, and then with Ryan, Diego and Alicia. It was why their lack of faith in him had hurt so much.

Alicia was the one and only woman he'd ever worked with who he'd had an intimate relationship with. He wasn't the kind of douchey guy who checked out his female coworkers as if they were sex objects or something low like that. But the first time he and Rory were introduced to Diego, Ryan and Alicia in a tactical planning room at the ICE attaché office in Panama, he couldn't take his eyes off her. He remembered thinking, "Me being on this black ops crew isn't going to work." Because how could he ever concentrate while working with the most beautiful woman he'd ever seen?

It hadn't taken long for him to figure out she was so much more than that. She was a genius. Smarts-wise and tactically, she was one of the most well-rounded operatives he'd ever worked with. She'd made him look forward to getting out of bed each morning. Watching her work, fighting alongside her, making love with her every chance they got had been the two best years of his life.

"You said McCaffrey recruited you?" she asked.

He took a deep breath, swapping the memory of her and how they used to be together for a different set of bitter memories, those of him and Rory as blood brothers. "Yes, Rory and me. We'd just come out of a tough deployment in Afghanistan looking like heroes, setting records with number of kills and towns reclaimed for U.S. control, so we were in the spotlight, which I guess is how we caught Logan's eye.

"Rory and I had to unlearn a lot of army thinking

that differed from black ops, and there were a lot of laws and regulations we hadn't needed to know before. After Logan showed us the ropes, we were assigned a black ops handler and were placed with you, Ryan and Diego."

The story he'd been told at the time was that their crew's last solo sniper had burned out fast and returned to his old job with the FBI, so the idea of a sniper team had appealed to the team's leader, Diego.

"How did you find me with Logan's crew?"

"I saw Rory's boat in the bay. Then I saw you get in the van with Logan." Shaking his head, he brushed the handprint bruise on her arm with his fingertip. "I'd assumed you were working with him. But he hurt you."

She moved her arm away from his touch. "I was the one who engaged him in hand-to-hand combat, and I got plenty of hits in on him. It was an even matchup."

Testy, testy. Whenever she got like that, as if she had to prove her strength and skills were equal to or better than others', his imagination always brought forth an image of what she must have looked like as a blond-pigtailed child, asserting her stubborn independence, determined even back then to do everything on her own.

"Then how did you end up cuffed and at gunpoint?"

"I had the upper hand until the rest of his crew showed up."

He rubbed his chin. "His crew. That was news to me. Logan had never mentioned he was running his own black ops unit."

"We're being hunted by our replacements, of all the warped ironies."

He huffed. "The universe has a wicked sense of humor."

"Tell me about it. Here we are, together—and you're the last person I ever wanted to see again."

"Don't be shy. Tell me how you really feel."

"You should've walked away when Logan gave you the chance. No, let me start over—you should have never interfered in my business in the first place. Now Rory's on the loose and you and I are both wanted criminals."

He turned and faced her. "Is that your way of saying thanks for saving you? Because you suck at it."

"You're such a fool."

Without thinking about it beyond how ticked off she made him when she belittled him like that, he stepped her back up against the wall, caging her between his arms. "Any more names you want to call me today? Why don't you go ahead and get it out of your system."

She met his glare, not breathing, her chin held high like she was a princess and his stable-boy touch defiled her purity. What kind of freak was he that something like that would turn him on? But, oh, man, was he feeling it with her something fierce, just like he always did.

This time, though, his lust and longing for her swirled with angry frustration for what they'd had and lost, for his own out-of-control feelings for her that just wouldn't fade away no matter how hard he'd tried, and for the terrible mess she'd gotten herself into—and him now, too, it seemed.

Damn it, he was pissed off at her and at himself and how they'd let everything they'd had fall apart. If they could only step outside the bounds of time for a moment so he could concentrate on how she felt pressed against him, how beautiful she was and how much he loved holding her in his arms. His gaze dropped to her lips.

She must have noticed his change of focus, because she wrenched her face away. "I have to find Rory." Her voice was distant.

"Why are you doing this to yourself?"

"I can't let him get away with what he did to me."

John's heart sank at the hint of vulnerability in her tone. He hated Rory for what he'd done to her, for the physical and mental pain that must have come from being shot point-blank in the chest by someone you trusted. He had no idea what miracle had spared her life, but the miracle was wasted if she couldn't find a way to truly live again. "He didn't get away with it. He was going to rot in an ultramax prison for the rest of his life. To me, that's worse than death."

"It's not the same."

He wasn't buying it. Revenge was too pat an answer for someone as complicated as she was. "This is about more than getting even for you. I'm now a part of this mess you've created, and I deserve the truth."

She didn't answer, and he knew that silence was all he was going to get for the time being. But he wasn't ready to release her yet.

"Okay, new question. Are you the least bit curious how I got to St. Croix after you left me stranded in the Caribbean? Weren't you even a little worried for my safety, out there in the open ocean without even a piece of driftwood to hang on to?"

She rolled her big green eyes over to look at him. They were the most beautiful eyes he'd ever seen, so sophisticated, so cool and collected that he struggled against the desire to kiss the composure right off of her face.

"You're a big boy. You can take care of yourself."

That he could, even if he was getting damn tired of her minimizing him. A boy, a fool, a sidekick, never the alpha. She talked a tough game, but branded on his soul was the sound of her whimpering his name— *whimpering,* damn it—begging for the pleasure that only he could give her, murmuring praise about just how much of a man he was.

He curled his hand around her hip.

"Don't touch me." Her eyes were pure ice as she stared vacantly over his shoulder, her tone flat and clinical in a way that made his jaw tight with aggravation. But he was a *no means no* kind of man and let go of her immediately.

He pressed his knuckles against the wall next to her arm. "There was a time you couldn't get enough of me touching you."

She flicked a glance at him. So impertinent. "Right up until you helped Rory try to kill me."

It took every ounce of his self-control not to cup her chin and urge her to look him in the eye. "No. Never."

"How do I know? Rory said—"

"I know what Rory said. I read it in the deposition transcripts. You would believe him—" he screwed up his mouth, hating that she had the power to make him so infuriated "—over me. After everything we were together."

"What were we really to each other besides a little stress relief?"

He threw his head back and chuckled. "Right. Stress relief. Of course. Because our relationship has been so stress-reducing. That's why I fell in love with you. Because it helped me reduce the stress of the job. Sure, let's go with that."

She drew a ragged breath. Then he saw it—passion in her eyes. It was a look of the same torment that was tearing him up inside, but anything was better than the chilly distance she fell back on to keep people at arm's length. Along with the heat in her gaze, life had returned to her skin in the form of pinked cheeks and a slight sheen of perspiration. No longer the refined femme fatale with flawless looks and nary a hair out of place, but a real woman. His woman.

He touched her cheek, fully expecting her to demand he remove his hand.

But she didn't. Instead, her eyes drifted closed on another tremulous breath. "I hate you."

"I know."

He cradled her cheek in his palm. Pulse pounding, he ignored all the reasons he shouldn't be doing what he was about to, then leaned down and pressed a kiss to her closed mouth.

She didn't open her mouth or kiss him back, but she didn't protest it, either. Stepping another foot over the line in the sand she'd drawn, he touched her hip again. This time, in response, she settled a hand on his neck. Keeping his eyes closed and his lips pressed lightly against hers, he pulled her up against his body and let his hands explore her, coaxing her stiff joints and muscles to relax, to give up the fight and let him into her soul.

This was how it always started, with the feeling that he was standing naked and vulnerable before a locked, heavy door, banging on it with his fist, demanding entrance. And her with the power to either grant or deny him. Such a princess…

When knocking on the door to her soul wasn't enough, he decided to kick it in—destroy the whole damn door to get to her, his Phoenix. He slipped his fingers under her shirt and splayed his open hands over her sides and ribs, the power and strength of her swathed in soft, feminine skin. With a sharp inhale that parted her lips, she finally gave up her defenses and yielded to him.

He took her mouth with the hunger of a man who had something to prove—to himself, to her. Hunger for what they'd lost, the love, the endless wicked nights that would forever live on as the best of his life. Her hands plunged into his hair, holding him close, kissing him back, letting him take as much as he wanted.

When the fire in his veins threatened to consume the last of his dignity, he pulled away, breathing hard. "The next time you want to make a dig about me being a boy or a sidekick or whatever name you're tempted to lob at me, you remember this—there isn't another man in the world who knows you like I do, who makes you feel the way I do. Don't you ever forget that."

"As if I could," she whispered.

Wiping a hand over his mouth, he took a few swift steps back. It wouldn't do, being that close to her, even if it got him the confession he wanted. The bitter hurt was too much to bear.

She stayed rooted against the wall, but followed him with her gaze. "What are we going to do now?"

There was that *we* again.

"*We* aren't going to do anything." He pushed the back door of the bar open, but turned in the doorway to level a hard gaze at her. "I'm going to check in with Eugene and you're getting back in that car and leaving."

"You're going to leave without me?" It wasn't said with panic or fear, but something else he had trouble putting his finger on. Incredulity, perhaps. As though he'd be an idiot for striking out without her.

"You're a big girl. You can take care of yourself." God, he hoped he was right. He'd hate himself if she got taken into custody all over again. He released the door to swing closed behind him and followed the sound of ragtime jazz toward the main room of the bar, but over the music he heard the smack of Alicia's hand moving to hold the door open.

"Wherever you're going to look for Rory, I'm coming with you."

Halfway down the hall lined with closed doors labeled as restrooms, the kitchen and supply closets, he stopped short. What game was she playing now? "No, you're not. I think you'd better go back to concentrating on keeping yourself safe because the next time Logan and his crew catch up with you, they'll be better prepared and I won't be there to save you."

She'd probably rather throw herself off a cliff than take his advice or be reminded that he'd saved her hide, but he had to try to help her see the dire situation she'd created for herself. "When Logan's crew catches you, you'll go to prison for a long, long time, if they don't shoot you outright. Disappear until everything blows over. I'll handle Rory."

She took a stilted step toward him, then stopped, her fists tight. "How dare you tell me what to do?" Her nostrils flared, probably with the effort it took for her not to slap him.

The jazz in the main room clicked off abruptly. Sporting a toothy grin, Eugene appeared at the entrance to the hall. "Hey, it's John the Glove. That's the best surprise I've had all day. Why are you lurking in my hallway? Where you been hiding?"

After his world fell apart, John had thrown himself exactly one pity party. It just so happened to have been at the very establishment in which he now stood and had involved a stunning number of rum bottles, a mess of locals and live-aboard boaters and Eugene's massive collection of Michael Jackson albums, which happened to have been John's favorite musical artist in his previous life as a somebody.

John didn't remember much about that night, but the story he'd heard was that sometime around one in the morning, John had dressed up in the coconut bikini top worn by the giant wooden parrot on the patio, a pirate hat and a black glove someone had rustled up, then executed a passable rendition of Michael Jackson's "Bad" routine. That sounded exactly like something John would've done in his heyday, back before music and dancing lost their appeal.

"I've been making the rounds to the islands, killing time."

"You still rockin'?"

"Not so much anymore."

Eugene waved them into the main room of the bar, then poured rum into three lowball glasses. "Man, that's too bad. You ought to come back here sometime and entertain my customers. You were on fire that night."

"So they tell me."

He held out two of the glasses to John and Alicia. "Are you going to introduce me to your friend?"

"No. She was just leaving."

Alcohol was another of life's pleasures that had lost appeal for John, but part of cultivating an informant relationship with bartenders meant drinking, and overpaying for their liquor. He fished a hundred-dollar bill from his bag and set it on the counter. "I hope this is the good stuff."

"For you, always. You tell me when you're ready to borrow Cheeky's ensemble again." He nodded toward the wooden parrot.

John thought about waiting for Alicia to leave before questioning Eugene, but he had a feeling she wasn't budging. "I need some information."

What made Eugene such an ideal friend and informant was the enormous number of family members he had throughout St. Croix and the other Virgin Islands. John had only made use of Eugene's connections once, when he'd heard a rumor that an ICE bigwig had arrived on St. Croix—it turned out he'd been there on vacation, not looking for John, as he'd feared.

"I already figured that because you're back to looking like your soldier self. Did you finally decide to rejoin the living?"

He almost said no, but that wasn't true. He'd made the subconscious decision to rejoin the living the moment he'd decided to pursue Rory so he could clear his name. Funny how life could change at the drop of a hat like that. He sipped the rum and was surprised anew by the rush of enjoyment it brought him. He'd thought his ability for pleasure had been dimmed beyond repair. "I did. And now I'm looking for a man. An escaped convict."

Eugene offered him a smile of dismay. "You and every U.S. authority in the Caribbean."

John glanced at Alicia. She cradled the glass of rum in both hands but had made no move to drink it, riveted as she seemed to be by their conversation. "True, but how many of them have come to talk to you?"

That insight earned him a laugh as Eugene poured himself a shot of less expensive rum. "Not one of them thought to see what some old bar owner knew until you showed up."

"Then they're all idiots."

Eugene held his glass up. "I'll drink to that."

John took another sip of rum. Dang, that was good stuff. What else had he convinced himself he'd lost his taste for? He lifted the rum to his lips again, but realized as he tipped his head back that he was already starting to feel its effects and set it back on the counter without taking a drink. It was one thing to reacquaint himself with the glories of rum and another to get tipsy in the middle of a manhunt. He'd done that on a mission once, in Egypt. Not pretty.

Eugene downed his rum in one swallow, then set the empty glass on the counter. "I may not know much about who you were before you came here or what your job was, because even when you were drunk you didn't say nothin' about nothin', but my gut's telling me that you stand a better chance than the police of getting this man before he hurts someone or messes up my island. What do you want to know?"

"This man, Rory, he was my sniper partner until he screwed me and a bunch of people over. He arrived via speedboat on St. Croix a couple hours ago. I need to know if he's still here and how he might get off the island undetected."

Eugene rubbed his chin. "I think I know who to call about this, but it's going to cost you." A smile broke out on his face.

John knew from the spark in Eugene's eyes what was coming next, but he was grateful enough for the information to wait for the punch line. Standing next to him, Alicia pinched her brows in confusion.

"You owe me a Michael Jackson encore."

Yup. "Couldn't I just buy a bottle of that rum?"

"Naw, man, you can't bribe me. I've got standards."

"Michael Jackson standards?"

"You owe me one."

Busting out with a song and dance number in front of Alicia might make John feel as if he were dying, but technically it wouldn't kill him. "Fine. It's a deal—but this time I'm not wearing the bird's bikini."

Eugene's rumbling laugh cut short at the sight of a car pulling up out front.

John drew his gun. Alicia did the same. Without a word, they exchanged a look with Eugene, who was already sliding their glasses of rum out of view into a sink full of dishwater, then sprinted back through the hall. These might be bar customers, but then again, they might be U.S. authorities, and John and Alicia were in no position to take chances. Going back out through the alley door they entered from wasn't an option because any law enforcement agency worth their salt would station an officer out back when conducting a search to prevent the quarry from ducking out the rear exit.

Instead, John put his hand on the first doorknob he came to, the women's restroom, as the sound of multiple male voices grew louder.

"Welcome to The Salty Parrot," Eugene said in a booming voice. "How about some rum on this fine afternoon?"

"No rum today, thanks," one of the men said. "We're searching for two men and a woman. Americans. Armed and extremely dangerous."

With a quick prayer that the hinges didn't squeak, John yanked the door open, took Alicia by the arm and pulled her into the darkness.

Chapter 7

In the women's restroom, John held the door ajar so he and Alicia, huddled near the opening, could listen in on Eugene's conversation with the officers.

"What did these Americans do to bring you all the way out to St. Croix?" Eugene said.

"One of them is an escaped convict and the other two are his accomplices."

The man's accent sounded American, as well. Definitely not Logan, but it could have been a member of his crew or someone from any one of the other U.S. agencies or branches of the military gunning for Alicia, John and Rory. Whoever they were, they had an oddly warped version of reality. Alicia and John as Rory's accomplices? Okay...

"As you can see, they're not here," Eugene said, cool as a cucumber.

"Sir, there are three armed and dangerous criminals loose on this island. They destroyed the rum distillery in Frederiksted and one of them shot and killed a health clinic nurse in Christiansted. We think one of them must be injured because many of the clinic's first-aid supplies were raided."

John heard Alicia's breath catch and knew she hated that the man she'd set free had committed murder of a civilian within hours of his escape. John hated it, too. If he'd taken the kill shot on St. Thomas or on the boat when he'd had the chance instead of trying to keep Rory alive so he could interrogate him, then that nurse would be alive still. Rory was a desperate man and was clearly willing to take desperate measures, including murder, to ensure his freedom. Just like that, finding Rory took on a whole new level of urgency.

"Witnesses have reported to the local police that they saw the suspects' silver, two-door car circling Teague Bay. We're running a thorough check of the entire area. Any information you can share with us will help us get these three off the streets before they kill again," the officer added.

"I haven't seen anything out of the ordinary, but if I do, I'll call the police right away."

"Thank you for your cooperation. If you don't mind, we'll take a peek out back."

Footsteps sounded in approach.

John eased the door closed. He didn't release the breath he'd been holding until he'd locked it. He sensed Alicia next to him, flattening herself against the wall near the door's hinges.

Smart plan. If the unexpected visitors got curious about the locked door and convinced Eugene to unlock it, their best position would be behind the door as it opened. He took position next to her and withdrew his gun, accidentally brushing her shoulder with his arm before she shifted away from the touch.

The only light came from the sliver of space beneath the door. John looked past Alicia's legs and outstretched gun, his eyes on the light as shadows cut through it with the rhythm of feet walking. The door was heavy, the walls thick. Eugene and the men weren't talking, so the only sound John could hear besides the beat of his pulse was Alicia's shallow, steady breathing.

There was no time to contemplate how surreal the moment was, being alone with Alicia in the dark, them working as a team. Like old times. He cut off the thought. Forcing himself not to catch her scent on the air or think any more about the heat and tension rolling off her body, he returned his full focus to the door.

The shadows passed again on the other side of the door. Still, he and Alicia waited. It felt as if they stood there in the dark forever, breathing, not touching, their fingers near the triggers of their guns.

After several long minutes, John allowed himself to tilt his face toward Alicia and breathe in. She didn't smell like anything except the battle they'd both waged that day—dirt, sweat and gunpowder residue. The scent unsettled him and made him aware of a painful kind of emptiness in his heart. Loneliness. It was the only way he could describe the sensation.

The two of them had been in all kinds of combat and training situations together in which they'd both emerged smelling of gunpowder, dirt and adrenaline. If anything, the scent made Alicia more beautiful. It spoke of strength and grit, of a woman who didn't hold back from being powerful or getting dirty. It was perfect for Alicia because in everything she did, she went all in, every time.

He inhaled again, this time willing the hurt to wash through him rather than sink in him like a heavy stone. At least he didn't feel numb anymore, as he had in Frederiksted a year ago. Even loneliness and hurt was better than that.

After a couple minutes of silence, one set of shadows stopped in front of the restroom. The doorknob rattled as though being unlocked. John and Alicia both raised their guns, ready to strike.

The door opened a foot or so, then the light flipped on. Moving in synchronization, John and Alicia stepped out from the wall and adjusted their aim to the head coming into view.

As soon as John registered it was Eugene, he lowered his weapon. Alicia didn't.

Eugene startled at the sight of their guns. "Relax, relax. They're gone."

Alicia wasn't buying it. "How do we know you're telling the truth?"

Eugene grinned at John. The opening notes of Michael Jackson's "Bad" drifted through the air. "John the Glove, I think it's time you introduced me to this lovely, yet lethal woman you've brought to my establishment. And then, you dance. I'm ready to see your moonwalk."

Alicia's gun lowered and her expression lightened as she studied Eugene. "But Michael Jackson doesn't do the moonwalk in his 'Bad' routine."

As always, John was impressed by Alicia's knowledge of random factoids and statistics. She'd been a kick-ass partner in Trivial Pursuit.

"I used to add it in. Crowd-pleaser." He shifted his attention to the hall. "But I don't dance anymore."

He felt vulnerable having said that, letting her in on how fundamentally he'd allowed her and ICE's accusations to change him. Squeezing past Eugene, he walked into the main part of the bar, giving himself space to think, away from Alicia's scent and warmth and skin.

Eugene followed, looking concerned. Behind him walked Alicia.

Eugene eyed her, considering. "I take it you're another ghost from John's past?"

"More like a business associate," Alicia said.

John failed to suppress a snort of surprise. Eugene's brows flickered, letting it be known that he saw the lie for what it was, too. "On with the introductions, then. Alicia, this is my friend Eugene. Eugene, meet the woman who ripped my heart out and crushed it beneath her stiletto boot."

She dropped the hand she'd extended in greeting to Eugene and glared at John. "That's how you're introducing me?"

"Just calling it like it is."

Eugene's broad smile showed off his straight, white teeth. "She's the reason you came to the islands that first time."

"More or less."

She raised a brow and leveled a searing glare at John, impertinence painted on her beautiful face. "That's one hell of a story you're telling yourself, because that's not what happened."

John couldn't think of a single thing to say that

didn't rehash the same argument they'd had in the alley out back. He walked to the front of the bar and scanned the bay and parking lot for any sign of the law enforcement officers.

"Well, heartbreaker, it's nice to meet you. Are you hunting that criminal, too?"

"My name's Alicia. And yes, John and I are going to hunt him together."

So they were back to that, were they? "Eugene, give us a minute, would you?"

Eugene nodded toward the front door. "I could use a smoke, anyway."

As soon as Eugene disappeared around the corner on the front patio, Alicia angled her body into John's line of sight. "I meant what I said before. I'm coming with you."

"And I meant what I said. There's no way that's going to happen, so feel free to stop begging."

Predictably, her lips flattened into a straight line at the word *begging*. She might know all of his buttons to push, but he knew hers, too, and it was high time he put her on the defensive for a change. He made to turn his back on her, but she grabbed his sleeve.

"You're not thinking about this right," she said. "We stand a better chance of hunting Rory down together than we do apart."

He bristled. So that was her angle. Alicia might be one of the most tech-savvy operatives in the world, but John had a few tricks up his sleeve, too, the most critical being that he knew these islands like they were his motherland—every cove and quirk, local customs and criminal elements. He had no doubt he'd find Rory first, because street smarts went a whole lot further in the islands than technological know-how—and apparently Alicia realized that, too.

"You want to use me to get to Rory so you can guarantee a kill shot."

"Yes," she said without hesitation. "But you'd be using me, too. Like how we used each other for—"

It was absolute BS that she was going there again. "You say *stress relief* one more time and I'm out of here. There's nothing sayin' I have to stand here and listen to your lies."

She bit her lower lip. "Rory deserves to die for what he did to me. And what he did to that nurse," she added quietly.

"I know. I get it. You deserve revenge and he deserves to die. He absolutely does, after what he did to you. But you two aren't the only ones who deserve something. I deserve a chance to clear my name."

She released a hard peal of laughter. "You think Rory's going to help you with that?"

The chance was iffy at best, but he had to try. And how dare she look down that princess nose of hers at his plan. He flexed his pecs, then cracked his neck to the side and allowed his gaze to settle on her lips a fraction longer than would be polite. "Phoenix, you of all people should know that I can be very persuasive."

A flicker of awareness crossed her features before she put her game face back on. "ICE is looking for us, along with probably every other federal agency and branch of the military. I can hack into their systems and throw them off track. I can create a false digital trail for us, rearrange ferry and flight schedules, tap into local police radios—more than you can imagine."

Oh, he could imagine it, all right, because her claim

was far from an empty brag. He'd seen firsthand just how mind-blowing her computer skills were. "If you've got it all figured out, then why do you want my help?"

"*Help* is such an unpleasant word." He was pleased she felt that way because he'd chosen the term on purpose. "I think we should work together on this hunt because you have one skill that I don't."

"Only one?"

She ignored the loaded remark. "You know these islands better than I do, and you know Rory better than anyone. If we work alone, we probably wouldn't be able to outsmart the authorities and find Rory before he does any more damage."

John could. Piece of cake. Except he couldn't get it out of his head that ICE or the military would catch up with Alicia again. And next time, he wouldn't be there to back her up. It was a threat that would not only dog her while she tracked Rory, but for the rest of her life. She was now a marked woman, a dangerous criminal in the eyes of the law. The thought turned his stomach. "And after you kill him? What then?"

"What do you mean?"

"Your life, Alicia. What are you going to do? You're a criminal on the run now. What's your plan?"

"None of your concern."

She was right; what she did wasn't his concern. Except that now, after that kiss and the accompanying rush of old feelings that came with breaking down her emotional door, and after ruminating on the potentially life-threatening consequences of the terrible situation she'd put herself in, he found that it very much was. Damn it all.

Determination hardened her features. "You and I

will work together to get Rory. And when we do, you take what you want from him, then get out of my way so I can kill him."

It struck him then how it would feel if Alicia witnessed Rory's admittance of the lies he'd told about John's guilt—what it would feel like to be exonerated in front of the person whose opinion had mattered most to John once upon a time. He couldn't resist the fantasy that he might glimpse regret in her eyes, that she might want him again.

No. Not that. He didn't want her anymore. Or rather, he didn't want to want her. He'd allow himself the rest of the dream, along with the peace of mind that came with being able to protect her again, if it came to it, but there was no such thing as forever between them. There was no *we* anymore.

"All right. You've got yourself a deal." He thrust out his hand for her to shake, feeling instantly ludicrous with the gesture. "We'll be business associates," he added with a sarcastic grimace.

She gave a sharp nod. "Yes. Business associates."

When she shook his hand, he couldn't help but feel that they'd both just jumped down a rabbit hole from which there was no return.

The kiss made her do it. Alicia had never claimed kissing as a defensive argument before, but there was no getting around it today.

Sure, John had skills that she didn't, skills that complemented her own. And true, they'd find Rory faster by working together, which was of the utmost importance because they'd released a volatile, violent criminal into the world—yes, *they,* because she would have killed Rory if John hadn't interfered—and they had a duty to neutralize him before he caused any more harm. But though her guilt over the clinic nurse's death would haunt her for the rest of her life, that hadn't been the only reason she'd pushed for an alliance with John.

It was that kiss.

She hadn't been kissed like that since the last time John kissed her.

Okay, she hadn't been kissed at all since the last time John kissed her, so maybe that had something to do with the toe-curling bliss of his lips working their magic on hers and his huge, solid body making her feel delicate and small and oh-so-desirable. But that didn't change the fact that it had happened, and though she'd fought the feeling at first, deep down she'd wanted it to happen.

No man got under her skin like John. None before him, and she knew for certain there'd be none after him that could melt her defenses so thoroughly and exquisitely. John had been right when he'd said that no other man made her feel like he did. That should have been one more reason to hate him, not invite him to be her business partner, but it was a little late now to figure that out.

She was shaking his hand, still marveling at the weirdness of them being business associates and temporary partners, when boots thumped over the wooden front patio at a speed that told them someone was running their way.

John tensed. He made to grab Alicia's arm, but she was already ducking for cover behind the bar. He scrambled after her.

"John, Alicia, where are you?" Eugene's voice was

breathless. "I have a lead for you on your criminal, but you don't have any time to waste."

They emerged from behind the bar, holstering their guns.

"You were only outside for a few minutes. What could've happened?" John asked.

"My friend Harry was driving by, going way too fast. I flagged him down to see what was wrong, and he said someone called him because they saw one of his floatplanes take off. Someone stole it. So I thought, could it be this criminal John is looking for? Can this Rory man fly a plane?"

Alicia wasn't sure if this was good news or bad news because it meant that Rory had slipped off the island for points unknown.

"Not sure if he's ever flown a floatplane, but yes. He has his pilot's license," John said. "Thanks for this tip. I think you're right about Rory stealing your friend Harry's plane. The question is, did any of the law enforcement officials on the island notice?"

"I don't know about that. Harry said his wife's on him about calling the police, but he said he's going to go after the plane himself."

Alicia leaned in and set a hand on Eugene's arm as an idea occurred to her. "You said one of his seaplanes. He has more than one?"

"He owns an aerial tour company. He has three planes. Two now, I guess."

John rubbed his palms together. He must be considering the same idea Alicia was. Showtime. She hadn't been aware that Rory had his pilot's license, but he and Diego hadn't been the only two members of their crew with that skill. Alicia held that honor, too.

She didn't fly all that often anymore, but she'd piloted a floatplane and was willing to take the chance of tracking Rory in the air. What other option did she have?

"Where are we going to find your friend Harry?" she asked. "And how much do you think it'd cost to rent one of his other planes for the rest of the week?"

"Harry's business is called Flights of Fancy. It's across the bay, about a mile or so east. I told Harry that wherever he follows that stolen plane, he's going to be there a while because the weather's turning. Hannah's on her way."

"That's right. Hurricane Hannah," John said. Hands on hips, he cursed under his breath and walked to the window. "With all that's happened, I forgot about that."

Alicia hadn't, though she never expected to still be in the islands when it hit. She'd chosen today to break Rory out of prison specifically because of the hurricane's imminent arrival. Her idea had been for the hurricane to wash away her trail, help conceal the location of Rory's body and delay the military and Feds' search for him.

Her initial assessment had been correct, for all the good it was going to do her—Hurricane Hannah would definitely delay the search for Rory.

"I told Harry it's too risky to go flying into a storm to follow an armed and dangerous criminal, but he is determined to do this. Maybe you can convince him to let you two track the plane instead."

"We'll give it our best shot," Alicia said. Hope bloomed inside her. If they could convince Harry not to alert the police, and if they could convince him to rent them a plane, she might just have a chance at getting the vengeance she needed to close the book on the most painful chapter of her life.

John dropped his bag on one of the small, round tables dotting the room. He rummaged around, moving aside a gun or two, and withdrew a stack of cash. Hundred-dollar bills by the looks of it. He held it out to Eugene. "For not giving us up to those Feds and for the rum. And because good bartenders are hard to come by."

Eugene pocketed the cash without glancing directly at it. "Thanks for that. Stay safe, John the Glove. Watch out for the weather—and don't forget you still owe me that moonwalk. The money doesn't get you out of that obligation."

The men exchanged side hugs and back slaps. "You know I'm good for it."

Alicia offered Eugene a smile. "Sorry I kept you on the business end of my Glock for so long."

He waved off the apology and offered his hand to shake. "Not the first time. Probably won't be the last."

She took his hand, then leaned close and kissed his cheek. "Thanks for the lead."

John was already in front of the bar, scoping out the bay. Alicia adjusted her computer bag and followed, her mind reviewing the procedure to get a floatplane into the air.

"Hey." It was Eugene again. She turned just inside the threshold of the patio. "You take care of him."

It was an odd thing to say. Of course she was going to take care of Rory. That's what all this was about. Failure was not an option. "We'll take care of him as fast as we can. Hopefully before he does any more damage."

"Not Rory. John. He's a good man and I don't want to see him get hurt again. It wasn't pretty last time."

In the months after John had reached out to her, she often wondered, on nights she couldn't sleep, where he'd gone and what he was doing. If he was as tormented by the past as she was or if he'd moved on, carelessly, callously. No one told her and she was too stubborn to ask or research him online. Knowing now that he'd suffered didn't bring her nearly the comfort she'd once imagined it would.

"I'm not playing him. And, despite how he introduced me, I didn't break his heart." *He broke mine.* "I guess he never mentioned that he tried to kill me."

The words rang hollow. When had her conviction about his guilt wavered? She still believed it, didn't she? *Did you ever really?* a little voice inside her asked.

Eugene didn't flinch at the incendiary declaration. He folded his hands across his chest and leaned back against the bar. "John said a lot of things about you the first time he was in this bar. Not one of them led me to believe he had designs on killing you."

What did he say? She was too proud to ask, not that she had the time to stand around gabbing. John was probably already halfway around the bay. "I've got to go. Thank you for everything."

Without waiting to find out if Eugene had some final retort or piece of advice, she jogged down the front stairs and onto the single-lane road that ran along the bay.

The air crackled with volatility, like an electric charge was swirling all around her. Ever darkening clouds rolled nearer to the island, pushed along by the wind that had kicked up in the span of time since they'd been in The Salty Parrot. Alicia hadn't had the pleasure of living through a hurricane, but to her untrained eye, it didn't look two days away, as the original forecast had predicted. The first chance they got, they needed to find a weather update.

John was several blocks ahead of her, not running, per se, but not exactly waiting for her, either. In a way, she appreciated the space to catch her breath, replay her conversation with Eugene and look her fill at John.

He afforded her a brief sidelong glance, then kept going. His long legs strode with purpose and his eyes scanned his surroundings. Muscles and bones, mind and limbs and torso, his whole body, all worked in total harmony—like a highly evolved predator, which he most certainly was. Twice now, she'd witnessed him in action today. Both times, he'd taken her breath away in awe of his technique and power. She'd always thought him an exceptional soldier, but now his skills were extraordinary. It was as though he'd done nothing but train for this mission for the past year and a half.

Maybe he had. Maybe there was more to his motive than she'd considered. Point of argument: he'd found her and Rory on St. Thomas almost instantly. How had he known?

Her steps faltered. Okay, yeah, that was a huge question that somehow hadn't occurred to her before. But now that she had the time to chew it over, how *had* he found her so fast on St. Thomas?

She quickened her step but realized almost immediately that given his fast pace, she wasn't going to catch up with him unless she ran. So she did, bridging the distance between them just as an old plastic sign reading Flights of Fancy came into view up ahead.

"Hey," she called.

He looked her way, his expression one of uncompromising focus. "There are still two planes in the water, which means Harry hasn't left to chase after Rory yet. I don't see any police cruisers out front of his shop, either. We might have a legitimate shot at this."

"How did you find me so fast on St. Thomas?"

He blinked, processing. His steps slowed. "What?"

"This morning on St. Thomas. How did you get there so fast? How did you know where I was? Because now that I'm thinking about it, it can't be a coincidence."

"We don't have time for this." His stride lengthened again.

He was right, but a familiar and unwanted vulnerability had crept into her consciousness, and she couldn't see taking one more step on their quest without pulverizing it and recapturing her sense of control. After the shock that Logan's team had been tracking her every move, she had to know what John's angle was. "I say we do."

He let out a hard chuckle. "We already shook on this partnership. Isn't it a little late to be second-guessing my motives?"

"I'm clear about your motives. It's your methods I'm questioning."

John scowled but was prevented from answering by the sound of a door banging open.

A short, thick man with a bushy orange-and-gray beard stepped down the front steps of Flights of Fancy. He carried a double-barreled shotgun, the kind best used for hunting birds and small game, and wore an absolutely livid expression on his face as he strode toward the dock where two floatplanes were moored.

John sprang into motion. "Harry? I'm a friend of Eugene's. I think he mentioned me to you. Can we have a word?"

The request was met with a grunt as Harry unlocked the metal gate barring access to the dock. When the lock clicked, he opened it with his shoulder, sending a withering look to John. "You tell Eugene to mind his own business. He can't stop me from going after my own property."

John reached into his pocket and withdrew his HK45, pointing it at the ground, his finger nowhere near the trigger. The gun got Harry's attention fast.

"He told us someone stole your plane," John said. "He sent us over here because we can help you get it back. My name's John and this is Alicia."

Harry's attention shifted to Alicia, so she followed John's lead and withdrew her own gun in a show of affinity. "You want the plane. We want the man piloting it." She caressed the side of the Glock and offered Harry a confident smile. "I'd say we're a match made in heaven."

He squared up to them at the top of the ramp leading down to the dock. "You have thirty seconds."

John swung his bag forward and rummaged inside. "Good enough. The fugitive who stole your plane is armed and dangerous. You shouldn't go after him alone. My colleague and I are trained in combat to handle men like him. We can help you get your plane back, and if that's not enough incentive..." He pulled out another stack of cash, making Alicia wonder anew exactly how much money he was carrying around. "Maybe this will make it worth your time."

He held the stack out to Harry, who shifted his rifle to his left hand and wrapped his fingers around the money.

"I didn't know U.S. soldiers carried around cash bribes." He didn't sound suspicious, more like impressed.

John smiled his old smile, the happy-go-lucky one he used to wear when he listened to music or told a good story about his days in the army. The one that showcased his straight white teeth and masculine chin. The one that took Alicia's breath away. "We're not your average U.S. soldiers."

Speaking of twisting the truth... At least Harry seemed to be considering their offer now, if the way he was lovingly running his thumb over the edges of the crisp one-hundred-dollar bills in his hand was any indication.

"Have you called the police yet?" Alicia asked.

Harry tsked. "By the time the police get their act in gear, my plane could be halfway to South America. And if, miracles of miracles, the police did recover it and claim it as evidence, I might never see it again. No, thank you."

"How are you planning to track the plane?"

"Your thirty seconds are up. It's time to fly." He turned and plodded down the ramp with wide, swift steps. Alicia and John exchanged a look, then followed. Harry glanced at them over his shoulder. "This isn't my first stolen plane. There are a lot of punks who think it'd be fun to go for a joyride. Most of them have no idea how dangerous landing a seaplane is. The last one, I had to fish it out of a reef off Buck Island. After that, I fitted all my planes with GPS locators and added a video camera to my dock." He gestured to a wooden birdhouse sitting on the shingled roof of his business office.

GPS tracking and video confirmation that Rory was the plane thief? Jackpot. As if reading her mind, John said, "Mind if we take a look at that tape?"

Harry pocketed the cash and waved his smartphone at them. "You can do that in the air."

Chapter 8

No doubt about it, the plane thief was Rory.

After John had watched his fill of the security video, he'd passed the phone to Alicia with a simple, "It's him."

Alicia hadn't even known Rory had the skills to pilot a plane. But from what she could tell on the tiny screen of Harry's smartphone by the way Rory ran a quick visual inspection of the Otter floatplane, then ferried it to open water and out of the camera's view, he knew his way around a plane just fine.

She watched the footage three times, stewing over the mess that had become of her operation, then walked the phone up to the cockpit and dropped it in the empty copilot chair. One thing was certain—it was time to stop kicking herself for not pulling the trigger on Rory when she'd had the chance. Instead, she needed to concentrate all her energy on righting her mistake.

The plane they were presently riding in was the largest floatplane she'd been on, with six passenger seats broken into three rows, each seat hugging a window to maximize the view. Alicia knew from experience that the area they were flying over boasted a magnificent view of the great arcing chain of lush, green Caribbean islands sitting like jewels in a vibrant blue sea. Today, though, the view was only of storm clouds and rain, with the teeth-rattling turbulence to match.

Given the deteriorating weather, she'd expected Rory to puddle jump to the next closest island. Maybe Virgin Gorda or St. Kitts, but instead, he pointed the stolen plane southwest. According to what they could see on the GPS receptor, he was hugging the Antilles, never deviating into open ocean. Maybe he didn't know where to land and was hoping to find a cove that suited him, or maybe the plane didn't have much gas. Whatever his thinking, Rory didn't seem to be landing anytime soon.

For the most part, Harry, John and Alicia sat in silence. Harry, with his hands and mind busy piloting the plane, and John and Alicia at a loss for what to do or say and busy keeping themselves from bouncing around too hard from the turbulence. They sat on opposite sides of the aisle, John in the row behind her.

Whether it was her imagination or real, she felt his eyes on the back of her neck, assessing her every move and sound, and the way she looked. She was too stubborn to turn around and confirm the hunch.

"You were right."

John's voice was low, as though he didn't want Harry privy to his words. Her heart started pounding at the sound of his voice and she knew it was going to take some time to adjust to the reality that he was a real live person, close enough that she could reach out and touch him, that she could hear his voice and know with absolute confidence that it wasn't just another dream. She turned her head in his direction, not enough to see him, but for him to know she was listening.

What was he doing? Was this a confession? An apology? "Right about what?"

His clothes rustled softly as he moved into her line of sight and sat sideways in the chair across the aisle from her. Still, she kept her eyes on the faded blue carpet next to his boot.

After a long pause during which the pressing weight of his steady gaze on her became almost too much to bear, he said, "You wanted to know how I found you and Rory this morning."

Oh. She tried to think back to what she would have been right about, but couldn't get past the thumping of her heart or the sight of his hands in her periphery, sitting loosely on his thighs.

"You were hunting me?"

His hands shifted, his fingers weaving together between his knees. "Not hunting, but I was keeping tabs on you. I had an agreement with Logan that he'd update me whenever there was a new development involving you—when you moved, when you quit ICE, that sort of thing. Who knows now how much of it was lies, but he was telling me the truth this morning when he emailed me that Rory had escaped and you were missing."

She wasn't sure how she felt about that or if she even dared ask him why he'd done it. "I set everything up specifically so I wouldn't appear to be missing. I had what I thought was an airtight alibi, but I underestimated how closely ICE was tracking me." She lifted her focus from his hands and feet to his face and challenged his granite stare. "Or you."

Some emotion flared behind his eyes, but he shuttered it almost instantly. "Logan never let on to me that he had it out for you or that he thought you were dangerous. Not ever."

That was a consolation, if John was telling the truth, which her gut said he was. "Yet he told you where I'd be this morning?"

"No. That was all me. Though there was a measure of luck involved."

"I don't see how luck could be involved. You found me even before Logan did. How?"

"Up until this morning, I was living on Jost Van Dyke Island, just north of St. Thomas. Given the timing and all the various options Rory had to get off Puerto Rico, the ferry to St. Thomas seemed like a good bet. Since it was close, I decided to start my search there. I saw you get out of a car and walk down the beach."

The faintest of chills washed through her. He'd been watching her for more than an hour. "Why didn't you show yourself sooner?"

There it was again. That flicker of some volatile emotion playing just behind his eyes. "Seeing you was…" He swallowed, his eyes narrowing. "I decided it was a cleaner, more manageable plan to stay out of sight and bide my time. Unlike Logan, I wasn't after you. I was after Rory."

She wrenched her face to the window and stared at

the gray beyond the plane's wing. She'd spent twenty months visualizing John's betrayal. Every sleepless night, she reconstructed the events leading up to that day, to that moment during their final mission in Panama when Rory stood in front of her, aimed his Ruger at her chest and pulled the trigger. All while John was out of position, off radio, totally unaccounted for while his best friend tried to kill her.

Both men had been taken into custody immediately, she was told after the fact. But while she hadn't read transcripts or seen video of John's interrogations and interviews because those hadn't been allowed by the judge into evidence in Rory's trial, Rory had been adamant about John's involvement. Because she didn't see how he had anything to gain from insisting on it, she'd believed him.

Of course she had. Because John had let Rory's accusations stand. He let her believe in his guilt without fighting for her. They had but that one brief encounter two months after the shooting, when she was fragile after a discouraging physical therapy appointment in which she'd learned how far she'd fallen physically, when she believed, despairingly, that there was no pushing past the physical and mental pain of what had happened because there was no end to it. There was just pain and loneliness and disability.

And he let her believe that.

Until today, she'd believed it with a fervor—because the alternative was too much to carry. Because if she'd allowed herself to consider that Rory had been lying about John, that her instincts, as well as those of their other black ops crewmates, Ryan and Diego, were wrong about John, then how would she ever forgive herself for doubting him? How could John ever forgive her?

No, she wouldn't beg forgiveness, even if she had been wrong. Because that was yielding her power to a man, a move that had nearly killed her in the past. Even if John was innocent, they could never go back to what they were. She had a plan for herself, and John didn't fit into it. There was no space for love in the world of black market assassins.

She returned her focus to him, not his face but his body, no longer caring if he knew she studied him the way he hadn't stopped studying her since the plane took off. He'd always been ripped, in peak physical shape, but there was a hard angularity to his body now. Every inch of him was muscle and steel and virility.

No softness at all or hint of the gentleman who used to whisper her call sign as if it was a term of endearment. He'd called her Phoenix even when they were alone. Because she was resilient and strong, he used to murmur in bed. Like the bird, and like the desert city she grew up in. Like the sun. No man she'd slept with could pillow talk like John. He'd elevated it into an art and she'd been hypnotized by his charm, those sweet words and even sweeter moves that seemed to have given way to a cold, hard warrior.

She allowed her gaze to rise up to the lips that were the window to his emotions and so, so talented at turning her boneless and carefree. At least they remained unchanged. She missed a lot about her former life, but she especially missed being kissed by John. Every kind of kiss, from the ravishing, up-against-a-wall, *I'll die without you* kind of way that he'd proved again today he was a master at, to the slow, tender kisses that made her feel as cherished as a rare jewel.

A pang of longing and loneliness hit her right in the heart.

"You're staring at my mouth."

She raised her gaze higher, to his dark, unyielding eyes. "It's the only part of the old John you have left."

"Would that be a compliment or criticism?"

A criticism. But she didn't need to let on how much she'd missed him, despite everything. "Take it as you will."

He leaned closer, his hand propped on her seat back. "It that an invitation?"

Her attention lowered, returning to that one familiar part of him. But far from being soft and sweet, a hint of a sardonic smile teased the edges of his lips. She longed to press her lips to his and erase the defensiveness and bitterness from them. "You don't want that from me. You're just trying to make me squirm."

"What I want and what's good for me are rarely the same. And I'd never mistake you for the kind of woman who squirmed when her back was to the wall."

She couldn't decide if he meant to plant that image in her head or if it was a Freudian slip, but imagining her back against the wall, with John and those lips ready to take what they wanted, sent a low-down heat sliding into her belly. She turned her head toward the seat back and brushed her closed lips against his knuckles. He gripped the fabric harder.

"I've got you now, you bastard!" Harry's voice boomed through the cabin.

John and Alicia pulled apart, breathing hard, and turned their attention straight ahead.

"What have you got?" John said, his voice showing only the slightest strain.

Harry tapped the GPS display. "Martinique. That's where he landed."

"Guess I'd better brush up on my French," John muttered, squinting at the blips on the GPS screen.

Martinique. Interesting choice. She could pull a few facts and stats out of her head about the French-owned island, but she didn't know much about it beyond that it exported sugarcane, sported an active volcano that was responsible for what many had dubbed the worst volcanic disaster of the twentieth century and, despite that, was a popular destination for rich European tourists. She wondered if Rory knew enough about Caribbean geography to make the decision deliberately or if random factors like the deteriorating weather or low fuel had mandated a landing. For all they knew, Rory wasn't even aware of which island he was seeking refuge on.

Twenty minutes later, they started their descent through the clouds, first to check if the authorities had beaten them there, then to follow the GPS's coordinates and get a visual on the stolen plane before landing somewhere nearby and backtracking on foot. Harry explained that all the planes in his fleet were amphibian, meaning they could touch down safely on both water and land. They had no idea if Rory was aware of that, but the GPS did show that he'd landed on the southern coast of the island.

While Harry concentrated on the plane's descent, John busied himself with guns and other defensive tools from his sports bag, offering Alicia a backup .22 to replace the weapon Logan had lifted from her ankle. The tension and desire that had, earlier in the flight, sucked all the air from the narrow cabin was forgotten as she and John took positions at windows on the left side of the plane, ready to search for not only the stolen plane and Rory, but any signs that the U.S. government had picked up his trail, too.

Harry began a low, slow flight around the island's edge to make sure they were free from worrying about tangling with U.S. authorities, starting at the eastern edge of the island where the green volcano reached into the clouds above them. Despite the GPS locator's insistence that the plane had touched down on the south side, she kept her eyes peeled for Rory, too, because she knew better than to trust a machine on blind faith. There was nothing saying Rory hadn't found the GPS and deliberately led them on a wild-goose chase.

The first major harbor they flew past was, according to John, that of Fort-de-France, Martinique's capital that perched on the Caribbean Sea like any number of European coastal villages in Alicia's memory—with cobblestones and whitewashed houses jammed together in disorganized splendor. Except this time there was the distinctive tropical flavor of palm trees and panga boats and an outdoor marketplace with cart after cart of large, gorgeous offerings of tropical fruit. The harbor was packed with boats of all sizes and even a smattering of floatplanes, but no Rory and no military activity whatsoever.

They continued around the west, then the southern side of the island, where the landscape was dominated by sprawling resorts and gated communities of massive estates that Alicia assumed were vacation homes for the world's millionaires and billionaires.

John was the first to spot the plane floating in a shallow inlet on the Caravelle Peninsula, rocking in the choppy surf, exactly where the GPS showed it to be. Only then did Alicia release the breath she'd been holding. They saw no sign of Rory, not that they were expecting to see him waving up at them from the pilot's seat or from the nearby beach.

"Don't land here, and don't slow down," John said, dropping into the copilot's chair. "If our quarry's still nearby, he'll bolt if he senses someone's on his tail."

Alicia angled her head for a last look behind them as they flew past. "It looks like he tied it to a mooring buoy, then swam to shore. Maybe he's planning on returning."

The swim in the salt water must have been excruciating for Rory's gunshot wound, or at least Alicia could hope.

Harry huffed. "This whole area will be battling hurricane force conditions in the next couple days. My plane will be destroyed if we don't get it out of there."

"Then that's what we need to do," Alicia said.

In the next cove, Harry brought the plane down. With the wind and rough surf, the landing had Alicia visualizing emergency evacuation procedures for sinking planes, but thankfully it didn't come to that. There were no mooring buoys in this deserted cove, so Harry ran the boat aground and staked a rope from the plane into the dry sand. It would probably hold if the wind didn't worsen or change directions, but leaving the plane like that for any length of time would be a huge gamble.

"Harry, you stay with this plane. Inside it, in case Rory's nearby and comes to investigate. John and I need to make sure the area's safe before we call for a tow."

"Like hell I will. I'm coming with you. That's my plane he took and he has to answer to me."

Before she could think better of it, Alicia turned to Harry and unbuttoned her shirt low enough that the tops of her bra cups showed. So did the puckered, jagged scar in the center of her chest that still looked angry and damaging. The mark of her vengeance. She didn't look at John because she couldn't stand to see how the scar affected him. But she felt his stare. "Rory Alderman might have stolen your plane, but he did this to me. And this is what he has to answer for. Trust me when I tell you that he won't be getting away with anything."

Harry nodded and looked as though, for the first time, he understood the kind of dangerous criminal they were dealing with. He held up his hunting rifle. "You've got ten minutes, then I'm coming after you."

The inlet Rory landed in was bordered on the side closest to the mooring buoy by a thick, unstable-looking rock jetty and the other by a white sand beach that was the backyard of several closed beachfront bars and what looked like a time-share complex. No one was on the beach, and no time-share employees, locals or tourists were in sight as far as Alicia could see in any direction. Shielding her face from the bits of sand flying in the wind, she followed John along the tree line. It hadn't started raining yet, but she could smell it coming in the thick, damp air.

The plane looked empty. The side door was un-latched and swung open and closed with the rhythm of the waves. She stopped at the base of the jetty, the toe of her boot inches from three red-brown drops. "I've got blood here."

She scanned the length of the jetty, picking out a dozen other blood drops. Rory's leg had to be killing him. Because of that, he couldn't have gone far without transportation, unless he stole a car from the time-share, convinced some unsuspecting local to give him a ride, or flagged down a cab, which didn't seem likely because not a single car had passed on the frontage road the whole time they'd been there. She also doubted he'd stolen a car. That had been a risky, high-profile move on St. Croix that Alicia would bet he wouldn't try again unless he had no other options because whoever he stole it from would likely report it, creating yet another trail for any number of the people and organizations hunting him to follow.

John peered over her shoulder. "He's long gone."

"That's what I'm thinking, too."

John's attention swung to the trees and the jungle beyond. "There are a lot of places to get lost on this island. Even if he patched himself up on St. Croix with the medical supplies he stole, he needs to get off his feet and recuperate. He can't keep running like he has been."

"We need a base. Private enough that we don't have to look over our shoulders every two seconds, but with access to Wi-Fi. Somewhere I can start to dig for information online." *Like a hotel room.*

Tactically, that was the most logical choice, but she didn't seem to be capable of suggesting aloud to her former lover, who'd already curled her toes with a ravishing kiss that day and who'd almost done so again in

Harry's plane, that they seclude themselves together in a hotel room indefinitely.

"Agreed. But first we need to help Harry secure this plane. I'm not comfortable leaving him alone to handle it in case Rory returns."

Yeah, leaving Harry to face the possibility of going up against Rory without their help would be a terrible way to repay the man for locating Rory and transporting them, even if helping him took them off Rory's trail and was bound to be a slow, tedious process. Though hitting the pause button on their mission made her feel tense and panicky, she knew this was the right thing to do.

John motioned his head back the way they'd come, then started up the beach. "I'm sure Harry's on his way here. Let's intercept him before he gets to the beach, in case Rory's nearby. For all we know, he's watching us right now."

Alicia hadn't considered that possibility. She scanned the surrounding beach and trees, not expecting to see anything. Still, a shiver crawled up her spine. She set her hand on her Glock, then jogged through the sand to catch up with John.

More than an hour later, Alicia stood next to John and waved goodbye to Harry as his plane skimmed the water, then took off into the cloudy, misting sky.

It hadn't been easy convincing him that they'd personally make sure his plane made it into the private airport they'd contacted for a tow, but it was a favor they'd insisted upon performing as soon as the weather began to deteriorate more rapidly. Harry had realized that if he didn't get in the air soon, he'd lose the window of opportunity to get home to his wife in St. Croix before Hurricane Hannah hit.

It was the way Harry had talked about his wife, the worry and love in his voice, that convinced Alicia that they needed to put their hunt on hold to help him, despite everything she stood to lose if Rory disappeared. That part of her—the part that could love, that was capable of giving herself up to another person body and soul—had died inside her when she was shot. In dark moments, she still grieved over that loss, and somehow, helping Harry get home to his love made her feel a little better.

John must have had his own reasons for going along with her plan to take care of Harry's plane, because he didn't put up a fight about it or suggest they split up so he could continue the hunt.

The tow was slow in coming and even slower in getting the plane to the airport, a private runway ten miles outside Fort-de-France. But reach it, they did. After two hours that felt more like ten, they sat in the tow truck, with Alicia itching to crack open her computer and get busy on her search for Rory.

Maybe the airport had Wi-Fi and a quiet room she could use.

The island of Martinique proved a colorful, fascinating distraction from her impatience as they drove along a two-lane highway past poor neighborhoods, luxury resorts and clusters of ultra-pricey vacation estates. There was a distinctly European influence obvious in the details of the island culture, from the French that the tow truck drivers spoke to the white-washed houses and the haphazard layout of the cobblestone streets, but the heart and vibrancy of the island seemed to have risen from the immigrants from all over the world and the descendants of slaves who—John explained—had been brought over to work the sugarcane fields centuries ago.

Alicia was enthralled and, for a few minutes, set aside the pressure she was under and danger she was in, and simply took it all in—from the lush greenery of the land; the three women wearing colorful wraps and walking on the side of the road, baskets of fruit and other foods balanced on their heads; a father and young son on a moped pulling a makeshift trailer holding a bucket of fish; to the occasional luxury cars racing by and pricey, monogrammed wrought-iron entrance gates that led into what looked like private jungle oases.

At the airport, while John was making arrangements to store the plane, Alicia interrupted as politely as possible given her impatience. "Is there a lounge or sitting room at this airport? I'm looking for a place to charge my computer."

"We have a lounge for our members," said the man wearing a name tag that read Luc. "If you're looking for a powder room, there's one behind you."

"This lounge. Would you mind if I...?"

Luc wrung his hands, looking uncomfortable. "It's usually only reserved for those who pay for use of the airport."

John was on the job, though. Before Luc could say any more, John pulled his hand from inside his bag and slipped him a folded fifty-dollar bill. Once again, Alicia was grateful for John's understanding of how the islands operated.

"But with the incoming storm, no one's been in or

out all day," Luc said, a smile suddenly brightening his face. "Please be my guest. It's the door to the right of the powder room."

She nodded her thanks to Luc, then John, but she was already busy thinking about what to look up first once she'd tapped into the airport's internet connection. Looking for Rory was going to take a lot more ingenuity and patience than she'd have time for here, so she decided that a better use of her time would be to figure out what Logan McCaffrey's vendetta against her was all about and what intel was floating around ICE about her and John.

She was still having trouble wrapping her brain around the truth that ICE had known she'd disappeared and where she'd gone when she left. She just couldn't see how that was possible. She'd been so careful with her plans, so careful to make sure she seemed at home in Arizona, from credit card usage to phone calls made on her land line at home, which indicated, on paper, that she hadn't left her house in days.

That was a puzzle for another day, though. After Rory was dead and she was halfway around the world, safe under a new identity. She'd flirted seriously with the idea of faking her own death, and a small part of her still wished she'd gone through with the plan—or at least a different, comparable plan after her conscience had persuaded her against following through with her grand scheme.

It only took her a few minutes to sneak into ICE's secure network through the virtual window she'd left open for herself before she'd left the agency and discover that her and John's names were listed along with Rory's on their posting of the ten most wanted criminals. Right up there with cartel leaders and terrorists. *Armed and dangerous,* the descriptions read. *Neutralize using whatever means necessary.*

That caught her off guard. She stared at the words, not quite believing them. If Logan's crew found them again, their instructions were no longer to arrest them, but kill them. As she'd decided during her first run-in with Logan at the Ammaly Resort, she ought to get used to that. Given the career she was trying to break into, having a price tag on her head was going to be her new reality.

But now that it was happening, now that John had been dragged into the fray, it didn't seem as acceptable as when she'd imagined it during the innumerable hours of physical therapy and training. What had she gotten herself into? What had she done to John?

Refusing herself the luxury of dwelling on her trepidation, she tiptoed to Interpol.

A couple minutes later, she looked up when the door opened to find John slipping in. He closed the door behind him. "Hey."

"Hey, yourself," she answered.

"What have you found so far?"

"I haven't started searching for Rory. That's going to take a more secure location given the ideas I have, but this storm is going to buy us some time. Weather forecasters are predicting that the hurricane will hit with full force by late tonight or early tomorrow. The airport and ferry companies are closed. Unless Rory has a death wish and braves the open ocean in a stolen boat or plane, he isn't leaving this island anytime soon."

"Good. I take it the authorities haven't figured out which island we and Rory are on?"

"Not that I could tell, but get this. ICE has us on their Most Wanted criminal list. They still think we're on St. Croix, so there's that. But they've sent notice of the situation and our profiles to Interpol and all branches of the military, FBI, Department of Homeland Security and the White House. According to them, we're armed, extremely dangerous, harboring national secrets, and all agencies have been given the go-ahead to neutralize us using whatever means necessary."

She scrubbed her hand over her face. "It's not easy to read that about myself." *And about you.*

"What did you think was going to happen after this stunt of yours, busting Rory out of prison so you could kill him?"

She erased her trail on the internet, royally irked at John's choice of words and the venom in his tone. "It wasn't a stunt. This is my life we're talking about. I thought this particular part of my operation would be over by now. I was supposed to be in Europe by the time the Feds figured out Rory was missing. Instead, the attempted murderer and traitor I sprang from prison is running amok. He's already killed that nurse. Who knows how many more in his desperation to flee? It wasn't supposed to happen like this."

He walked to the cola vending machine on the side wall and fed coins into it. "Didn't you have a backup plan?"

The accusation in his tone got her back up even more. She snapped the laptop lid closed and stood.

"I had a few. None of them involved you messing everything up."

He set his hands on his hips and leveled an unflinching gaze at her. He didn't look angry, but intensely serious. Like he was looking right into her heart. "You're scared."

Without answering, she turned and faced the decorative mirror above the sofa. Her hair was tangled and her clothes soiled. She reapplied her lucky lipstick that she always carried in her jacket, then raked fingers through her hair to smooth it back into place. There was nothing she could do about the scuffs on her clothes, but there was nothing like red lipstick to make her feel put together again and back in control.

Her gut reaction was to deny John's assessment. Opening up about her weaknesses wasn't exactly natural for her. Most of the time, she gave herself a break about that. Unwavering composure and a focus on strengths was a good thing in her line of work— lifesaving, even. Besides, joining the CIA as a teenager and hacking into the computer infrastructure of foreign countries on behalf of the U.S. government by the time she was of legal drinking age hadn't remotely resembled a normal coming of age.

Not that she regretted the choice. If she had it all to do over, she'd join the CIA again in a heartbeat, but every now and then, her inability to connect with people on an intimate soul-to-soul level made her feel like a prisoner in her own skin. It wouldn't kill her to open up to John; perhaps it would make her feel less alone.

"Yes," she answered softly. "I'm scared."

He had the good graces not to look surprised by the admission. "Me, too."

He collected his cola from the vending machine, then stood next to her and cracked it open. He offered her the first sip, but she shook her head. He set it on the coffee table, then performed his own cursory sprucing up of his appearance in the mirror. "But the way I see it, scared is good. It means we understand the stakes."

Scared didn't feel good to her. "No, it means we understand the stakes and they're too much. We have to find a dangerous criminal who's on the loose before U.S. authorities do. Meanwhile, we have the air force, the navy, Interpol and an ICE black ops team hot on our tail like we're the dangerous criminals—and those are just the groups gunning for us that we know about. We can't let them catch us, and we can't let them catch Rory."

"We *are* dangerous criminals. We're dangerous because of our skills and the national secrets we know from our years working for the government. And any way you slice or dice it, we're criminals because you broke a national traitor out of prison. As for me, when I saved you from Logan, I attacked federal agents and released the person they'd taken into custody, not to mention aiding in your escape right now. And, even though it was to save our lives, I still blew up a rum distillery. I'm culpable now, same as you. Knowing I'm right morally doesn't make me any less of a criminal."

At least they had morality on their side. She might be a dangerous criminal, but she would never hurt a civilian or use her skills for anything except to make the world a better place. Then it hit her. That was a lie. She'd released Rory back into the world and he'd already killed one civilian that they knew of.

She picked up her laptop. "We should go. Find a more secure location to regroup and track Rory down."

He didn't move toward the door, but instead teased at a spot of dirt on his pants with his fingernail. "Why were you planning to go to Europe?" He speared the finger in her direction. "Don't say sightseeing."

She shoved her laptop in its case, not willing to run her plans by him and impatient to immerse herself in tracking Rory. "We need to get out of here."

She walked to the door and had it open an inch when his hand appeared near her ear and pushed it closed again. "Why Europe? What's there?"

Fine. If he really wanted to know, she could tell him a harmless piece of her plan. She turned to look at him. "Not a what, but a who. Ryan."

His jaw stretched tight behind the thin, flat line of his lips. He gripped the can of cola until the aluminum buckled slightly, a move that flexed his forearm in a way that rippled up through his shoulder and made his pectoral muscle jump. "You and Ryan, then. That's how it is?"

Ah. Jealousy. It shouldn't have given her a thrill, but it did. A dizzying, knee-weakening thrill. Jealousy meant he wanted her for his own, which she should have already figured out from that kiss behind The Salty Parrot. She could practically smell the testosterone oozing from him, the primal roar building in his chest. Maybe he'd flex again—or maybe kiss her—if she let him keep believing she and Ryan were an item. Maybe he'd prove to her who she really belonged with.

A knot of desire tightened low inside her. It was ridiculous. They'd been business associates for only a matter of hours and she was already considering letting lust dictate her actions, letting John control her. It simply wouldn't do.

She gave herself a mental smack, then tossed her hair and forced a smile to her lips. "Simmer down. Ryan's engaged. He and his fiancée are operatives-for-hire in the south of France. I thought I'd start there, contract with them for a few jobs to get my feet wet and get my reputation up and running."

"And what is it you're going to do—intel?"

"Sometimes."

"And the other times?"

She shrugged. "Whatever needs doing, if the price is right."

He nodded like he'd figured her all out. "That's what this is about—you killing Rory. It's not just revenge. It's your way of introducing yourself to the underworld you want to be a part of."

"Precisely."

"And you think you have it in you to be a black market operative?"

She huffed and turned back toward the door. "Go to hell."

His hand held it closed again. "No, I'm serious. You don't think it's going to kill your soul to do that?"

"Don't you dare take a moral high road with me."

"Why not? I'm allowed to be worried about you."

"No, you're not."

Behind her, he was silent for a beat, then he said, "I always liked Ryan, but if he doesn't give you the same warning I just did, then he's not a very good friend."

She propped a shoulder on the door and sent him a sidelong look. "And you, who wanted to kill me, are?" It felt odd saying the words because she was almost certain she didn't believe him guilty anymore, but it was the only weapon in her arsenal at the moment.

His tongue poked against the inside of his cheek and he looked away, nodding. Then he downed the rest of the cola and tossed it in the wastebasket near the door. "You were right. Let's get out of here."

Then he bullied her out of the way, opened the door and strode out.

It pissed her off, him ending the fight. It pissed her off because how was he ever going to prove to the U.S. government that he was innocent when he couldn't even be bothered to prove it to her?

She raised her face to the ceiling and willed her frustration aside, then followed him through the door. He was leaning against the reception desk, cool as could be, chatting in perfect French with Luc. She understood the language much better than she could speak it, and she caught the gist of their conversation.

John asked him for a restaurant and hotel recommendation and for a taxi to be called. It was a savvy move of misdirection, because they'd never actually take the man's advice as it would leave a blatant trail to their whereabouts, but it didn't make her any less aggravated at his evasion of her demand to explain himself.

"Un restaurant romantique?" Luc said, offering a broad grin to Alicia.

"Oui," John answered dryly without sparing Alicia a glance.

She grabbed a brochure on snorkeling from the counter and walked out the main door, leaving him to his charade. It wasn't raining, precisely, but misting enough to keep her under the eave. Not that the shelter helped. With every gust of wind, a fresh flurry of mist enveloped her.

Her eyes stung. She tried not to wipe at them, lest her mascara run, but vanity was a tough sell. It'd been too long since she'd slept. Two days, and long ones at that. She sidestepped along the office wall until she was out of view of the glass doors, affording herself at least the illusion of a moment of solitude. Then she rubbed her fingertips against her temples and took a deep, steadying breath.

She never lost her cool like this. She was a consummate professional. Even when everything went sideways in a mission, which it did more often than not, she maintained total composure honed during fifteen years of service in covert ops.

Rory was here. She could feel it in the thick, humid air. The seas were rough enough and the forecast grim enough that his options to leave the island were shrinking. Add to that his hurt leg and she had a feeling he'd be settling in to wait the hurricane out.

She'd grown up in Arizona, where summer monsoons were standard, but they had nothing on the destructive power of hurricanes. Some of her fondest memories of growing up were of spending rainy summer days at her dad's house, watching afternoon cloudbursts from the spa on his deck. He was a teacher, and so off work during the summer, and she didn't appreciate until many years later how extraordinary and selfless of her mom it was that she got to spend summers with him, though it wasn't an official part of their divorce settlement.

She'd only experienced a couple hurricanes in her life, and they'd awed her with their force. It was hard not to feel as if she was a speck standing on a tiny rock in the middle of a vast, deep ocean, surrounded by forces trying to take her down or hurt her.

It was at that moment that one of those forces materialized at her side, his arms folded across his chest, his eyes on the horizon. Without turning her head, she studied him out of the corner of her eye. He stood stiff and still, every inch a warrior, from his physique and the cut of his jaw to the way he'd shuttered his emotions behind a stony, blank expression.

She didn't want to be ignored by a warrior right now. She wanted to talk to John. Her John. And that he'd so deliberately closed himself off from the conversation like they had nothing to discuss—*like he owed her nothing*—made her burn with frustration all over again. She wanted to howl at him louder than the wind, shove him in the chest and demand the answers he'd denied her for far too long.

She crushed the brochure in her fist. "You won't even try to defend yourself," she said under her breath.

"This isn't the place." He didn't even look at her. Didn't even afford her that courtesy.

She wrenched her gaze back to the horizon. There was never going to be a good place or a good time. They were on a manhunt while they themselves were being hunted.

Then again, she never should have brought up the topic, not because she should've waited until the right time and place, but because what if she got the answer she dreaded? What if he was guilty?

What would she do then? She needed his help, and an admission of guilt would make working together to find Rory inconceivable. She could tip off Logan's crew about him and set him up to get taken into custody, but she'd already flirted with that idea several months ago and decided against it. She didn't want to consider what it would be like to live with the knowledge that she'd destroyed John. Even if he was guilty. She just didn't want to go there.

The truth was, more and more, she was doubting her conviction about his guilt. Probably, she'd already subconsciously decided he was innocent because she wouldn't have suggested they partner up otherwise. No person in their right mind would put themselves in prolonged, intimate contact with one of their would-be murderers.

Then why wouldn't he defend himself?

Why was he letting her hang like this, without enough information to understand and accept the truth so she could move on from the hold he had on her heart?

Frustration and anger surged inside her anew. Why would he toy with her emotions like that? She squeezed her toes in her boots to stem the adrenaline and anger-induced quivering of her limbs.

She dropped her voice to a low hiss. "Where were you when Rory shot me? The report I read said you weren't in position, so where were you?"

He swallowed, but he still wouldn't shift his gaze from the horizon.

"Look at me, damn it."

He jerked his head in her direction. His eyes were dark, as if the blue in them was eclipsed by his black mood. The storm in his expression paralleled the intensity of the storm that was descending on the island and made Alicia's ribs tighten. She was so taken by the look on his face, by his larger-than-life presence, that she couldn't think or breathe.

As she watched, the flat line of his lips contorted into a sneer. "So you're finally ready to hear the answers I tried to give you more than a year ago and you're demanding them right now? That's pretty ballsy in my book, princess."

He'd only ever called her princess in bed, as a term of endearment, far removed from the sharp, bitter insult that the word was today.

"I'm not demanding. I'm asking. I want to know why you won't fight for..." She bit her lip. Why had she almost said that? She didn't want him to fight for her. Not anymore. Twenty months ago, she would've given anything for him to not give up on her, to fight for her to see the truth. To defend himself. But there was no going back and changing the past.

A flash of bright yellow caught her eye. A taxi appeared that Alicia hadn't heard coming over the racket of wind and her own tumultuous emotions. Before it had rounded the circular driveway and rolled to a stop in front of them, John's entire facade had morphed into that of a smooth operator, perfectly at home in any environment, without a care in the world. He even smiled.

Alicia took a breath and forced her shoulders and posture to relax. She painted on a smile of her own and leaned closer to him, allowing their shoulders to brush like a real couple might. She tensed at the feel of his hand sliding along her back to curl around her side and had to force herself to relax all over again as he coaxed her body closer in a gesture that was intimate in its casualness. It was such a convincing imitation of tenderness that Alicia's heart squeezed.

They stood like that, snuggled together like Academy Award-winning actors, while the taxi driver opened a black umbrella then jogged around to open the back passenger door. John released her with a nudge forward.

Alicia smiled sweetly at the driver, swung her computer case around to hold in her arms, and ducked into the backseat. John followed her in.

"Le restaurant de L'Auberge Priori," he said to the driver.

"Oui, oui. Bon choix," the driver said, bowing as he shut the backseat door. "Very romantic," he added in broken English. If he noticed how disheveled they both looked, then he did an excellent job of hiding it.

"Yes," John said, patting her hand. "That's exactly what we're going for."

Chapter 9

John and Alicia crowded onto the bench seat of the compact car, not speaking, not touching. Alicia cradled her computer case, John that enigma of a sports bag.

The air was stuffy with the windows closed against the drizzle. Alicia peeked at the dash and didn't see an air-condition option. It was hard to breathe; she didn't know where to look, what to think about.

She should be thinking about Rory and how she was going to find him, but she'd done nothing but think of him and her revenge since the day she woke from a medically induced coma in the hospital two weeks after the shooting, and Rory-fatigue was setting in. She closed her eyes and tried not to think of anything at all.

As the taxi pulled to the curb in front of the hotel, Alicia had just started wondering how they were going to pay for the ride when John pulled a stack of euros,

Martinique's currency, from his bag. Of course he had euros in his bag. What didn't he have in there? And what in the hell would she have done if he hadn't agreed to work with her to find Rory? The realization was staggering.

She watched the driver jog around the taxi to open their door. John unfolded from the car first, tucked a large bill into the man's palm, then offered Alicia a hand out. Refusing the gesture wouldn't have fed into their cover story, but she didn't want to take his hand. Shaking it had been painful enough.

She took it, anyway, gritting her teeth behind her smile.

The driver walked them under the umbrella to the revolving glass door of the hotel. It was a swank hotel, evident in every detail of its Moroccan-themed interior of lush carpets, thick drapery and gold leaf wallpaper. They were underdressed by a long shot, but thankfully it was practically vacant, probably due to Hurricane Hannah's approach. Nearly all the other people there were workers busy boarding up the windows in preparation for the storm.

The doors to the restaurant sat near the main entrance, and beyond it sat a mostly empty lounge and bar area. The glow of candles on tables in the dimly lit dining room shone through the wall of windows like fireflies. It was utterly romantic and exactly the kind of restaurant Alicia loved.

Loneliness wrapped around her heart. How long had it been since she'd gone on a date? She'd never dreamt of a normal life, with marriage and children and a house. But she did dream of love and not being alone. It was a pie-in-the-sky fantasy given the career she'd chosen—and it certainly didn't mesh with life on the run as a wanted criminal. But a girl could dream.

John remained holding her hand and led her to the receptionist desk, flashing the woman behind it an easy grin. Clearly, he had a plan in mind, one that seemed to involve the two of them planning a romantic evening, so Alicia followed suit. She stood behind him trying to look seductive, like a lover waiting for her companion to arrange the details of their night of pleasure. She kept her eyes on John, watching his mouth as he spoke.

In beautiful French, he told the receptionist in so many words that they needed a room close to the ground level because they feared the coming storm and wanted an easy exit in case the power cut on the elevator during the night, and that they also needed an eight o'clock reservation at the restaurant. When she asked his name, he said it was Jonah Carmen. He even had a passport to back up the alias and enough cash to pay for the room in advance.

Normally, Alicia found John speaking in any one of the several languages he was fluent in sexy as hell—except that this time she understood how calculated the act was. That beneath that dashing exterior was a man who was absolutely furious with her.

When a bellhop asked after their luggage, John took Alicia's hand and kissed the back of it slowly, his lips lingering over her skin as his gaze lingered on hers, before admitting they didn't have any. Flush-cheeked, the bellhop showed them to the elevator, where John pulled Alicia up tight against his body, then slipped the poor embarrassed worker a folded bill and bid him farewell.

He pushed the button for the third floor with the

back of a knuckle, then crowded close to her, a hand braced above her shoulder and the other on her hip, most likely for the benefit of the security camera mounted in the corner of the elevator roof. He dipped his face close to her ear but didn't say a word. He just breathed on her ear and neck, deep, ragged breaths that spoke of his restraint and tension, the simmering volatility beneath a threadbare composure. If anyone was watching the tape, they'd look like lovers who couldn't wait to get to their room.

But the thought of being alone with John in a hotel room, with him brooding and angry and her frustrated by the way he'd shut her questions down, by the lack of fight in him, was only the stuff of dread. No matter what happened next between them, it wasn't going to be in this hotel—this was just a show to lead their would-be followers astray—but somewhere near here, in some other room with a lock and John and a bed.

She uncurled her fist over his chest, where the curve of his pec muscle gave way to a hard, flat stomach heaving with the effort of each breath. He was so strong and solid, yet hot to the touch. Under the guise that she was acting for the benefit of their ruse, she nuzzled his hair. He smelled like a man, the very way she liked John best—sweaty from a mission, amped up on adrenaline and ready to bully right past her defenses and personal boundaries.

The elevator dinged open on the third floor. John pulled back and twisted to check the illuminated floor number, then grabbed her hand and dragged her through the hall to the room. It was a move that could have been that of a lover impatient to get his paramour behind a closed door so he could ravage her. But if this ruse was anything like the ones they'd executed when they were black ops teammates, they'd be back out in the rain in a minute or two, tops.

With the storm, hotel workers would notice a busted window, and she preferred slipping away elegantly and unnoticed down a staircase instead of rappelling down the side of a building in the rain. She was all for thrills and adventure, but anytime she could have adventure without compromising her hair and makeup, so much the better.

He set her against the closed door and pulled the key fob from his pants pocket. She slung an arm around his neck and pressed kisses to his jaw as he dunked the key fob into the slot on the door, then opened it gradually, giving Alicia time to catch her balance.

She took a quick inventory of the space, then reached behind the door for the Do Not Disturb placard, careful to hold the door open just enough so that the hotel's computer system would only register that they'd entered the room, not left it again. The interior was even more gorgeous than the lobby—sensual reds and golds and a bed made for the classiest of fantasies or the soundest of sleeps.

Thank goodness she and John weren't spending the night there together. He'd taken her to a room like this once, in a hotel every bit as posh and Moroccan themed on the coast of Spain.

"Nice room," she said.

John swept past her then methodically emptied the mini-fridge's contents into his bag. He didn't look up or acknowledge the statement. She hadn't expected him to, honestly, but she'd hoped for some kind of reaction.

Some fire in his eyes that wasn't anger, but passion—or at least fondness at the memory.

The next instant, he was striding past her again, through the door and out to the hallway, all pretense of the passionate lover gone. Even if the hallway security cameras were being monitored, she and John would be gone before hotel security could react.

She closed the door, cutting off the memory.

With her hand on the gun in her computer bag, she sidestepped behind John down the hall toward the staircase, watching their backs, determined not to get caught off guard again by Logan or his team.

The afternoon was dark, the mist from earlier now a steady stream of rain. They walked with swift, economic steps along the sidewalk, all pretense of romance gone. Three blocks away, they found an older motel that didn't a require photo ID to rent a room. It didn't have Wi-Fi, which was fine because it was surrounded by cafés and hotels. One of them had to have a Wi-Fi signal she could tap into.

John preceded her up the stairs to their second-floor room. The silence between them was taking its toll on her nerves. There was no facade of sexual tension or anticipation, just the impenetrable barrier of his broad, stiff back as he climbed the stairs, then opened the door to room 227.

He did hold the door open for her, which was an unexpected gesture given how furious he clearly still was. She set her computer bag on the bed and was almost afraid to look up or make eye contact with John. He stood near the closed door and she could feel his eyes on her.

"I killed three men trying to get to you," he said in a tight growl of a voice.

She turned, her throat tightening as she caught sight of his half-lidded, hard-jawed expression, his body quivering ever so slightly in a way that she wasn't sure how to interpret. It had to be restraint, like blunted pain. Mixed with the anger at her that he'd suppressed for too long. He had every right to hate her, and yet, he'd saved her from Logan's crew. He'd agreed to work with her to find Rory and he was still sticking with her. Why?

She smothered that line of thought. It didn't matter why. Nothing mattered except finding Rory. John was a means to an end. Nothing more.

He'd killed three men to get to her. "When?"

"During the RioBank operation. You asked me what I was doing when Rory shot you."

Alicia's breath caught. She'd never heard what happened on that day from his perspective. His interviews while in federal custody had been sealed and none of the strategies she tried to hack the system had worked. "Who? Where? Why weren't you there for me?"

She bit her lip and wrenched her gaze to the curtained window. She hadn't meant to say that last part aloud. It made her too vulnerable. It reminded her that she wished, deep down inside, that he'd protected her, that he would have stopped Rory and saved her.

It reminded her of the fairy-tale cartoon movies she'd watched when she was nine—the ones her parents plunked her down in front of to get her out of the way during the long, hard year their marriage crumbled. Tales of knights on dashing horses and heroes riding magic carpets, of kisses that broke curses and adventures in battle and across distant lands that made her long for a hero of her own. Tales that hinged on the hero saving his woman so they could live happily ever after.

And that wouldn't do. She didn't want to be saved. And she certainly didn't want to be reminded that John had already saved her today and that her future success hinged on him coming through for her again.

It was a bitter pill to swallow.

He walked past her, dropping his bag on the bed along with the HK45 from his pocket, and sat in the room's only chair. "Had no one told you that?"

"No. Your interrogation and interviews were sealed once the judge decided there wasn't enough evidence to charge you with a crime. I read Rory's deposition and the investigators' testimony, as well as Diego's and Ryan's. That's all. No one from ICE reached out to me about you specifically, not even off the record. Sometimes I got the feeling that ICE suspected me of wrongdoing, too. Our whole crew, really. It didn't make sense logically, and I didn't have any proof of that until Logan McCaffrey came after me on St. Croix, but I got the feeling more than once during the trial that we were all being looked at as possible coconspirators with Rory, so no, they were pretty tight-lipped."

He winced, shaking his head. Then he wiped his palms on his thighs and sat back. "My post during the RioBank operation was stationary monitoring of the perimeter of the bank building from the building across the street while you and Diego escorted the asset inside."

She didn't remember a lot about that day, but she knew that part from Diego's and Ryan's testimony.

"Ryan was stationary lookout in the bank lobby and Rory was mobile perimeter detail in the van. He went off radio less than a minute after you entered the building. After trying to reach him for five minutes, I left my post to go mobile, planning to cover both my and Rory's zones while I looked for him."

She seemed to have lost the ability to move her limbs. All she could do was lean against the side of the bed and hold the gaze John directed at her.

He gave a tense shake of his head. "I'd barely taken ten steps from the building I was stationed in when I was grabbed, my mouth taped shut, and dragged into an alley by the three men I mentioned. And they were ready for me. Professionals. I held my own, but they kept me busy. It's clear to me now that Rory arranged for them to keep me out of the way. Because, right after that, Rory surprised you and Diego up in that bank. It happened so fast. I couldn't get the tape off in time to warn you over the radio."

Her mouth went dry. "You heard it happen?"

His mouth screwed up like he'd tasted a bitter lemon. Propping his elbows on his knees, he curled his right hand into a fist and wrapped the other hand over it. "The whole thing. I heard Diego say, 'What are you doing out of position?' and then there was the buzz of the stun gun and I could tell by the way Diego roared that he was the one who got stunned." He winced again and shook his head. "Then I heard the gunshot. And I knew. Before you made that sound you did, I knew it was you he shot because of course that's what he'd do. He'd take out Diego, then he'd take out you."

"I made a sound? No one mentioned that to me."

"It was a gasp like nothing I've heard before or

since. I had nightmares about that sound for months. Dreams of me getting pummeled in the alley and hearing you get shot." His voice was strained, his hands pressed together so hard that the veins in his biceps popped. She was struck by the urge to wrap her arms around him to remind him that she was all right now; she'd escaped the terror of that day and made a full recovery.

Instead, she willed her feet to unstick from the ground, shook the lead from her legs and walked to the window to stare at the rain soaked road. "You said you killed the men."

"At the moment I heard the shot, I was going fist to fist with the guy who seemed to be the ringleader, but hearing what happened to you, I was filled with some kind of supernatural strength—you know how it feels when adrenaline does one of those mega spikes that makes you explode with power—and I almost crushed his face in. When I went for his gun, the other two jumped on me, but I kept repeating in my head…"

His voice trailed off, so she turned, searching his face. "Repeating what?"

He stood and shook out his arms. "It doesn't matter anymore. I killed the other two men with one of their own guns, then I started running." The emotion had drained from his voice, leaving his tone flat and cold.

He walked to the window and stood next to her, his eyes on the road. "I caught up with Diego, Ryan and Rory outside the bank. Diego was turning Rory into raw meat with his fists and when he saw me, he commanded Ryan to subdue me. I was so out-of-mind afraid for you that I let him do it. I just wanted him to tell me what happened to you and where you were now. ICE officials took me into custody right there in front of the bank, and, uh, I didn't see the sky for two months."

Two months. That was about how long it had taken Alicia to get out of the rehabilitation wing of the hospital. She remembered the night he approached her on the street not long after that as she was coming out of physical therapy. He'd been too thin, but still strong, with desperate eyes that had raked over her body.

"You must have come to see me right after your release."

"Yes. And you'd already tried and convicted me in your mind."

She'd still been rife with anger that the charges against him had been dismissed, and seeing him had triggered an avalanche of emotion inside her. Pain of the heartbreak she'd suffered because he'd conspired to kill her, panic of being alone with one of her would-be killers knowing she was still too weak to defend herself should it come to that. Fury because—for a split second on seeing him—her heart had lightened and she'd longed to touch him.

She'd poured the hate, fear and heartbreak into her words to him that night. She winced, recalling all she'd said. He hadn't lingered long after that. She couldn't remember his expression, his reaction; she was too caught up in the storm inside herself. She didn't even remember him speaking. He must have, but the words had ricocheted right off her defenses.

"Unlike the Feds," he continued. "They couldn't find any conclusive evidence that I was innocent—not even any bodies in the alley—but they also couldn't find evidence to support Rory's claim that I was with him when he met with the mercenaries who hired him to take our unit out or that I'd helped him get into the bank undetected by the rest of our crew. They couldn't find any because there was none. Because I would never, ever do that. To anyone. Especially not to you."

Rory had accused John of so much more than that in his official statement, and Alicia had let herself believe it all. How had she reasoned that trusting Rory's version of the events made her more in control? Whether or not he was right about John, she'd still believed him unequivocally and without proof, in essence letting herself be manipulated. Why had she not been able to see that at the time?

"When I was released from custody, it was made abundantly clear that I was no longer welcome in the United States." His voice was a raspy monotone, like the effects of his quivering restraint had tightened his throat. "I had to see for myself that you were okay, and after that, the Virgin Islands seemed like a good place to go on a bender. It turned out that they're also a great place for a man to disappear in."

She battled against the compassion and tenderness building inside of her for the man her universe had once hinged on. She was on a mission. John was a means to an end. If only it were that simple. But she still had to try to force them back to the job at hand before she got irreversibly swept away in memory and feeling.

"Like Rory," she said.

He turned to face her, the ice gone from his eyes, replaced by the same fire that burned bright in them when he'd rescued her from Logan's van. "He's not going to disappear. We'll find him. You said at the airport that you wanted me to fight for my good name. This, going after Rory, keeping you from killing him first—" his heated gaze traveled the length of her body in a slow perusal "—torturing myself by being this close to you. This is me fighting with everything I have, at the limit of my endurance and skill, for my good name and my life back."

Torturing himself being this close to her. He wasn't the only one who was tortured by it.

She reached out and touched his cheek with her fingertips. He never tore his eyes from hers, that smoldering gaze that threatened to consume her.

"That's not what I meant. When I wanted to know why you wouldn't fight." God, could she say this out loud? Could she be that vulnerable? The thought made her heart race and her head dizzy. But John had been absolutely open with her. He'd exposed everything he'd felt and everything he'd gone through, so the least she could do was share a little of herself with him, even though it terrified her. "I wanted to know why you wouldn't fight…for me. If you were really innocent, then why didn't you try to make me understand? You left so fast. You didn't even give me a chance to process it all."

He seemed to shake himself awake, blinking, his brows furling.

Then he was in her personal space, pulling her close, making her aware of nothing but him and the flood of testosterone and need rolling off his body. A knot of delicious tension gathered in her belly as he slid a finger along her jaw and around her ear.

His fingers plunged into her hair and brought his forehead to hers. "I need to hear you say it." She shivered at the sound of the husky pillow-talking tone she remembered well. "Tell me you believe I'm innocent."

Panic knifed through her, sharp and painful. It was one thing to wonder why he hadn't fought harder for her to believe him, but it was another to take that extra step. She couldn't go there. She'd already given more than she thought she could bear. Because *there* was a slippery slope of exposure and weakness, so much more than she was capable of giving.

It meant acknowledging her loneliness, confessing that she needed John and had missed him so badly that she woke in the middle of the night aching, she wanted him so far beyond what was healthy for her—or him. He deserved so much more than being the lover of a black market assassin and one of America's newest Most Wanted.

Closing her eyes, she brushed her lips against his. "It doesn't matter what I believe."

His hand tightened around her waist, in her hair. The knot of tension in her belly morphed into white-hot lust, battling hard for supremacy over her fear. She'd lived like a monk since being shot, her sole focus on transforming herself, body and mind, into a fighting machine. No sex—not even self-pleasure. Like she did with her loneliness and anger, she harnessed all her base needs and sexual frustrations and transformed them into power and purpose. And after a while, she'd realized that the sexual part of her soul was dead. Gone with that single shot of Rory's gun.

But if that was true, then why did she feel so weak with John's hard body pressing into her, raw virility radiating from every inch of him? Why couldn't she transform the urge to bring his skilled lips to hers into something productive and functional?

There isn't another man in the world who knows you like I do, who makes you feel the way I do.

He was right, damn it.

He backed his face up. She tore her gaze from his lips and met his iron stare. "Of course it matters." The pillow-talk silkiness of his previous words was gone, but the growl remained. "Phoenix, I need you—"

Seizing a handful of his T-shirt at the collar, she pulled his lips to hers—to shut him up and end that slippery slope of a conversation…and because she couldn't help it. She needed so badly to be kissed, touched. She needed John and his wicked lips and tongue and body. She'd been so lonely without him. So empty, alone with her pain. How was it that only now she was realizing that revenge was a cold, cruel bedmate?

He tensed, bringing her tighter against him with the movement, his hands clamping onto her backside, his chest pressing her upper body against the window. She groaned, wantonly, but she couldn't help it. The feel and taste of him were too much and not enough all at the same time, leaving her dizzy and overwhelmed— and recklessly aroused. She wrapped a leg around his thigh and he took over from there. Grabbing her behind her knee, he ground his hips between her legs and stroked his tongue into her mouth with a low, deep guttural sound that told her he'd been starving for her the same as she had for him.

With sure, steady fingers, she unfastened the top two buttons of her shirt. When he noticed, he broke the kiss, pushed her hands out of the way and ripped her shirt open, spilling buttons over the floor.

Breathing hard, he molded his palms to her breasts and pressed his lips to her scar, kissing it as if it was a thing of beauty, a pleasure point. It lit up the scar's sensitive nerve endings in a way that was—shockingly, unexpectedly—euphoric. She had no idea it could feel that way, as that part of her had never been touched in any way other than clinical or as a symbol of her vengeance. She arched forward, holding his head to her chest while his hands mapped her breasts with slow, reverent movements.

"Do you believe I'm innocent? I need to hear you say it."

But she didn't want to go there right now. She didn't want to talk at all, because talking meant admitting she'd been wrong. It meant handing over even more power to him beyond her current blazing lust, beyond needing him to find Rory and evade Logan. Lust that demanded she let him take her hard and fast against the wall like he had during their last time together on the balcony of her condo in Panama while the rest of their black ops unit members slept inside.

She dropped her hand to the button fly of his jeans and peeled the buttons open one by one until his cotton-clothed erection pushed into her hand. "It doesn't matter anymore."

He lifted his head and gaped at her, his nostrils flared. He pushed his hips forward, thrusting into her hand. This time, it was he who kissed her, aggressive and deep, demanding her surrender. She gave it to him—at least, everything she had to give. Not her power. She'd never surrender that to anyone again. But her body, her heart, her loyalty from this day forward, she gave it all to him.

He gathered her tighter against him, sliding his hands from her breasts around her ribs to her back, kissing her so ravenously that she had no more room to worry about her fears and fantasies. There was only room for John and the way he made her feel.

Then, with a startling abruptness, he released her body and mouth and pushed away from the window, away from her caressing hand. His shoulders hunched; his lips contorted into a scowl as he refastened his pants and drilled her with a fierce look. "It might not matter to you, but it matters to me. *You* matter to me. And there isn't a damn thing I can do about it."

He spun away and strode to the bed, where he picked up his gun, checked the magazine and chamber, then stuffed the gun in the back of his waistband. "I'm going to check the perimeter. Stay here. I won't be long." He stared at his bag and, after a moment's hesitation, pulled out a white T-shirt, which he tossed to her.

Speechless, her mouth still open and dewy from his kiss, she held the shirt in front of her chest and watched the play of his shoulder blades as he left.

Chapter 10

By the time John returned to the room less than an hour later, Alicia had followed the wisdom of her idol, Elizabeth Taylor, and had poured herself a drink, put some lipstick on and pulled herself together.

The white T-shirt he'd intended for her to wear smelled like him, so much so that she'd buried her nose in the fabric and had taken a moment to imagine what the two of them would have been doing right then if she hadn't panicked. But she had panicked and she'd been unable to tell John the one thing he wanted to hear—what she now knew, in her heart, to be true. She put the shirt on and eyed the scattered buttons on the floor. If she had the time later, she'd sew them back on, but for now she had work to do and a quarry to catch.

While her computer warmed up, she'd reapplied her favorite red lipstick and just that simple act made her feel more grounded. She found mini bottles of alcohol in John's bag, which she hadn't been able to keep herself from taking a look inside. She'd forgotten that he'd cleaned out the minibar in the last hotel, but was grateful for the accidental discovery because she was famished and in need of some liquid courage. She popped the top on a can of mixed nuts, emptied a mini vodka into one of the glasses she found on the bathroom counter and returned to the bed to snoop through the bag.

There wasn't anything remarkable inside it that didn't make sense for a warrior to carry: cash and IDs, spare ammo, guns, grenades, a compass, rations and all kinds of other survival kit odds and ends. If she'd been hoping to find a tattered photograph of her, like a corny movie cliché, she would've been disappointed.

With a fond smile, she picked up the only personal effect in the bag: a copy of Michael Jackson's *Bad* album—John's talisman and good-luck charm. That album was the sound track of her life for the two years they'd worked together in black ops. He'd played it every time he drove and in every hotel they stayed at. Sometimes, he sang along or broke out in dance.

Her heart ached, thinking of the ice in his eyes, the hardness he exuded now. He said he didn't dance anymore. She believed it. And she knew, without a doubt, that she'd had a hand in destroying the man he'd been. Because of Rory.

She held the cool plastic of the CD to her chest and let anger toward Rory wash away her regrets. He was going to pay. Not only for what he did to her, but what he did to John, too. She set the CD on the bed. Maybe she'd put it on later tonight during the long hours of internet surveillance and let her mind wander back to old times when their black ops crew was together and happy.

After a halfhearted attempt to put his bag aright, she set up her computer and tapped into the Wi-Fi of the restaurant next door, then got busy hacking into the St. Croix police department network to see if they'd yet discovered that Rory had left their island.

Before she'd barely cracked through the police network's security, John returned with a plastic bag filled with what looked and smelled like curry takeout. His attention zeroed in on his bag on the bed, then her. "You're still here."

He sounded genuinely surprised. As if he'd expected her to take his bag and disappear, which she supposed would have been a viable option, if, one, it had ever entered her mind, and two, if she had no integrity at all. But they'd made a deal to be business partners, a deal she'd insisted upon, and after giving herself over to the mercy of his kiss and touch, she knew now that she still cared about him the same way he professed to caring about her, as much as that terrified her to admit.

"We're business partners, what did you expect?"

"Business associates, was the term you used."

Yeah, okay. Rather than debate the semantics of being associates versus partners, she changed the subject. "What do you have in the bag?"

"Colombo curry, the island's specialty."

"Has the storm started ramping up yet?"

"Still just light rain, but I talked to some old-timer locals while I was getting dinner. They said it'll be here by midnight."

She tapped the top of her laptop screen. "I'm in the St. Croix Police Department network and it doesn't look like they've figured out that Rory isn't on their island anymore. The next place I'm going to look is the NSA."

"You can get into NSA's secure network? I thought they'd outfitted it with an impenetrable force field, or whatever you computer geeks call it."

"You were close. It's a firewall. And it's not impenetrable because I made sure it wasn't before I left ICE."

He set the food on the small round table near the far wall and fixed a curious expression on her.

"What?"

He shook his head, a bemused smile on his lips and, perhaps, a hint of admiration. "Way to go, partner."

Not long after nightfall, John stared at the satellite image of Martinique that Alicia had pulled up on her computer, trying to use his knowledge of the island and Rory to figure out where their quarry had gone after landing the floatplane. The options were staggering. Even more so because John was familiar with Rory's methods and knew he was a huge fan of misdirection. The plane's location wasn't going to lead them any closer to finding Rory than his boat did on St. Croix.

John rested a hand on the back of Alicia's chair, careful to avoid touching her hair or making the move overly familiar, despite that being overly familiar with her was exactly what his body and heart wanted to do at the moment. Good thing his head was back in control now, because finding Rory was going to take every bit of brain power he had.

Alicia had transformed the narrow, wooden desk

near the window into a high-tech surveillance head-quarters. After tapping into ICE's network, she'd made it look like child's play to keep tabs on Martinique's police department as well as all the traffic cameras and cell phone towers on the island.

John was amazed, as he always was, by Alicia's computer skills, the singular passion for and the creativity involved in her science. That alone would've been impressive enough, but she was also a lethal operative with a commanding physical power and weaponry skills that rivaled the most elite soldiers. He had no idea how many eighteen-year-olds got invited to join the CIA, but she had to be one in a billion.

Maybe that was key. She was eighteen, a child still, when she'd thrust herself into a world of espionage, warfare and politics, where she was taught to doubt everyone, trust no one. Maybe he ought to cut her some slack about her lack of trust in him. She'd never had a normal dating or young adult life. No regular college experiences and friendships like John had enjoyed before joining the army as an officer.

Her unique history and sharply honed genius were two of the things he'd always found intriguing and sexy about her, so he could hardly hold her extraordinary life against her now.

What he really needed to do was stop thinking about that last kiss, about the way the flesh of her chest had felt to his lips and hands, so he could concentrate all his energy onto finding Rory, because the sooner they found him, the sooner they could each move on.

Moving on. What a strange concept. How could he move on from Alicia when their relationship felt unfinished in every way?

When she'd admitted that she wished he would have fought for her, it felt as if he'd grabbed hold of a live wire, it was such a shock to his system. Like his heart and mind finally woke up after hibernating for a year and half. She was right. How had he never seen the collapse of their relationship from her perspective? It was almost as if he'd expected her to turn him away and when she did, he gave up. Since when was he the sort of man who gave up? Scrappers didn't give up. Underdogs relished the chance to prove people wrong. But he'd just up and left without a fight.

What the hell had he been thinking?

Even if she'd wanted to contact him, he'd totally checked out and went off the grid. He hadn't given her any spare chances; he didn't fight. She'd never even heard the truth about what he'd gone through and done on the day she was shot. He'd been devastated that she didn't have blind faith in him, but she came of age in the CIA, for pity's sake. She'd been taught not to have blind faith in anyone. Had he really expected a whole life of learning and conditioning would go out the window when it came to the way she processed their relationship and his motives?

She still couldn't admit out loud that he was innocent, but maybe it wasn't too late for them. Just maybe. But nothing was going to happen until she could verbalize that she trusted him and believed in his innocence. And his gut was telling him that wasn't going to happen as long as Rory was on the loose.

This meant one thing: that finding Rory was no longer just about clearing John's name. It was fighting to lay the past to bed once and for all so Alicia could move on. So she could be free from all the things that were weighing her down and poisoning her outlook on life and John could find out if there was something between them worth fighting for still.

John paced behind Alicia's chair. They'd spent hours at the computer but still hadn't found the needle in the haystack that would lead them to Rory. While it was comforting to know that the hurricane would keep U.S. authorities off the island and Rory on, that same storm would eventually demand that he and Alicia hunker down to wait it out, rather than search for their quarry.

Though they hadn't discussed their strategy for surviving the hurricane, John knew they wouldn't be able to do so in this hotel room unless they took up residence in the bathroom because one bad wind gust and flying debris could shatter the window in a heartbeat.

He stopped walking and braced his hands against the back of her chair. "We're not getting anywhere and our window to search before the hurricane hits is only getting smaller. If I were Rory, what I'd do is hole up and let my leg heal while I waited the storm out, betting on a power failure and general chaos in the days afterward, then take a ferry or hire a boat to take me to St. Lucia or Barbados. Or all the way to Panama or Colombia. From there, disappearing indefinitely would be a piece of cake."

"Any one of those plans would require a lot more cash than he could've found in those wallets and purses he stole from the Ammaly Bay."

Her voice faded off and he could tell a lightbulb had just gone on in her head.

"That's it," she murmured, typing so fast that the click-clack of the keys mimicked the sound of the rain beating on their window. It was one of the most comforting sounds to John that evoked memories of lying in bed listening to her type—cracking codes, hacking into corporate networks, doing her computer genius thing.

"Talk to me, Phoenix."

"Well, tracking petty theft is nearly impossible, especially in touristy places like the Caribbean where tourists are getting ripped off all the time, but I bet those people from the resort who got their purses and wallets stolen reported it to the St. Croix police. If I can find the police report, we'll have a list of names and stolen items."

"Then what?"

She twisted in her chair and smiled at him. "Rory needs cash, right? So what if he's hitting ATMs here using the stolen debit cards? I can look for ATM usage by the names of the people who had their wallets stolen. Do you think Rory would remember the PIN code cracking techniques I taught our black ops crew during your first year with us?"

Genius. No wonder she was smiling so big. This plan might actually work. "Definitely." Alicia had taught them all how to crack PIN codes in case they ever got in a pinch for cash while on a mission. More than 50 percent of people use the five hundred most common four digit PINs for their ATM cards, not just in the U.S., but internationally. Since Rory stole whole wallets, including passports, phones and photo IDs, he'd know people's birthdays and names of family members, too, which were other common passcodes.

"Good. That's what I hoped. I'm already in the St.

Croix police system, so now I'm just running a search for references to the Ammaly Bay Resort from today."

"I know you're a genius and all, but I'm thinking that Logan's crew is going to reach this same conclusion sooner or later, especially if Logan has a techie like you on his team."

"He does. I'm sure of it. How else could he have tracked me so efficiently?" A new window popped up on the computer screen. She scrolled through the new information, her eyes narrowed in concentration. "Most of the debit cards have been canceled, but I can work with that, too, because I can pull up the networks of different banks on the island and see if there's a high volume of rejected cards at any one ATM."

After a few more minutes of furious typing, more windows popped up and John, who'd been attempting to figure out what she was doing, gave up and backed away from the computer.

He lay sideways on the bed, hands threaded behind his head, and closed his eyes. He let the sound of typing and Alicia's muttered words to herself carry him into the memories of how they used to be. From that rosy view that filled him with equal measures of peace and sorrow, it was impossible not to wonder what the future held for them after they caught Rory.

What if he fought for her now? Would she let him in to her life? Did he even want to try? Could he be with someone who'd once thought him capable of plotting her murder and who still couldn't admit aloud that she knew he'd never hurt her?

The typing stopped, leaving the only sound in the

room being the rain and wind against the window and creaks and footfalls in the building beyond their room. He waited for the typing to resume but it didn't. As the silence stretched on, he opened his eyes and looked her way.

She was looking at him and seemed flustered that he'd caught her at it.

"I was trying to decide if you were asleep."

"Just resting my eyes." He pushed up and sat on the edge of the bed, stretching his arms overhead. "What's up? Did you find something?"

"Not yet." She picked up the now-cold takeout and lifted the fork. "I have all the data in place and all my search options open. Now, we just have to wait for Rory to make his first move. Who knows when that will be?"

"Great. A digital stakeout. Your favorite."

"You remember that time in Lebanon when we were tracking those artifact smugglers? We sat in that gnarly, roach-infested room for three days waiting for a hit from all those different agencies I tapped."

"I thought you were going to shoot your computer."

Her expression morphed into fake incredulity. "Why would you think that? I mean, just because I was waving my gun at it, that doesn't mean anything."

He fought a smile at the memory. "And yelling, 'Chime, you bastard or I'm going to kill you and your brother!'"

"Both my laptops were being difficult on purpose. And I thought threatening might help. I can be pretty persuasive when I want to be. I just wanted the damn thing to chime so we could get out of that nasty room."

"I'm sure it had nothing to do with the fact that you're a very impatient person."

"Moi?"

Reminiscing about old times, joking with Alicia— it'd been a long time since he'd thought about the past and his time on the black ops team with anything but bitterness. It was a shocking reminder that beyond lust or love, he *liked* Alicia. He liked the way she took on the world as if every new day was a problem to solve or a battle to fight. He liked her sense of humor, her impatience and her mind for totally random trivia.

The good memories, the room, the reminder of how compatible they were, the sight of her wearing his shirt—on top of everything else that day, it was too much, especially after more than a year of feeling nothing at all.

He couldn't decide what he wanted to do more— storm from the room again or gather her up in his arms and carry her to the bed. Given the war of emotions battling inside him, it was even money, but either way, he wasn't getting anywhere by sitting on the bed. He stood with a stilted abruptness, his composure so close to snapping that he couldn't quite get his limbs to work right.

Alicia drew up tall and stiff. Her expression shuttered except for the hint of anxiety in her eyes, as if she could tell how close he was to kissing her again. She might have even stopped breathing. That made two of them.

He forced himself to draw breath. *Don't go there, man. Remember patience.*

"I'm going to take a shower."

"Oh."

The part of him that was still a gentleman knew he should've offered her first shower, but he wasn't feeling very polite at the moment. More like a caged animal. He ripped his shirt over his head and tossed it on the bed, then rubbed a casual hand over his chest and abs. He wanted her to look. It was vain and stupid, but so what? Let her see what she was missing because she was too proud and scared to admit that she believed in his innocence.

Holding her gaze, he walked her way, toward the bathroom door to the left of her desk, unlatching the fly of his jeans as he moved.

He stopped in the doorway, leaned his shoulder against the molding and grinned at Alicia's flushed face and chest that wasn't yet moving again.

"Don't forget to breathe, Phoenix."

Sucking in a breath, she offered him an almost convincing eye roll. Almost. "Oh, please. Egotistical much?"

He hooked his thumbs in the waistband of his briefs and pushed them and his jeans to the floor. "Little bit. Is that a problem for you?"

She kept her eyes on his, matching his stare of challenge. "You don't have anything I haven't seen before." He could tell she was going for exasperated sarcasm, but he didn't miss the thin unsteadiness of her voice.

It stirred his body to life, knowing she was forcing herself not to look lower than his face. And knowing that as soon as he turned around, she'd drop her attention to his backside. Knowing that she wanted him and was having to hold herself back the same way he was holding himself back from giving in to his basest need.

The animal inside him growled for release. Instead,

he spun on his heel and walked to the glass shower. And yeah, he did feel her eyes on him. He never did know how long she looked, but after he washed his hair, he cleared the water from his eyes and turned to the door only to find it closed.

Chapter 11

By the time the cloud-covered sky lightened the next morning, John was ready to hold a gun to Alicia's computer and threaten it with violence if it didn't chime with news of Rory's movement soon.

Finally, at 0800 hours, while John was on shift in front of the screen, an alert chime sounded. He had no clue what he was looking at, but all he knew was that when a chime sounded, he needed to wake the sleeping beauty that was snoring in the bed.

It had definitely been weird sharing a room with her, especially after he'd nearly lost control the night before and made love with her. He'd ruined her shirt, for pity's sake. Then he'd paraded around naked on his way to the shower, daring her to look. As if he had zero command over his actions. As if he was back in college trying to get a squeal out of the girls in his dorm.

He had to admit, it had been satisfying to watch Alicia try and fail to keep her eyes on his face.

Her stubborn refusal to capitulate and admit he was worthy of her trust was getting old, and he was certain it would come up again real soon, but not this morning. Because that alert chime meant they had a lead on Rory.

When they were lovers, he used to kiss Alicia awake, but today he needed to concentrate on their mission, so he wasn't getting any closer to her than the foot of the bed. Through the comforter, he wiggled her big toe until she roused.

"We got a chime. Time to roll."

She flopped onto her back, let out a groan-slash-sigh that spoke to how exhausted she still was after the scant couple hours of sleep she'd allowed herself, then rolled out of bed to her feet.

One look at her bed-tousled hair and soft-sleepy face and John had to avert his eyes before he did something stupid. Like kiss her or hold her. Or tell her how lovely and relaxed and real she was first thing in the morning and how much it made him miss seeing her like that when he was her man.

He turned to the little table that served as a coffee station and prepared two cups while she plunked into the desk chair and squinted at the screen.

"We have a hit. It's one of the theft victims from the Ammaly Bay Resort who didn't cancel their debit card. It was used four minutes ago at an ATM machine in Fort-de-France to withdraw two hundred euros. It's across from the Catholic church along the harbor about four miles west."

"That's where he is right now? Real time?"

She stood and strode to the boots she'd lined up near the door. "Yep. I don't have time to pack my computer because he's not going to linger long. Are you ready?"

Wow. She made illegal internet surveillance look like child's play. "Go ahead and say 'I told you so.'"

She wiggled into her boot and looked quizzically at him. "About what?"

He was ready to go, boots and all, and handed her a coffee in a paper cup before slinging the strap of his bag over his shoulder. "I would have found Rory without you, but this, us together—you with your mad computer skills—is much, much faster."

She grinned. It was a hell of thing because, outside of his daydreams, he hadn't seen her smile in twenty months. He'd forgotten how hungry he used to be to see that smile, to watch her face lighten, especially when it was directed at him.

"I told you so," she said in a singsong voice that made his heart ache. He'd forgotten about that, too. How he used to crave hearing the flirty lilt her voice took on when she teased.

He looked away and ran a quick pat down of his pants and shirt, doing an inventory of the weapons on his person.

He opened the door. "We have to hurry. Logan's crew is going to pick up Rory's trail soon, if they're not here already."

Alicia set the coffee cup on the table by the door, then pulled a stun gun from her computer bag. Poetic justice, John assumed, since Rory had used one to neutralize Diego before shooting Alicia.

She gave the air a test zap with it, then smiled again. "Let's end this thing with Rory once and for all."

Speed took precedence over personal ethics this morning. Rather than try to hail a cab or jump-start a stolen car, John sprinted to the closest idling car at the nearest intersection, flung the door open and ordered the middle-aged male driver out at gunpoint.

He hated pulling stunts like that, scaring innocent people and stealing their vehicles. The poor guy was probably on his way to work and John was leaving him stranded in the road with a hurricane bearing down on the island. It was a jerky move, for sure, but a worse move would be allowing a murderer to stay free for one second longer than necessary. For all he or Alicia knew, Rory had already committed more murders or was planning to.

He shoved a stack of cash at the terrified man, then dropped into the driver's seat as Alicia slid in on the passenger's side. Rather than wait for the light to change, he flipped a U-turn and sped off along the waterway.

When they were close enough that they could make out the cherubs adorning the church spires rising above the surrounding buildings, the rain turned into a downpour with wind gusts that pushed against the car and threatened to dislodge awnings on the buildings and the palm trees.

They saw more than one person with bags of groceries, braving the storm for last-minute supplies as merchants, drenched to the bone, hustled to cover windows with wooden boards. People were scrambling to batten down their belongings and get off the street, covering themselves against the worst of the rain and wind with colorful tarps, made even more vibrant by the churning gray sea licking up against the concrete wall separating the sea from the pedestrian byway lining the harbor.

John drove by the church at a crawl, looking for anything that resembled an ATM. Alicia spotted it first, across a side street from the church and tucked inside a glass enclosure attached to the outside of a bank.

They didn't see Rory on any of the surrounding sidewalks or streets, but shielding his identity wouldn't be hard in the storm. All he'd need was one of those tarps like the locals used as umbrellas.

John parked a block away on another side street up a hill from the frontage road and took the keys with him. They hurried along on foot in the direction of the church.

"We need height," Alicia called through the noise of the storm, pointing to a set of stairs leading to a second-floor restaurant's patio that overlooked the harbor. The restaurant was closed and boarded up, with not a single chair or table on the patio and the awning rolled up tight and strapped down.

The patio sat at an intersection, with great views in all directions along the flat road skirting the harbor. John debated whether or not binoculars would be effective, given the rain, and decided against it. First he needed to figure out which direction to look.

Where would Rory go after getting money? To get a fake passport, to pay for a hotel room? He scanned the businesses, most of which were closed and locked. For all they knew, he'd stolen a car and was long gone, but John's instincts told him Rory was still close by. Then he saw a market a block past the church that was still open, one of those general stores that looked as if it had a little of everything. It looked crowded inside with citizens and tourists making last-minute purchases. A man turned the corner toward the market, hunched under a blue tarp and resembling Rory's build and height.

"I think I got him. The blue tarp at nine o'clock."

She ran to the edge of the patio and squinted in that direction. "I think you're right, but I can't tell for sure."

There was no one on the sidewalk in front or behind the suspect, so if John could get his sniper rifle set up in time, he'd have a viable shot—if the man turned so John and Alicia could see his face and confirm it was Rory.

John dropped his bag and pulled out his Remington and a 7mm magnum cartridge. He set it against the patio rail and loaded the ammo, but it was all for naught. The man kept the tarp pulled tightly over his downturned head until he was in the store, out of sight.

"We've got to go on foot. This is it, John. I can feel it."

John could, too. He cleared the unspent ammo, shoved both into his bag, then followed Alicia back down the stairs.

"I'll cover the back door. You cover the front," she said.

It was a good idea in theory, but John had the feeling that if Rory ran out the back door, Alicia would kill him on the spot rather than honor their agreement. It wasn't a chance he was willing to take.

"Let's stick together."

At the base of the stairs, she turned and stopped him with a hand to his chest. "The only way that makes sense is if you don't trust me."

They didn't have time for this. "Okay. I don't trust you."

She looked as if she wanted to either argue about it or slap him, John couldn't decide, but she stopped herself. "Fine. Let's see what we can see through the store's window, then go from there."

John blinked water out of his eyes as he noticed a man leaning against a wall a few stores down from the store Rory had entered. It was the man on Logan's crew who'd sat in the passenger seat of the shuttle van, looking casual and unaffected by the fact that it was raining cats and dogs, with one hand on a closed long red umbrella and the other in his pocket, probably gripping a gun.

John and Alicia crouched on the stairs, scanning the nearby buildings for the rest of the ICE unit. They couldn't be far away. After all, Logan's rule was to always have backup.

"How did they find us so fast?" Alicia whispered.

The woman who'd been driving the van was the next John noticed. She stood under an eave of the church, her eyes glued to the alley behind the row of buildings that housed the market.

Knowing what he did about Logan's crew's objectives, they were staking out the store with one sole purpose: to trap Alicia by using Rory as bait. Which meant there was at least one operative at each possible exit point for the store—the woman on this end of the alley, someone on the other side and probably a stationary sniper. At least, that's how John would've played it if he'd been a crew leader.

"If the man under the tarp is Rory, then there's no

easy way for us to get to him before Logan's crew does," Alicia said.

"They're not here for Rory."

Her eyes brightened with understanding. "We can't just leave. We can't let Rory slip away."

John pulled his handgun. "Then let's see how we can add a little confusion into their plan."

They sneaked up behind the female operative, with John electing himself as the bait. He walked right up to her, gun ready, waving. As soon as she set her hand on her own gun, Alicia stepped from the shadows with her stun gun and zapped the woman good.

She crumpled to the ground. John grabbed her firearm and stuffed it in his pocket while Alicia bound her wrists and ankles, then he and Alicia jogged across the street and flattened against the wall around the side of the alley. Alicia kept a lookout on the street side, in case Rory or one of Logan's operatives appeared. John peered around the corner of the alley, searching for the stationary sniper.

John and the man saw each other at the same time. He recognized the man as the operative who had been sitting in the very back of the shuttle van. Today he was standing in an open floor-to-ceiling window in the second story of a building across the alley.

He moved his aim from the rear door of the market to John's head, just as John aimed at his. "One hostile. I've got him, Phoenix. You keep your eye on that front market door for Rory or Logan."

He was perfectly happy with the sniper in the alley not realizing Alicia was present for as long as they could pull that off.

"Set your gun on the floor, then get your hands up

where I can see them," John bellowed. He had zero expectation that the man would comply, but it was worth a try.

"You're in no position to be making demands against Damian." It was Logan, walking out of a door into the alley below his sniper—named Damian, apparently—a handgun aimed at John. "Where's Alicia?"

What did he expect John to say to that asinine question? "Behind you, moron."

Logan smiled indulgently. "You're outmanned two to one, here, John. It's time to set your gun down. If you cooperate with us about finding Alicia, I can promise you lenience when I take you into custody."

"What a tempting offer, but I think I'll pass." He smiled at Damian. "I'm going to shoot you first, just so you know."

Logan laughed. "Even if you got that shot off at Damian before he fired on you, do you really think you can make a shot that tough? You've been working on your tan at the beach for too long. The sun's warped your judgment."

Boom. There it was. The sweet spot—John's comfort zone of being underestimated by his opponent. He stepped into full view and shrugged. "You have a point there. Damian and I are a hundred meters apart at a seventy-degree angle with high wind conditions and rain. That'd be a tough shot for any man."

Alicia cleared her throat.

"Or woman," he added. "But I must say, I'm glad you noticed my tan. I think it complements the blue in my eyes, don't you?" He winked at Damian for emphasis.

At the exact second the man's focus shifted to John's

eyes, John squeezed the trigger, aiming at Damian's knee. He hit his mark. Damian hit the deck, shooting. Shots rang out from Logan's gun, too, but John was already ducking back around the corner, out of range.

Logan fired again, the bullet ricocheting off the cinderblock near the corner where John stood. Bits of cinderblock and white paint crumbled onto the rain-soaked cobblestones. John pulled his rifle around from his back and started spraying bullets in Logan's direction. After several shots, he chanced a look. Neither Logan nor Damian were visible.

"What's happening on your side, Phoenix?

"Everyone's fleeing the market. They must have heard the shots, but I haven't seen Rory."

John looked in the alley. Still no Logan. Movement on the roof caught his eye. Bingo.

"He's on the roof. Rory. Running scared."

Alicia got close to him and followed his line of sight to the roof. Rory was running in the opposite direction along the flat roof of the building. Bad plan, Rory. But then again, between John and Alicia and Logan's crew, they'd pretty much had all the street level exits blocked, so it was hard to blame him for getting creative.

Once, when John and Alicia's black ops crew was in Athens, Greece, they'd engaged in a rooftop chase, except that they were the team of five and the scumbag art thieves they were chasing down were the party of two. The thieves had stolen a critical artifact from a museum that had been on loan from Egypt and would've caused an international incident if it couldn't have been recovered on the down low, but there they were chasing them over rooftops and jumping buildings to keep up.

"You know what this has me thinking about?" he asked.

She smiled. "Athens."

"Exactly."

They tapped the sides of their guns together. "Let's roll."

After a boost from John, Alicia scaled the fire escape ladder first. Wet and caked with dirt, it was tough going, but she managed fine.

John waited for her to start on the second ladder before starting the first in case it couldn't hold their combined weight.

In minutes flat, they were two stories aboveground on the building's flat roof deck. The rain was hitting the deck so hard that it gave the illusion it was raining upside down. Alicia wasn't entirely convinced that a particularly strong gust of wind wouldn't blow them clean off the roof. Judging by the angry sea to their right and the swirl of black clouds above them, Hurricane Hannah's arrival was imminent.

Rory was four buildings in front of them, but in another seven or eight buildings, he'd reach a dead end where the block stopped at the cross street.

With Alicia in the lead, they took off in a sprint as fast as the uneven roof and rain-slicked patches of tar or tile allowed. From the looks of it, Logan and his team had flanked the buildings, with Logan running along the street and the man from the passenger's seat of the van running through the alley, keeping pace with John and Alicia and chancing an occasional shot. Whether they were aiming at her, John or Rory was unclear, but if Logan's history held true, he was after her, and her alone. To be on the safe side, she kept one eye on Rory and the roof and the other on Logan.

Sure enough, while she watched, Logan ground to a stop and turned his gun in her direction.

She was in the process of hitting the deck when John's arm pushed her down and she hit the roof hard. Gritty water splashed in her eyes and mouth. John dropped on top of her as though shielding her with his body as he unloaded his firearm over the edge of the roof, returning Logan's shots.

As soon as the gunfire stopped, she shoved him off, spit out the grit and wiped her eyes with the hem of the T-shirt. "Thanks for that, but I know how to duck and cover all by myself."

"It was a gut reaction. Sorry."

Logan must have ducked out of range of John's shots because she didn't see him and so took off running toward Rory again. John ran by her side, holding her pace though he could probably go much faster if he wanted to. She wasn't sure why it irked her that he didn't.

"You didn't have those kinds of gut reactions when we were teammates," she said.

"True, but in all fairness, this is the first time I've been on a mission where you're the asset. It's throwing me off."

She smacked his arm as hard as she could. "I am not the asset. I'm your business partner."

"Whatever you say."

As a woman who'd worked in a world of men since a week after her high school graduation, Alicia knew that no man ever said "whatever you say" and meant it. The throwaway line was passive-aggressive man code for "You're delusional and can't be reasoned with so I'm not going to try."

They scaled a short chain-link fence separating a roof maintenance area from the tiled facade on the other side. Alicia made sure she hit the ground on the other side at the same time John did.

"You're not in this to protect me," she said. "We're in this together to catch Rory. I can take care of myself. And I'm just as good an operative as you are."

He looked taken aback. "I know that. Like I said, I've never had an asset before who was—"

"For the last time, I'm not the asset."

"Okay."

Ahead of them, Rory struggled to maintain his balance, slipping and grabbing at ledges. Alicia slowed as he did in approach to what looked like a pretty substantial gap to the last building in the line. She was so intent on watching him back up and take a running leap across the gap that she didn't see the change in the slope they were traversing. Her feet flew out from under her and she dropped her gun, intent on breaking her fall with her hands.

John caught her midfall, wrapping his arms around her middle until her momentum stopped. Then he set her back on her feet and handed over her gun.

"Don't say it," she said.

A light shone in his eyes. Tender and knowing, taking the fight right out of her. He nodded.

They both turned their attention to Rory, who had reached the dead end and had ducked behind an air-conditioning unit in the center of the building that looked to be a boutique hotel. The only wild card Alicia could see in the equation was what Logan's crew would do now.

She got low and peered over the edge into the alley. No Logan. John was performing the same check on the street side.

"Anything?" she called.

"Nobody here."

"Interesting."

They both took stock of the nearest roof access points. There were three, which wasn't unmanageable. This was the scenario they'd ended up using in Athens against those artifact thieves, because every rooftop chase ended in a dead end, which forced the criminal into a pressure situation that caused them to make stupid mistakes.

But Rory was no ordinary criminal. Neither were the thieves in Athens, though, and Rory and John had surrounded them at gunpoint while Diego and Alicia had extracted full confessions, then took them into custody and recovered the artifacts without a single shot fired. She loved days like that.

John knelt near the edge of the building facing Rory and took his sniper rifle from his bag. Alicia got close to him, but instead of watching Rory, she had her eyes on the roof access points.

"You're hurt," John called to Rory. "There's a hurricane coming and ICE has a new black ops team on your tail. You need to surrender to me and Alicia before this gets any more out of hand."

"So you can kill me?" Rory shouted back.

It was Alicia's turn to try. "We could kill you right now, and we could have killed you before you walked into that market. But we didn't. We want to talk to you." She almost couldn't get that half-truth out, but her vengeance would have to wait until John had a shot at getting the answers he needed. "I can't guarantee that Logan's team will be so interested in what you have to say."

Rory laughed. "Boy, oh, boy, this is golden—you two working together to get me. Alicia, I hope you're sleeping with one eye open so he can't kill you while you dream."

John's jaw rippled. His eyes narrowed.

"I slept just fine, actually." Which was the truth. She'd slept like a baby for the first time since she could remember.

"Don't engage him on that," John said quietly. "He thinks his best chance of getting through this standoff alive is to pit us against each other so we're distracted. He knows that when you and I are working together, we're unbeatable."

She agreed with him about Rory's strategy, though she'd never thought about the two of them like that. He was right, though. They did make a great team. "I know."

"Alicia," Rory continued, "you have to ask yourself—why would I lie about John? I was already going to prison for the rest of my life."

"Don't fill her head with lies. You've done enough damage."

Nobody was filling her head with anything except herself because she wasn't some passive, malleable weakling. Not like she was before when she took Rory's, Diego's and Ryan's word for John's guilt. Now she didn't only have John's version of what happened, she had the man himself.

She had John, who'd rescued her from Logan and freely admitted he was scared about what was going to happen to them. The man who'd kissed her like his life depended on it and who hadn't abandoned her though she couldn't tell him what he wanted to hear about her belief of his innocence.

"Alicia, I can tell you don't know what to think," Rory said. "But I'm telling you the truth. John and I were partners. Blood brothers. You know that. Sure, he was too chicken to pull the trigger when it came to getting you out of the way, but he was more than happy to let me do the honors."

John steadied his rifle, keeping his eye in the scope. "You sound like a desperate man, which is good considering we're about to kill you if you don't surrender yourself to us."

But Rory was unfazed. "John, she's playing you, too, you know. She doesn't give a damn about you, never did. Not like you cared about her. She used you."

John lifted his gaze from the scope and stared across the gap to Rory. "You mean like you used me?"

Rory laughed. "I didn't use you. I was trying to show you a new path away from that life-sucking, low-paying team of bureaucrats we were a part of in ICE." He was unconsciously inching out of the safety provided by the air-conditioning unit. She bet John could execute an accurate kill shot now with no problem. "Even the army screwed us over. They paid us a pittance to risk our lives for half-baked operations run by a bunch of suits in Washington. I was trying to help you take control of your life."

John shook his head. "By killing the woman I loved?"

Only Alicia's professional experience kept her from flinching or showing any outward change in expression. He'd been in love with her? Since when? Her thoughts returned again to the night he'd come to her two months after the shooting, the desperate hunger of his expression. He'd wanted to see for himself that she was okay. Thinking about it now, she knew he'd loved her then. Did he love her still?

"She didn't love you. You know that. She was holding you back, just like she's doing right now. I knew you wouldn't realize your true potential unless I took her out of the equation, but I underestimated the hold she had on you. I thought we were blood brothers, but you screwed me over, so I screwed you over."

"What is my true potential, do you think? Joining you on the dark side and becoming rich, evil bastards together?"

Rory moved fully away from the air-conditioning unit, sneering. "You could have been somebody, John. Now you're just a nobody, same as you ever were. You're like one of those filler characters in a thriller movie—the kind they don't bother giving a name to. Schmuck Number Three. The guy who always dies first. At least if you'd stuck with me, you would have had money and power to help you grow a backbone."

Rory sounded a lot like Alicia had when she'd first talked to John on St. Thomas. She'd called him a side-kick. The Robin to Rory's Batman. God, what a fool she'd been. This whole time, since the moment she'd initiated the sequence to break Rory out of prison—no, further back, from the moment he and Rory joined their ICE team—John was the one who'd kept his honor intact. He'd never wavered, and he'd never compromised about who he was and what he stood for, no matter what vitriol and lies had been flung at him.

And then, this week, he'd sacrificed his freedom and future to help her. He was the best man she knew and she loved him.

My God. She loved him and yet she'd nearly followed through with setting him up to take the fall for the deeds she'd committed this week. It made her tremble, thinking about the monster she'd narrowly avoided becoming. No better than Rory.

She touched John's shoulder. His expression was hard but she sensed his compassion and goodness behind the stone mask. This man, this warrior, was no follower, nor sidekick. Rory was a sociopath and murderer. That she'd believed his word over the man who loved her, who treated her like a precious asset, was something she'd regret for the rest of her life.

"Do you have this shot?" she asked.

Sadness flashed in his eyes. "Yes. But there has to be another way."

"You have to take the shot. Please. Logan's crew is going to catch up with us any second. If he gets taken into custody, neither one of us will get what we want. And if he escapes and kills another civilian, that blood will be on both our hands."

"I could shoot to wound, like I did last time."

She set her hand on his back, stroking. "He's never going to tell you what you want to hear. But I can."

It was time to tell the truth and say what needed to be said—that she believed in his innocence and that she loved him. It didn't compare with proving his innocence to the rest of the world, but it would have to be enough. This conversation was twenty months too late, but it was all she had to offer him.

She drew a deep inhale and opened her eyes, ready to come clean about the way she felt. Then all hell broke loose.

Chapter 12

In John's periphery, he saw movement on the roof of the parking garage across the alley. Logan and his two remaining operatives positioned themselves along the roof's edge. One operative trained his automatic rifle at Rory, the other at John, and Logan's gun was aimed straight at Alicia.

John pulled her to the ground. She could insist all she wanted that she wasn't the asset in this mission, but sometime between waking Alicia up that morning and spotting Rory from the restaurant patio, John had made peace with the truth that his mission was no longer to capture Rory. He was there to keep Alicia safe. To keep her from getting captured by Logan or shot by Rory or taken into custody by any one of the wolves at her door trying to destroy her.

Whether she could admit he was innocent or not,

he couldn't live with himself if anything happened to her under his watch.

"Is it Logan?" she said.

"And two of his friends."

"What are we going to do now?"

Good question. He peered over the edge at Rory, who stood in the same place, raising his arms in the air like Logan was presently instructing him. "I still have the kill shot."

"Then you have to take it."

Could he really shoot the man who he'd gone to war with—his once-upon-a-time blood brother and best friend for more than a decade? He set his eye on the scope and slid his finger to the trigger, his heart warring with his head. Rory wasn't his best friend anymore. He was the man who'd tried to kill the woman John loved. One shot would be all it took.

Then all the yearning and betrayal, all the pain and hope that someday Rory would reverse his position, the threat he posed to Alicia, her quest for vengeance would be over in seconds, and he and Alicia could both move on with their lives, even if he'd never have the chance to prove his innocence. Even if killing the man who'd once been his best friend in the world— whom he'd spent holidays with, whom he'd been the best man for at Rory's wedding and his shoulder to lean on when that marriage ended—was something John would never recover from.

But even as his heart and mind warred, Alicia's body pressed against him, her hand stroking softly over his back, reminding him of feelings he couldn't repress, try as he might. Reminding him of what he wanted from her, what he'd dreamed of with her—the life, the love, the adventure of having her by his side.

On an exhale, he steadied his aim and prepared to make the hardest decision of his life.

"I know you're on that roof, John and Alicia. Stand up slowly, your arms in the air, and we'll do this nice and peacefully. I swear on my life that I won't hurt her, John. If she turns herself in right now, I'll personally see to her safety in custody."

Sure, he would. Because Logan had already proved to be such a stand-up friend.

"If you two don't stand up and surrender in the next, oh, thirty seconds, then I have a grenade with your name on it ready to launch," Logan called to them.

A grenade, huh? Great idea, if not a smidge repetitive after the rum distillery incident. Oh, well. All was fair in black ops. He grabbed his M4 automatic rifle, made sure it was fully loaded, then screwed on a grenade launcher.

Alicia grinned and selected an antitank grenade from his bag. "We can't even take credit for this being our idea."

He handed the outfitted rifle to her. "I can live with that if you can."

They tapped gun barrels.

"You shoot that at Logan at my signal."

"Got it."

He took a fortifying breath, then stood, his sniper rifle aimed at Logan's chest.

"Are you crazy?" Alicia said in a harsh whisper, trying to pull him back down behind the protective lip of the roof.

"There's a good chance," he answered. He locked

gazes with Logan and called, "It's either him or us. You're going to have to choose."

His crewmates laughed.

"How about I choose D, all of the above?" Logan said.

John shook his head. "Getting greedy, Logan? I thought you knew better than that."

Logan's smile was malicious. "My people have guns aimed at you and a directive to neutralize you both using whatever means necessary and you're giving me a lecture on combat tactics? That's rich."

"Go ahead, Phoenix. I'm tired of listening to this guy."

"If I do it, he'll shoot you."

"No, he won't. He'll be too busy scrambling off the roof."

A loud crack filled the air as she fired. The grenade canister landed in front of Logan's feet and rolled his way.

Both of Logan's crew members turned tail and ran toward the stairs. With a fierce growl, Logan lobbed his own grenade in their direction.

As John watched the grenade spin through the air in his and Alicia's direction, time seemed to slow down. He dropped his rifle, grabbed Alicia's arm and helped her stand.

"You have to make that jump," he shouted, pointing to the roof Rory was on. It was the only idea he had to keep her alive. "Go!"

She was already running. He ran, too.

Together, they launched themselves over the ledge. John twisted in the air, watching Alicia. She'd gotten enough air, but her momentum was slowing too soon. Panicking anew, their eyes met and held. John stretched his arms out, one toward the roof, the other to Alicia, grabbing hold of her wrist as she grabbed hold of his.

The move slowed them both down more. They weren't going to make it. He dug deep, willing them to safety before the grenade exploded. Willing them not to fall two stories to the concrete sidewalk between the buildings.

His arm hit the roof edge. His fingernails scraped over the slick wet brick, losing purchase. Then Alicia's weight lightened.

"I've got a handhold," she called.

He looked down. She had a death grip on one of the decorative wrought-iron bars covering the window below him. He released her wrist and, as his fingers slipped off the last bit of roof, he grabbed hold of another wrought-iron bar, praying it held.

Above them, a roaring boom ripped through the air. John looked up as a fireball eclipsed the sky but passed right over them in a wave of heat and volatile energy. Bits of building crumbled around them, and the air clouded over with debris, but they were alive.

Alicia walked her hands across the bars toward the fire escape ladder. Neither spoke as they navigated the ladders to the ground, avoiding falling debris and spots that were slick with rain. John, for one, wasn't capable of speaking yet because he was still processing all that had happened and how narrowly they'd escaped death.

Had Rory been so lucky? What about Logan and the other agents? And worse, had any civilians been in the building and lost their lives? That last question was too dire to consider at the moment.

On the ground, John pulled Alicia into a tight embrace. She hugged him back and they just stood there, breathing hard and coming down off the adrenaline rush.

"Just launch the grenade, he said. It'll be easy, he said." He could hear the smile and relief in her voice.

"Next time, I'll give more consideration to your objections."

They shared a smile, then both turned their attention to the roof where Rory had been.

Alicia jiggled the ladder they'd come down as though testing its durability. "We have to catch Rory. We can't let a murderer stay on the loose."

"There's no chance he's on that roof still. He knows how to seize an opportunity to flee when it presents itself." Sirens sounded in approach. "Time's up, Phoenix. We're out of luck and out of chances. We need to get out of here before we're surrounded."

They rounded the corner to the street as fire engines and police squad cars sped to the scene. John didn't even have it in him to act like a shocked bystander. He slung an arm across Alicia's shoulders and kept walking.

"John." Her voice held a note of panic.

"What?"

"Is that… Is he… No."

He followed the direction of her gaze across the street, to what looked like a marina where Rory was sprinting over a dock toward a worker securing Jet Skis for the storm. They watched him knock the worker into the water, then grab a Jet Ski.

"He can't mean to go out on a Jet Ski. That's a death wish," John said.

Determination made Alicia's eyes shine bright. "We have to go after him."

John nodded. He figured as much. And, as she'd said before, they couldn't very well let Rory escape. "Let's rock and roll."

By the time they reached the marina, Rory was already skimming over the waves toward open water. Now that John was closer, the waves looked way bigger than they had from across the highway. Where the hell did Rory think he was going?

"Alicia, this isn't a good plan. The sea's too rough. We're in the middle of a damn hurricane."

But she was already on another Jet Ski, giving chase, leaving John with no choice but to follow. He jumped on the first Jet Ski he saw that had the key in it and revved the engine. At least Rory had veered left and was now running parallel to the shoreline.

They curved around Saint-Anne to the southwest side of the island, jumping waves and generally trying not to die a watery death. Alicia was so focused on the hunt, he doubted she even noticed the deteriorating conditions, but John had never felt so waterlogged, not even when he was hanging on to the outer rail of the speedboat Rory had stolen.

More than once, Rory looked over his shoulder at Alicia and John, seemingly furious that he couldn't shake them. After the last time he looked, he shot back toward shore, then swerved around a rock formation, then another, as though he hoped to get them off his tail by taking huge risks.

Alicia was relentless. She followed him every step of the way, though once she nearly overturned her Jet Ski. John stopped watching Rory and devoted all his brain power to keeping track of her movement in case she fell in the water.

In a rocky section of coast that had John's anxiety peaking, Rory swerved right, out toward open ocean again, straight at a massive, churning wave. He jumped it handily.

Alicia followed, but the erratic waves changed and swirled without warning, and John was relieved when she slowed down and maneuvered around the worst of it, though she'd lost a lot of ground on Rory. He looked over his shoulder at Alicia again, smiling this time like he was impressed with his own skills.

That was why he didn't see the huge jagged rock jutting out of the water ahead of him.

Hitting Rory with a bullet was an impossible shot, but Alicia had to try. The water conditions were getting too dangerous for them to continue on for much longer. It was too much of a danger to John. If anything happened to him because she'd insisted on this crazy chase, she'd never forgive herself.

She fumbled in her bra for her handgun, when she heard John shout something.

She looked up in Rory's direction and what she saw was like a dream sequence. His Jet Ski hit a massive rock, sending Rory into the air. A boom sounded as the Jet Ski exploded.

Alicia's arm dropped from the throttle. Did Rory just die before her eyes? Her heart pounded in her throat. John had stopped next to her as they stared at the burning Jet Ski, Alicia searching in vain for Rory's body. When, after a few minutes, she didn't see it, she decided to go in for a closer look.

She turned the throttle and sped nearer, searching the water, feeling very much like she was sleepwalking. She heard John call her name as though from a great distance, and then next thing she knew, a wave was crashing over her.

She had no idea what became of her Jet Ski because she couldn't even figure out which way was up, the undertow was so powerful. She pulled her arms through the water, trying to surface. Then an arm encircled her waist. John. She figured out the direction of his strokes and emulated him, helping all she could to get them back above water.

John pushed her above the surface before him. Alicia gasped and pulled on John to help him up, too. Once he was safely up, she spun in the water, looking for Rory.

"I'm getting you out of here," John called over the roar of the surf.

"Go without me. I have to finish what I started. There's no other way."

"There's always another way."

"If he's still alive…"

"I'm not going to lose you to—"

A wave smacked into John's side, throwing him into the rock behind him.

Alicia's heart sank. "John!"

She lunged through the water to get to him but couldn't see him in the dark, churning sea. Treading water, she turned in a circle, calling his name. Then one of his arms burst through the waves, stroking. She grabbed hold and pulled, helping him surface.

Her ragged cry of relief was swallowed by the roar of the waves and wind. She held on to him, catching her breath. He didn't seem to have hit his head too hard, but she'd never been so scared.

They clung together for a moment, foreheads touching, breathing into each other. "I thought I lost you," she croaked.

His gaze turned searching. "I thought I lost you, too."

She looked around her, past the tunnel vision for Rory that she'd had. The wind was whipping sand around the beach, the surf was higher than ever and they were surrounded by sharp, underwater rocks. John would never get out of the water without her, so to keep him safe, she'd give up her need for revenge. Because without John, who was she?

Even estranged from him, even though she'd cultivated a superficial hatred for him based on lies she'd let herself believe, he'd still been a huge part of her life. Thoughts of him had shaped her every choice, the way she processed the world, how she thought about herself and thought about love and laughter, happiness and pain.

It was John who she'd dreamed of, who she'd railed against when something went wrong, whose image she'd pictured during physical therapy when the pain started and she wanted to give up. Hate, heartbreak, love—it was all so mixed up inside of her, as though the lines separating each emotion were impossibly thin and fragile.

Sometimes, it had only been fury at him that had kept her going during her darkest moments. Fury and sorrow and the bittersweet wash of memories that hit her like an aftershock when she was lonely. She loved him more than life itself. More than revenge.

She blinked the water from her eyes. "We need to get to shore."

John nodded. "Good. Thank you."

Together, they swam to the beach, each pulling the other along, keeping each other afloat. They trudged through the surf until the waves licked at their knees.

Once they were on shore, though, she couldn't stop looking out to sea, at the rock Rory's Jet Ski had run into. There was nothing to see, though, but the rock itself; not even the Jet Ski remained above the churning seas.

"Don't even think about going back out there. He's not worth it."

She wrenched her gaze away, hating the lack of closure in not being able to confirm Rory's death. She glanced back to sea again as a feeling like grief washed through her.

"Listen to me, Phoenix. I won't let you back out there. I died inside when you were shot."

That got her attention. She turned toward him and hugged herself.

He stepped closer and touched her cheek. "I couldn't stand it when they took me into custody, not knowing if you were alive or well, but they wouldn't tell me anything and I was in that holding cell for so long." He rubbed his hands over his eyes in a futile attempt to push the water and sand from his face.

She was filled with a sudden and wholly consuming desire to comfort him for all he'd been through. She threaded her arms around his ribs.

"And then when you got out of the hospital, and it was clear you were going to survive what Rory did to you, you and I only talked that one time." His jaw shook with each bellowed word in the storm. "Check that, we didn't talk. You wouldn't talk to me. I saw it in your eyes that you believed him. Over me."

She deserved this. He needed to yell at her and she loved him enough to let him get it all out. "I'm so sorry I ever doubted you."

"I could have lived with the rest of the world thinking me a criminal, a traitor—but you? It killed me all over again. I died. Life over. Do you understand me?"

She'd known from the first time he ever made love to her that she held his heart in her hand. What she never realized until this day was that he'd held hers in his. And this control she thought she was protecting from handing it over to men? It was illusion. A cruel lie.

"I understand. And I'm so sorry."

John took hold of her face with both hands, cradling it tenderly. "I'm not losing you to this storm, even if you never admit that I would never hurt you. Even if it makes you hate me more than you already do."

She stared at his drenched shirt, then past it, to the strength and heart of the man beneath the layers. Her man. The love of her life. She swayed and the only thing keeping her upright in the wind and waves was John. Always John, with his unflappable conviction.

She'd thought he made her weak, as weak as the gunshot wound had. But how could that be true, when right now, it felt as if he was the only thing keeping her strong? How could she hate him for walking away from her before when, now, in her darkest hour, he was the only person who'd stayed by her side?

She turned her gaze to his fierce, passionate eyes that told her he'd be the anchor of her life, if only she'd let him. "I believe you. About everything. You're innocent. I don't know how I…"

His eyes closed. "Say that again. Please."

"I believe you. You're innocent. You didn't know what Rory was plotting and you didn't work with him to kill me. And I love you. God, John. I love you so much."

Nodding like crazy, his hands cradled her jaw as he pulled her lips to his. She clung to him and surrendered her body and heart to him.

A gust of wind knocked into them. They heard a crack and looked up the beach to see a tree branch hurtling over the sand. "I think Hannah's here," John said.

"We need to get off this beach."

It was John's turn to shift his attention to the rock in the distance where they'd last seen Rory. A dozen emotions flashed across his face—regret, pain, longing. Rory had been his best friend. A blood brother, John used to call him. As betrayed as Alicia had been by Rory, John had been a victim, too. Rory was going to die out there in the water, in the hurricane, and even if he wasn't, there was nothing they could do about him until the hurricane passed. Walking away now, not saving Rory's life in favor of keeping Alicia safe, ended his chance at redemption.

She pulled his face back to hers, kissing him with her whole soul.

When he ended the kiss, she followed his line of sight to the hill rising from the other side of the road, dotted with luxury estates.

"I'm going to get you up to one of those vacation homes on the hill." The way he said it, the husky, low-down tone of his words, sent shivers through her body.

He was going to find a shelter for them to ride out the storm in. He was going to make love to her.

She'd never wanted anything more.

His fingers brushed along her cheek, pushing errant hairs behind her ear. "Do you have it in you to go a little farther away from the beach?"

Knowing they'd be safe from the storm soon, knowing what he was going to do her, she had all the energy in the world. "Lead the way."

Chapter 13

Alicia stood in the doorway of what looked to be a home theater, her Glock drawn and ready, her ears listening for any hint that she and John weren't alone in the sprawling, hilltop estate that had seemed the surest bet in the long line of wrought-iron-gated mansions along the deserted residential street.

Most of the houses they'd passed had the feel of being empty, save for those in which the owners or employees were still braving the rain and wind gusts to take thirteenth-hour measures to secure the houses' windows and patio furniture against the coming storm. They'd selected this particular house—a white-and-blue two-story architectural triumph of angles and curves set amid a lushly landscaped tropical oasis and a pebbled driveway that had to cost at least eight figures—because it was the only one with its windows not boarded up against the storm.

John thought that probably meant the owners were away and, with the storm upon them, there was no way workers would be summoned to secure it now. Not that he and Alicia were taking any chances.

They'd hopped the fence, then circled the house twice. The garage door was hooked up to a keypad, which was perfect. It only took Alicia a few minutes time to figure out the 2-4-6-8 code. They closed the garage door behind them. With a crowbar Alicia found in a cupboard near a workbench, John muscled the door from the garage to the house open. After all the laws they'd violated in the past couple days, a little breaking and entering was the least of their sins.

An alarm buzzed, but disarming house alarms was something she'd been doing for sport since she was fourteen and discovered that the couple across the street from her mom's house—the ones with the state-of-the-art computer system that she couldn't afford—only wintered there three months out of the year.

Still not taking any chances in assuming they were alone, they'd made a sweep of the ground floor before separating. John crept upstairs while Alicia handled the basement.

This was the kind of house Alicia felt right at home in—luxurious and sparsely decorated, with top-of-the-line everything and not a single personal touch. Outward displays of people's private lives made her uncomfortable. She knew that was a messed up way of thinking, and one she couldn't even blame on her CIA training, but from having two separate bedrooms in two separate households after her parents split. Neither liked it when she talked about the other. She'd figured out fast that life was easier for all parties involved when she pretended that whatever parent she wasn't presently under the care of didn't exist.

Like, instead of going to her mom's house for the weekend, her dad somehow preferred to think that she merely powered off like a machine until it was his turn for custody again. And they both hated hearing about boyfriends or parties, especially if she'd had any fun when she wasn't with them. So she'd learned to keep the details of her private life private, her photographs off the shelves, everything inside. Now, doing any differently made her uncomfortable.

The CIA was perfect. It was as if her whole life had been training for that career.

The Krav Maga with her father, the secretiveness, learning all about breaking and entering to use her neighbor's computer. She was made for this life.

The home theater, which shared the basement with a large utility room that housed a washer and dryer and a fitness room, was dark and windowless and utterly cozy. Three rows of plush brown leather sofas with little tables on either side of them for drinks and food faced a massive viewing screen that nearly took up the entire wall on the far side of the room.

If the hurricane got bad and the house started to deteriorate, this was where she and John would probably stay to wait it out. A shot of lust rippled through her when she thought about passing the stormy night with John in this room, of all the many ways they could make use of the sofas, blankets and throw pillows here.

Despite that she could feel the emptiness of the space, she methodically walked the rows, her gun pointed at the ground, making absolutely certain they wouldn't be caught by surprise by some employee either using it as his own hurricane hideout or guarding the estate.

"So this is the room." John's voice was velvet-soft and deep. He stood in the doorway, arms crossed over his chest in a way that made his biceps strain against his shirtsleeves.

"The room for what?"

Rather than answer her, he prowled in her direction, stripping his shirt off. He tossed it on the ground.

She was suddenly, inexplicably self-conscious. It'd been twenty months since she'd had an orgasm. Twenty long months of denial, of feeling as if that part of her was dead. What if it really was? What if she couldn't be that easy-to-orgasm sexual being she'd once been to John and she disappointed him? Or even worse, what if he'd changed? So much about him had. Could she trust him with herself to let go and feel?

John's jeans fell to the floor, revealing a pair of wet, skimpy, stretchy blue briefs that had molded to his body's every contour. He always did like wearing sexy designer underwear and she loved the way it looked on him—reflecting not just the perfection and virility of his body, but his bold, self-deprecating confidence and humor, which were the traits of his she'd first been attracted to. Maybe this was a sign that he wasn't so different a man than he used to be. Maybe the old John was hiding under layers upon layers of armor. But what if it wasn't?

He slid his hands up her forearms. "You're thinking too much."

"How do you know that?"

"Because you always overthink this part."

He was right; she did. She could talk herself out of

pleasure nine times out of ten because the idea of letting go and losing control was terrifying. Worse than standing in a plane's open hatch with a parachute on, waiting for the signal to jump. Butterflies in her stomach made her shiver and her breath catch.

He stroked her arms with his thumbs. "Shh…easy there. Because do you know what one of my favorite things to do is?" His hands slipped down to cover hers. He lifted them and set her hands on his chest, pressing until her fingers splayed across his hard, hot flesh.

"What?" she whispered, closing her eyes, feeling so out of control that her whole body, from her legs to her neck and head, was tense with anxiety, turning her fear of being incapable of passion into a self-fulfilling prophecy. She knew, logically, that all she needed to do was relax and trust herself, trust John. But the message from her brain wasn't translating to her spirit. All she could do was cling to the loneliness, that hole inside her that told her that she could never love, not the way John deserved. She just wasn't built that way.

His lips found hers, brushing over them, then tugging gently on her lower lip. Then he kissed the tip of her nose before pressing his forehead to hers. She gripped his chest and squeezed her eyes closed.

"One of my favorite things in the world is getting you to stop thinking so much. I used to live for that moment when you let go and let me in."

"I don't know if I can let you in anymore." She opened her eyes and met his heated, determined gaze. "John, I haven't— I can't…"

He rubbed her arms. "You don't have to do anything you don't want to do."

"No, please. I want you. I want to…" She mashed her lips together. "I'm just…scared."

His brows drew together. "Of me?"

"Of myself." It cost her a lot less than she'd expected it to, making that confession, exposing her deepest feelings to John. It would be a learning process, but she'd never met a man more worthy of entrusting her true self to.

He nodded. "Let's start with something easy. I saw a washing machine down here. How about you let me take you to the laundry room and get these wet clothes off you and washed before Hannah takes out our power?"

She felt some of her fight evaporate. How did he do that? "Laundry as foreplay?"

"Exactly." Grinning, he took her hand and led her from the room.

He left the hallway light on but kept the laundry room light off. Standing before the washing machine, he took hold of her shirt. "Raise your arms for me."

Working slowly, tenderly, he peeled the layers of clothing from her. His let his touch linger on her shoulders and arms, on the curve of her hips and hair. Nothing pushy, nothing that ratcheted up her anxiety more than a low buzz of nerves.

She stood still, arms hugging herself, and watched him measure detergent, then start the machine, marveling over how sexy the chore was when performed by a totally naked, hard-bodied warrior that she could reach out and touch anywhere she wanted. To prove it to herself, she extended an unsteady hand toward his hip and ran her hand along the gorgeous, perfect V diagonal of his traverse oblique muscle, loving the way his flesh felt beneath her hand.

He held himself in place, facing the washing machine, hands braced against the lid, and let her explore, even flexing his abs in a way that nearly made her purr as she bumped her fingers along his eight-pack. "My warrior," she whispered in awe.

Before her nerves could stop her, she moved her hand to encircle his thick, hard length. He burrowed his nose and mouth in the crook of his shoulder and arm, eyes squeezed shut as he took the pleasure she offered.

When he opened his eyes and turned to face her, his smoldering gaze was gone, replaced by a full-fledged fire. He took hold of her waist and lifted her effortlessly onto the top of the washing machine. The metal was biting cold on her backside. But the temporary discomfort fled her mind entirely when he moved between her parted knees and brushed his fingertips over the strip of hair between her thighs. His light touch blended with the vibrations from the washing machine, sending a shiver of pleasure through her flesh.

Then he cupped a hand to the back of her neck, pulled her face to his and kissed her with a gentle, loving reverence. She threaded her hands into his hair and gave herself over to the moment, her fears temporarily forgotten.

"Before we get any further," he murmured, "I need you to know that I don't have protection. I looked in the upstairs bedrooms but didn't find any." His hands smoothed over her back, caressing, loving her. "Even if we don't get to do that part, there's still so much we can do. Being together like this, it's enough for me, for now."

The number one rule of being a female operative was staying on the pill to keep periods predictable or nonexistent, whatever duty demanded. Even so, there were a lot of reasons beyond an unwanted pregnancy to use condoms, and Alicia had never once had sex without one—even though she and John were lovers exclusively for almost two years. That would have been too much of an acknowledgment of exclusivity, too much of a bond.

Tonight, she wanted that connection with him. To trust him the way he'd always wanted her to. She palmed his erection as a deep need settled low in her belly. She couldn't believe how much she'd missed this sensation of wanting sex so badly that it made her ache, and the idea of bringing John pleasure, of giving him her body to use for his pleasure, was a heady feeling, indeed. If only she could be as sure about her own pleasure. What if she couldn't come? What if she couldn't feel any more than this?

She shoved her fear aside, determined not to let it stand in her way anymore. "I'm on the pill. And I want to do this with you. Raw, like this."

He released a ragged exhale and looked into her eyes. "I'm safe. Tested and fine. I would never compromise you like that."

"I trust you." It felt so freeing to say. "I haven't been tested recently, but I'm safe." She swallowed, gathering her courage, then added, "I haven't been with another man since you."

He looked concerned by the confession, like he worried over her well-being. "Why not? My ego's going crazy here. Tell me you didn't wait for me. Tell me that's not what this was about. What's going on with you?"

She could have lied, but she was done with that where he was concerned. "It wasn't about waiting for you, at least not at first. It was a tactical decision. I wanted to take every unwanted emotion I had—my hatred of you, my sexual frustration, my anger at my body—and transform them into power to help me heal. But as time went on, and my body grew stronger, I realized I wasn't interested in anybody sexually anymore. I stopped thinking about it at all. I felt…"

She shook her head. How could she describe it when she barely understood it herself?

"What did you feel, Phoenix? Talk to me."

"I felt nothing. I thought that even though I survived the shooting, that part of me didn't because I wasn't interested in sex. I couldn't think about it without thinking about you, so it was just easier to not think about it at all. And after a while I didn't even have to fight it. That part of me that could feel desire, feel like a woman, was dead inside me. And I'm afraid it's still dead."

She expected him to protest her words, to tell her that was all in her imagination. Instead, he didn't say anything, but placed his index finger in his mouth, wetting it, then used it to part her inner thighs.

At the first touch of his finger on her most intimate flesh, she arched, crying out. The feeling was exquisite—bliss so intense it bordered on pain. She looped an arm around his neck, holding on for dear life. She could feel her nails digging into his shoulder muscles but couldn't stop herself. She couldn't do anything but ride out the sensation evoked by his finger's slow rotation.

"Does that feel like nothing?" he murmured against her skin, his voice thick with gravel. "Does that feel like part of you is dead inside?"

"No."

"No. Not to me, either." His voice was thick, rough. His lips glided over her chest, pressing kisses to her scar and the tops of her breasts. His left arm was like a band around her middle, holding her steady like an anchor in a storm, telling her in his own way that she could let go whenever she was ready and he'd be there to keep her safe and steady.

His patient, loving finger dipped lower, gathering moisture, swirling in an unhurried rhythm, never pushing her too far too fast. She pressed her forehead to his shoulder, trying to relax as a gift to him. Trying to let go because he deserved somebody who trusted him enough to let go.

He slid a second finger next to the first, working them in unison in a way that was so masterful that it wrenched another cry from her. "You want to know what this feels like to me?"

With his magic fingers working and the vibrations of the washing machine, words failed her completely. All she could do was cling to him and feel and take whatever he offered, sexy pillow talk and all.

"When I touch you like this, when you wrap yourself around me and let me pleasure you, when you get wet because of me and you make all those sexy little noises that let me know how good I'm giving it to you, I feel like the most powerful man on Earth."

He punctuated that last word by slipping two fingers inside her.

She whimpered and arched her hips until his fingers were at the perfect angle to bring her pleasure and the washing machine undulations and vibrations rippled up her thighs. On the next noise she made, he captured her lips in a slow, deep, wet kiss.

"You are so beautiful, so alive, when you're giving yourself to me. Give yourself to me now, Phoenix. Because I remember how it feels for me when you come and it's even better than this. Even better than feeling like the king of the whole damn universe."

She was close to that now, so dangerously close. She concentrated on the feel of his fingers and the movement of the washing machine below her, his strong arm anchoring her, his lips on her neck and chest. He worked her body like he really was a god, every pump of his fingers inside her and every swirl of his thumb taking her higher, tighter, closer to the heavens.

Her every thought floated away and her body took over, rocking against his fingers until he took the hint that she needed it just a little harder and faster to get where she was trying to go.

Then his fingers moved, concentrating all their effort on her pleasure center, making way for his hard length, but she was too lost in sensation to fear this part anymore. All she wanted was to take the gift John was giving her, the gift of showing her that she could trust her body to do what it was designed to. Because of course he was going to make her come. Of course, this part of her wasn't dead because John had brought her back to life. She was alive and whole and in the arms of the man she loved…and everything was going to be all right.

She wrapped her legs around his hips as their bodies merged. His arm held her close as he moved, sinking deeper inside her with each thrust. There was never anything as right as this, as feeling the potent power and strength of his body, hard and huge and perfect, taking the lead, showing her what they were together, teaching her what it meant to trust, to be truly loved by a man.

Her fingers plunged into his hair, holding tight as she started to move with him, driving herself right to the edge of release until she was so close, her body tightened, desperate and reaching.

She snaked a hand between them and it only took the touch of her fingertip to bring herself all the way home.

Her release ripped through her, almost violent in its intensity and noise. Tears sprang to her eyes—tears of relief and release of so much baggage, she hadn't even known she'd been carrying it all or that it'd been so heavy on her soul. John drove into her hard and held himself there, gathering her so tightly in his arms she couldn't draw a full breath, his face pressed to her neck, his exhale tremulous as he joined her in ecstasy.

She stroked his sweat-dampened back and shoulders as he continued to pant against her neck, his body trembling slightly as he came down from his high, but she was too contented to ask him to loosen his hold. She listened to the faint sounds of the storm outside, John's erratic breathing and the washing machine as it clicked to the start of a rinse cycle. "We didn't even make it to the spin cycle."

He laughed a wheezy laugh and shook his head against her neck, then withdrew from her and worked his arm beneath her knees. "I'm going to take you someplace softer than this."

He lifted her into his arms. She laid her cheek on his shoulder, content to let him carry her into the home theater across the hall. What a change that was. She was content. Possibly for the first time in her life. It blew her mind what that meant. Previously, the idea of giving her power over to a man, of being vulnerable to another person, had been so terrifying to her that she'd never considered that love didn't work that way.

Love wasn't about losing control or becoming weak. It was about finding someone who made her stronger, better than she could be alone. Once upon a time, she'd put her absolute faith into her black ops crew. She'd thought that blind trust in others had nearly killed her, but that wasn't true. It had made her stronger, despite that her trust had been violated by Rory.

What it really came down to was that she couldn't let Rory's betrayal continue to dictate her choices and blind her from what she knew in her heart to be true: that she was going to be okay. That loving and trusting didn't make her weak or endanger her. And that her and John's connection ran deeper than either of them could control—but she didn't want to control it anymore. What she wanted was to spend the rest of her life with him.

With Alicia still in his arms, John lowered to the nearest sofa and grabbed a throw blanket. They snuggled in together, breathing and being. Alicia was happier than she'd been in twenty long, lonely months.

John nuzzled his nose into her hair. "I never did tell

you what it feels like to me, you letting go and coming for me." His voice had the oddest quality to it—tender, yet tired and with an undercurrent of deep, abiding emotion.

She lifted his head and looked at him to see the expression that would accompany such a voice.

His eyes were glassy and red-rimmed, and his face had lost the hard, icy edge from a few days earlier. He still wasn't the same John as before she was shot, but he wasn't the unfeeling warrior anymore, either. He looked worn-out, but lighter somehow. He looked utterly open and vulnerable, and she loved him all the more for it.

He tucked a strand of her hair behind her ear. "You, this, it feels like…" He shook his head, his jaw clenching so tightly that she could see the ripple of muscles in his cheek. "It feels like absolution."

"Absolution. I like that idea." A clean slate. A fresh start for the two of them to build on.

He pressed his lips to hers. "I love you, Phoenix."

Absolution. Forgiveness. The washing away of all their sins and transgressions, the doubts and fears and pain they'd caused each other. It was all gone. Rory was probably dead, they'd most likely be able to slip away from the island and disappear into the world at large before Logan's crew or any of the other federal agencies on the hunt for them realized where they were, and in his arms, he held his soul mate. It was a perfect new beginning.

The power had cut out while their clothes were in the dryer. It didn't return for two days. They transformed the home theater into their nest, lining the tables and counters with all the candles they could find and piling cushions and blankets on the floor. For two days, their world was candlelight and each other's bodies and the distant sound of the storm raging outside.

Every few hours, John walked the house, inspecting for storm damage, but other than superficial destruction and one time when a side door blew open, the house remained intact and solid, leaving him to concentrate on relearning Alicia's body, on cultivating her confidence and talking for hours on end about their lives and childhood and all the topics they'd never seemed to have time to broach before.

After the storm passed, after two days and night of love and laughter and planning for a future together somewhere overseas, the power and phone service turned back on. It was time for them to make a break for freedom and leave Martinique. Logan and his crew were probably still in residence on the island, if they'd survived the grenade explosion, but they had to take the chance. Harry's plane could get them as far as her condo in Panama, where they could replenish their supplies, secure quality fake passports and get on with their lives together.

It wasn't precisely an ideal future, because for the rest of their lives they'd be wanted criminals, looking over their shoulders, but that was the price they paid for the choices they'd each made. As long as they were together and free, he was prepared to live with it.

The first step? Returning to the beach for one last check for Rory's body, though the newscasters on the radio had announced that there'd been no fatalities reported on the island. After that, they were going to risk a trip back to their motel room to grab Alicia's computer. Not that she couldn't replace it, but the sensitive information contained therein would further implicate her as a criminal and John wasn't willing to chance it.

The residential streets surrounding the house they'd stayed in were littered with debris from houses, palm fronds, and ton after ton of displaced dirt and sand. Many of the windows were still boarded up, but people had emerged from their homes and were busy getting their lives back in order.

John and Alicia weren't the only ones on the beach. Families and solitary men picked their way through the piles of washed-up trash, probably searching for anything of value. John approached them and asked them if they'd found any bodies or injured people on the beach, but they hadn't.

He returned to Alicia's side with the news. She hugged herself and looked out at sea. He wouldn't say she looked regretful, but definitely pensive. He hugged her close. "Are you okay?"

"I am, actually. It would have been great to have the closure of seeing him for myself and knowing for sure that he was dead, but even if he isn't, his sins are going to catch up with him eventually. And I wouldn't be opposed to sending an untraceable message to ICE letting them know this was the last island he was spotted on. Honestly, I'm ready to move on. With you."

"Me, too. How about we get over to the motel and pick up your computer, then get to the airport? I can't wait to get out of the islands."

"I have a better idea that'll get us off Martinique even faster. I'll go to the airport and start a safety check of the floatplane while you get my computer. We'll meet on the runway."

He wasn't crazy about the safety concerns involved with splitting up, but the idea of going alone, of not having to worry about Alicia while he slipped into the motel, grabbed their gear, then slipped back out, was alluring. And maybe she needed a few minutes of space to catch her breath and acclimate to their new plan. He could respect that. They'd be together again soon enough.

"Deal."

They walked to the resort on the southern edge of the inlet and requested two cabs. The cabs trailed each other for several kilometers, then John watched the back of Alicia's head disappear in the rearview window as the road forked, with Alicia headed to the private airport and John to Fort-de-France.

The taxi let him off near a corner market, one of the few that had survived the storm without too much damage and that had the news playing on a battery-operated radio. From the radio and talking with the locals, he discovered that five lives were lost to Hannah, mostly in the U.S. and British Virgin Islands, none on Martinique. John's thoughts turned to Eugene. He decided to call and check in with him as soon as he got to the motel room.

He walked the three blocks to the hotel and stood in the doorway of a boarded-up restaurant, assessing the situation to make sure he wasn't followed or being watched. When he was sure the coast was clear, he walked across the debris-littered cobblestone street.

He smiled at the motel receptionist as he crossed to the stairs. Without letting down his guard, he made it safely to their room and locked the door, then checked everyplace he could think of where Logan or one of his crew members might be lying in wait to ambush him, but found no one and none of their stuff disturbed. He grabbed Alicia's computer bag from the floor near the bed, then did a double take.

Near the pillow sat his copy of Michael Jackson's *Bad* CD, as if she'd wanted it near her when she slept. Or maybe it was a lucky coincidence. The CD had been his good-luck charm for ages, since college. He thought he'd lost it along with the rest of his bag in the grenade explosion, but somehow, it had survived. Probably thanks to Alicia.

It was a sign of good things to come. It had to be. He tucked it safely in his jacket pocket, packed Alicia's computer and his police scanner in her bag, and was out the door in moments, anxious to get back to Alicia and on with their lives together.

He smiled again at the receptionist, then pushed through the revolving glass door, his head on a swivel looking for danger. Just as he was thinking this was too easy, and nothing in life was that smooth and simple, from out of the shadows of the boarded-up curry house next door stepped none other than Logan McCaffrey.

Chapter 14

John's gun was in his hand without him even realizing he was reaching for it. "Logan? And here I'd hoped I'd killed you. What a disappointment."

He glanced side to side, surveying the windows and road for any sign of the rest of Logan's crew. Though he didn't see anything suspicious, there was no doubt in his mind that there were multiple rifles pointed at his head at that very moment.

Logan looked relaxed, his hands in his pockets, probably on a gun or Taser or knife. "You can put your gun away. All I want to do is talk."

Oh, well, if that's all he wanted to do. Yeah, right. He grabbed a handful of Logan's shirt and shoved him backward through the door into the motel lobby.

"You son of a bitch. When are you going to figure out that Rory's the one you should be chasing, not us?"

A bellboy gave a start and scrambled out of the way as John threw Logan through the open door of the motel's empty café.

He stumbled over the closed sign before recovering his footing. His hands came out of his pockets, weapon free. "There are whole units of soldiers and federal agents tracking Rory. If he's still alive, he won't be for long. My team has only one job and that is neutralizing Alicia Troy's threat to national security."

"You just won't give up, will you?"

Logan folded his arms over his chest. "When you were on ICE, would you have given up?"

Hell, no. But that didn't mean he had to like it now that he was on the opposite side of the hunt. "Where's the rest of your crew?"

"They don't know I'm here."

"Sure they don't."

"I'm here as your friend." That last part was said with an appropriate amount of self-deprecation, like Logan and John were in on the same joke.

John forced a wry chuckle. "Great timing because I've been wanting to have a heart-to-heart with you, too. About how you set me up to lead you to Alicia."

It was Logan's turn to chuckle. "The past is the past, John. I think a better question would be how did I find you today?"

Good point. "I'm all ears."

Logan ran his tongue along the inside of his lower lip. Whatever bomb of intel he was going to drop on John right now was going to be a big whammy. "Alicia tipped me off."

Oh, please. "You're not even going to bother with a convincing lie? I'm disappointed."

"Why do you think she sent you here alone?"

He hated the logic in that. Impossible. She would never. She loved him as much as he loved her. He'd felt the truth in her declaration when they made love. For all the wrongs of her past, she'd never targeted him or set him up. Unlike Logan.

"Why would she do that? You're the only one who stands to gain from a lie like that."

"Not true. She's trying to strike a deal with ICE. She thinks giving you up and turning over Rory when she finds him will help her cause."

"Rory's dead."

"Are you sure?"

John's pulse pounded in his ears, loud and steady. There was a catch to this conversation that he couldn't wrap his brain around yet. He looked past Logan to the motel lobby. Any minute now, the rest of Logan's crew would probably burst through the door. Just in case, he set the computer bag on the floor behind him so he'd have the freedom to move unencumbered if it came to that.

"So, then, let me guess," John said. "You want me to give up her location first, as a goodwill gesture because, sore loser that I am, I want you to stick it to her? That's your logic? And I bet you'll give me leniency if I cooperate, right?"

"No, on both accounts. I'm not taking you into custody, John. Like I said, I'm here as a friend." He reached his hand around to the small of his back beneath his jacket.

John steadied the aim of his HK45 at Logan's chest, but all Logan did was withdraw a file thick with papers and hold it out to John. He didn't take it. "What is that?"

"Evidence I've been compiling against Alicia for a long, long time."

John nodded. "I think I get it now. First, you prove to me what a despicable traitor she is, then you turn me loose so I can lead you to her."

"That's more like it, except without the sarcasm." He waved the file in John's direction again. "Once you really do see how despicable she is, you're going to want to lead us to her."

John didn't want to look. He didn't need to read a bunch of fabricated lies about Alicia designed to turn John against the woman he loved. Logan should've known the bait wouldn't work on John. As the man who'd recruited and trained him, he should've figured out that nothing was more important to John than integrity. And part of that integrity was loyalty.

A sliver of doubt crept into his head. A week ago, his most stringent belief was that loyalty was his greatest weakness because it bred complacency—a false sense of confidence in himself, in his environment and in the people he trusted. Rory betrayed him. Alicia, Diego and Ryan had turned their backs on him and Logan had manipulated him to his own ends. He probably still was.

But now he knew that wasn't true. With all they'd been through together in the past few days, the battles, the intimacy, he trusted Alicia. He'd absolved her of her wrongs against him and she'd absolved him of his wrongs against her, so why was he standing there thinking about complacency? Why did he have a bad feeling about what was in the file that Logan held?

He transferred his gun to his left hand and reached his right out as if he was going to take the file. He grabbed Logan's wrist instead, yanking hard as he swung his gun around and clocked him in the side of the head as his knee connected with Logan's gut. Logan tried to get his fist up for a jab to John's middle.

It was a nice effort, and Logan was known throughout the agency as a mixed martial arts beast, but nobody could brawl like John. It'd been that way when Logan trained him, he'd bested Logan at the rum distillery, and he was ready for the battle today.

He was ready for Logan's counterattack and took hold of Logan's wrist, holding it down as he issued an elbow to Logan's face that sent him stumbling backward. But John wasn't done with the wrist he held. He yanked on it hard, pulling Logan forward, then sidestepped to give him room to fall. He sealed the deal with an elbow jab to Logan's spine as he dropped, then pinned him to the floor with a boot to the back of his neck.

He looked around, hands ready to fight off his next opponent, but all he saw were shocked, staring employees probably waiting for the cops to arrive. Unbelievably, Logan's crew was nowhere to be seen. The man really had come alone. It was weird because John never caught a break like this. Just one opponent, whom he'd subdued with only one sequence of moves? Some might say to never look a gift horse in the mouth, but that was effed-up advice because nobody ever died from being suspicious.

It all came back to complacency and a false sense of confidence—traps that John was determined to never fall back into again.

He trusted Alicia and he trusted himself. Period.

"Read the file, John. I'm not BSing you this time." Logan's words were slurred because the toe of John's boot was nudging his jaw, but he otherwise sounded totally unfazed by the fact that John dropped him like a fly. "Alicia set you up. She framed you for Rory's escape and she was planning to frame you for his death. Her death, too."

What kind of crazy lie was that? *"Her death?"*

"I'm not making this up. Read the damn file. Then take the deal I'm offering you."

"What deal?"

"Absolution. You'll be a free man and welcome to return to U.S. soil."

Absolution. Of an entirely different kind than he'd experienced with Alicia in his arms. But if the doors to freedom were really being opened to him, then why did he feel as if he was in a cage that was shrinking every second? Sirens sounded outside, giving him a matter of seconds to escape the building before life got a whole lot more complicated.

He lifted his boot from the back of Logan's neck and clubbed him across the skull with the barrel of his gun, knocking him out cold.

He grabbed the file and the computer bag, then ran through the café and into the kitchen. He burst out the kitchen's back exit and into an alley riddled with rain-filled potholes and broken palm fronds that must have washed up in the storm surge. Crashing through the water and debris, he came out on a frontage road.

What he needed was a place to hide and sort through his thoughts. The file felt like a toxic thing in his hand, radioactive and dangerous. Even considering opening it made him feel as if he was betraying Alicia's trust. Even if she never found out, how could he do such a thing as doubt her now, when they were so close to finding happiness together forever?

Then again, how could he not look? Blind faith was what got him into this mess in the first place. He could go on and on about how he trusted himself, but obviously his instincts had been so wrong so often in the past that there was huge part of him that knew he had to protect himself from himself.

He strode down the street, casual, looking around, trying not to draw attention as he dodged trash, downed signs and streetlights, and workers doing their best to put their lives and businesses back together. Four blocks from the hotel, he spotted a bar that looked open for business and ducked inside. It was dark and muggy, with four weary-looking customers sitting at the bar.

He ordered a rum straight up, dropped twenty euros on the counter, and without waiting for his drink to arrive, headed to the restroom.

He stood near the bathroom sink underneath a bare lightbulb hanging from the ceiling and stared at the file.

How had Logan found him? No way could it have been Alicia. She loved him. The more logical scenario was that she'd accidentally tipped Logan off to their location at the hotel during her computer surveillance. But that was before the hurricane. Had they really been waiting there the whole time for John and Alicia to return?

And where the hell was the rest of Logan's team? It was B.S. all the way that he'd come to John on his own, but for the life of him, he couldn't figure out Logan's angle this time. He'd let John beat the crap out of him while barely putting up a fight.

Alicia wouldn't have set him up to take the fall for Rory's escape and murder. She wouldn't have planned to fake her own death and frame him for it. She just... No. It was impossible.

With a curse under his breath, he ripped the rubber bands off the file and flipped it open. Time to prove what an idiot he was to doubt her.

There was nothing melodramatic in the file like a note or threat from Logan to John, just a thick stack of official federal documents by agencies from ICE and the U.S. Marshals to the NSA. There were screenshots of a faked plane flight manifest, retouched pictures of him on Fort Buchanan security cameras.

Following those were pages and pages of computer code that didn't make any sense except that stapled to the front was a summary written on NSA stationary that said, in essence, that these pages contained code found on Alicia's network of a program that had self-initiated on the morning of Rory's prison break that planted a false trail from the prison's power failure that led to his release to a manufactured IP address and identity in Florida belonging to John, but that had actually been created more than a year earlier.

There were pages and pages of proof that Alicia had put a lot of thought into framing John. If—and this was a huge *if*—they were real. Because Logan had already manipulated him once and there was nothing saying he was above doing so again, especially given how bloodthirsty he was to neutralize Alicia.

Feeling skeptical and guilty for betraying Alicia's

trust by reading the file, he flipped past the packet of code to the end. What he saw felt like a punch to his chest, knocking the wind clean out of him. He blinked and shook his head, then looked again at numbered ICE crime scene photos from Alicia's house in Phoenix along with a chem analysis of the room that found bleach on the floor and in the tub, trace amounts of her blood in the tub's drain and John's hair and fingerprints on the sink and shower curtain, the results certified by ICE's special investigation unit.

The last page of the document was an arrest warrant for John, citing Rory's prison break and murder, and Alicia's murder.

He sank to the ground and leaned his back on the door as his world started to spin.

She'd set him up. And not on an impulsive whim. She'd been planning his demise for more than a year. She'd faked her own murder and wanted John to rot in prison for it. She hadn't just been hungry for revenge against Rory, but revenge against him, as well.

He couldn't compete with that. What had she been thinking when they'd made love? Even then, was she plotting how she'd isolate him and contact Logan? Even if she'd changed her mind during the two days and nights they'd spent in each other's arms, that didn't negate this. The lies. The deception.

He really was a spineless fool, a follower and easy target for others to pin their sins on.

A patsy. Like he was when Rory's corruption came to light. Like he was when Logan wanted to locate Alicia. It didn't matter what John did or how much personal integrity he carried inside him, he couldn't escape this fate of being at the mercy of others' corruption. He was doomed to a life of being the fall guy. How had everything gotten so screwed up with him? How could being good and true and honest be such a flaw?

He loved Alicia with all his heart and she'd used him.

He clamped a hand over his mouth as pain, just as bad as the night she'd first accused him of working with Rory to murder her, rose up through his chest, closing his throat, making his sinuses tingle.

He crushed the file to his chest and gave himself over to a breathless, crippling pain worse than he'd ever experienced in his life. Did having an ironclad sense of honor really make him a sucker? Then again, thinking that bad things shouldn't happen to good people was a fallacy of the worst kind. Bad things happened just because bad things happened. And he got complacent. Fatal error.

A knock at the door startled him, followed by a man telling him in French to hurry it up because he'd been waiting in the hall for ten minutes. John hauled himself up and braced his hands against the sink.

"Juste une minute," he said. Drawing a fortifying breath, he looked at his reflection in the mirror. So this was what a loser looked like. *Always the sidekick, never the alpha.* A doomed man.

No, that wasn't true. And this was one pity party that had to stop immediately. He didn't have to play this game with these people. He didn't have to live this cycle of trust and abuse anymore.

He could walk away. He wasn't helpless or doomed to this fate. He could wash his hands of Alicia, Logan and Rory. Let them duke it out without him. He stared at himself in the mirror. It was time to go back into exile, this time for good. Far away from all the people who'd hurt him. He deserved better than this. Better than being a patsy for his lover, his best friends, his coworkers. It was time to retake control of his life.

He slung the strap of Alicia's computer bag over his shoulder. He felt so numb, so impossibly numb. Like that night on St. Croix a year earlier, on that balcony in Frederiksted. He felt nothing. He really was starting over, this time alone—as a wanted man, a true traitor of the government after his run-ins with Logan's crew and helping Rory and Alicia escape the consequences of their sins.

And he didn't have a friend in the world except Eugene and the other handful of islanders he'd cultivated acquaintances with during his stay. He opened the door, muttered an apology to the local shaking his head at him, annoyed by the wait, and turned to the back exit. This time, he was absolving himself instead of waiting for others to do it for him. He was a good, honorable man, and if this world couldn't handle that, then he didn't need this world. It was time for a new life and to find a way to be whole again.

He hailed the first cab he could find and directed it to the private airstrip. It was time to find Alicia so he could take one last parting look at the woman he'd loved with everything he had. And then it was time to move on.

The plane was still in the hangar and in good shape. Alicia would be able to fly them out of Martinique as soon as the debris was cleaned from the runway and the winds died down a little more.

While she waited for John, she spotted a corded phone on a table in the corner, sitting on top of a Martinique directory. What would it hurt to make a few calls and possibly find Rory—or at least his body? She ran a mental list of pros and cons, found the pros to be compelling enough, then flipped through the directory until she found a listing of local hospitals. It was a long shot, but there wasn't any danger in making an anonymous call from a business line.

After a look around the hangar to double check that she was alone, she picked up the receiver and dialed the first one. While it rang, she concentrated on the ideas of panic and fear, hoping to infuse her voice with both.

A hospital receptionist answered in French.

"Yes, hello. English, please?" She might've been able to pull off French, but not convincingly. Luckily, the receptionist switched to English and asked her how she could help. "I'm looking for my husband, who went out to buy some batteries before the hurricane hit and never made it back to the hotel. I need to know if a man that matches his description came to your hospital."

The woman was concerned and had a lot of questions about whether or not Alicia had contacted the police, the name of the hotel she was staying at and a physical description of Rory.

After all that, and a ten-minute wait on hold while the woman checked with the emergency room staff, the call was a dead end.

She poked her head out of the hangar opening but didn't see John yet, so she dialed the number of the next hospital in the phone book and repeated the story. On the fifth hospital, the receptionist returned in record time from putting her on hold to check for a man who matched Rory's description.

"Madame, a man was brought in yesterday and he has…how do you say…ah, *amnésie*. He cannot remember who he is."

Did she dare hope? She looked around, wishing John would get there so they could go to the hospital and check. "Oh, my God. I bet that's my Michael. I'll be there as soon as I can. Tell him his wife is on her way."

She hung up and chewed her thumbnail. What was taking John so long? Worry crept into her consciousness. Something might have gone wrong. It was ridiculous that they'd split up without a means to contact the other.

Any other man, she might've worried that he would've skipped out on her, but not John. She'd never met a man with more honor. Besides that, he loved her. They were going to spend their future together. Either he found Rory on his own, some local was having a problem and he stopped to help, or Logan found him. She just couldn't fathom any other possibilities.

She paced from the hangar to the front office and back, growing more and more worried. At the roar of an engine behind her, she turned around and nearly collapsed with relief to see him straddling a sleek black motorcycle.

She jogged his way as he parked just inside the hangar entrance. "The plane's in good shape. They've been cleaning up the runway all morning. There's just one new development I need to tell you about first, something that might change everything."

He had his back to her as he set his helmet on the

seat, so she didn't see the stone-cold look on his face until he turned around. "Funny, I have some news like that to share with you, too."

He pinned her with a look so frosty she stopped dead in her tracks. "What's wrong?"

"Everything, Alicia." He pulled a thick file from her computer bag and set it on the bike seat next to his helmet.

Confused and scared by his distance and coldness, she cupped his cheek with her hand. He flinched and pulled away.

"What's wrong? Are you okay? Does this have to do with the news you have to tell me?"

"Not long after I bought this bike, I figured out I was being followed by Logan and his crew. They thought I was going to lead them to you, but I took them on a wild-goose chase all over the island until I finally lost them, so you'll have plenty of time to escape."

"Logan? He found us?"

John nodded, but his face remained a blank mask. She wanted to pound her fists on his chest to snap him out of whatever weird trance he was in. "Yeah, he found me."

"How?"

His eyes flickered to the file on the bike seat, then his lips twisted into a sardonic grin. "He said you tipped him off."

Her heart sank. What lies had Logan convinced John of? "John, whatever Logan said to you, he's wrong. You know me. You know I'd never give you up like that. I love you."

"That's what I thought, too. Then he gave me this." He picked up the file and thrust it toward her.

"What's in here?"

"Proof that you had set me up to take the fall for Rory's prison break and murder. That you set me up as your murderer. Tell me that this isn't true."

A ringing started in her ears. Impossible. How had Logan gotten that information? She'd been so careful. No one was ever supposed to find out about the plan she'd aborted at the last minute. With trembling hands, she flipped open the file. Her stomach lurched and the ringing in her ears got louder. *This couldn't be happening....*

Amid several documents that Logan or someone on his team must have fabricated for the express purpose of making her look even more despicable, it was there—the brilliant, cruel plan she'd had for vengeance against John. She paused on the photographs of the crime scene in her house that she'd staged days before she'd left Arizona on her mission to kill Rory. Whoever had taken those photographs had disengaged her state-of-the-art security and sneaked in right under her nose, before she'd even left town.

There was no other possibility because the day she'd decided she couldn't go through with the plan against John, she'd stripped the bathroom down to bare walls and floors, ripping out the tub, sink and toilet. Then she'd torched the room because she knew she'd never be back and she didn't want anyone to accidentally find the trace evidence she'd planted.

They'd had this smoking gun the whole time they'd been chasing her and John. And they'd finally found the right window of opportunity to use it.

"John, you have to listen to me. Let me explain."

"Did Logan fabricate all this evidence or is this true? You owe me this truth, Alicia. No more lies. Not to me."

He was right. She did owe him that. After all he'd sacrificed for her, even though it probably meant she'd lose his trust permanently, she answered, "Logan was thorough in his research."

With a guttural growl, he pushed away and prowled to the far side of the hangar, bracing an arm on the plane's wing.

"John, listen. This file doesn't tell the whole story."

"What's the story, then? You have about thirty seconds before I walk."

"I couldn't go through with it. Not to you. I would have never been able to forgive myself. And then once I saw you again, once I admitted to myself that you were innocent and that I was in love with you, I couldn't believe what I'd almost done." She took hold of his shirt in both hands, needing him to understand that everything had changed. She'd changed. She'd become a better person for him. He had to see that, didn't he? "I almost ruined your life, but I didn't. Because I never followed through with any of these plans."

He squeezed his eyes closed then opened them wide and stood stiff and tall, facing her down. "I got so caught up in the fight to convince you of my innocence and find Rory, so caught up in the idea that I had something to prove, that I lost sight of protecting myself. I let my ego take over. Rory, Logan, you, our black ops crew—you all used me for your own ends, like my integrity was a weakness for you to exploit."

He removed her hands from his shirt and took a step away from her.

"Not anymore. I couldn't go through with it. John, please. You know me. You know I couldn't hurt you. Don't jump to conclusions and walk away without letting me explain."

Then he smiled, but it was the cruelest, most calculated smile she'd ever seen. She pulled back, feeling as though she'd been slapped.

"Like you did to me? Except you didn't just jump to conclusions and walk away. You planned to frame me for murder and being a traitor to my country."

What could she say to that? Yes, she had. But that was before. She'd changed so much since then. She'd let go of the bitterness and embraced her chance for love, for a new life with the man who had more honor in his little finger than she had in her whole body. "But I didn't."

It sounded like the flimsiest of retorts to her ears. A pathetic justification for the horrific thoughts she'd harbored and nearly acted on. A tear rolled down her cheek, with a million more behind it waiting to come out. She almost said "It wasn't my intention to hurt you," except that it had been. As much as she'd wanted to kill Rory to extract revenge, she'd wanted John to pay for hurting her, too.

"I've changed." It was the only real argument she had.

His sigh in response was deep and pensive. "Maybe so, but I don't think I have it in me to give my heart to someone who nearly ruined me after I'd devoted two years to our relationship, to loving and cherishing you with everything I had in me."

Nodding, she wrapped her arms around her middle. There was no argument to counter the truth in his words. She couldn't blame him for being unable to forgive her.

"With the plane, you should be able to get away safely."

She stared down at the ground. "This can't be happening."

"That was my thought exactly when Logan told me you tipped him off on where to find me so he could ambush me, then gave me this file."

He picked up the motorcycle helmet. Desperate and hurt, she rushed forward, blocking his bike from leaving.

"I love you. I know now that I've always loved you and I was just too full of pride to see that. I was too scared that loving you would strip me of control and power and all the things I thought I needed to thrive. I didn't tip Logan off about where you were and despite that I planned to frame you, I couldn't go through with it. Because I love you. And you love me. And if you drive away, there's nothing left of us and I'll die inside, John. Because I can't live without you. I don't want to."

He put the helmet on, visor up, and straddled the bike. She met his icy stare through her tear-filled eyes.

"I deserve better than this." His voice was husky, proving that behind the ice-deadened eyes lived the soul of a man she'd deeply hurt.

"Yes, you do. And I'm going to do better. I'm going to prove you can trust me, if you'll just give me a chance."

Lines of heavy sorrow settled over his face. He swallowed. He reached out, cradling her cheek in his hand. She closed her eyes and let the tears roll from her skin to his. Giving it all up, the pride, the control, the hard-hearted operative she'd become, the hate for Rory. Everything. For love.

"Please," she breathed.

Then the warmth and strength of his hand was gone. "Goodbye, Alicia."

Chapter 15

Alicia stood at the foot of Rory's hospital bed, watching him sleep.

Without John by her side, she was utterly lost, and her only anchor was this new purpose—to clear his name.

Impatient to get on with her plan, she unfolded her knife and pricked Rory's broken right arm just above the edge of his cast. In his sleep, he flinched, then groaned, looking absolutely helpless.

She smiled, dreams of vengeance coursing through her blood. Not for herself, but for John. What she'd figured out in the hour since he'd left her was that she needed him so much more than he needed her. He'd changed her for the better in fundamental ways, showing her that trust and love made her stronger, not weaker, that having a true partner didn't mean giving up control, but instead making control less important. Nothing, she learned from John, was more important than honor.

It was why she'd undertaken the most honorable course of action possible—to force Rory to tell the world the truth about John's innocence, then confess to every one of her sins and surrender herself to ICE.

Rory's eyelids fluttered open, then closed, then open again. Wide-open and terrified. He pushed back, pedaling up the bed as if he was trying to get away from her. Too bad for him she'd found soft restraints dangling from the bedframe and had secured them over his left wrist and both feet. "Alicia? How did you…"

So much for John Doe's supposed amnesia.

"I told them I was your wife." She scraped the point of her knife over the blanket covering his leg as she strolled up the bed. "It's fitting, don't you think? Our futures were bound together from the moment you shot me. It gives new meaning to the vow 'Till death do us part.'"

He settled back down against his pillow, feigning a casualness she knew was masking his fear. "If you're going to return the favor, then get it over with. Save the theatrics."

She smiled and got down low to his face, the better to hear his erratic breathing as she pressed the side of her blade into his neck. Not so forceful as to draw blood, of course. She couldn't have the nurses or doctors suspecting anything, but it was enough to watch him squirm in pain. "My poor, delusional husband. Actually, your doctors released you into my care. Isn't that wonderful news? Your discharge order should be coming through the hospital's computer network any minute now."

Before coming to stand vigil at Rory's bedside as the worried wife, she'd taken the time to do that part right, hacking into the computer's network and faking his doctor's discharge orders. If her code had executed as she'd designed it to, then a nurse would be walking through the door any minute to take out Rory's IV and bid them farewell.

He drew a labored breath, then futilely pulled his arms up, tugging on the restraints. "You put something on my chest. What is it?"

"Something you taught me to make when our crew went on a mission in Uzbekistan."

His facade of calm disappeared. "You strapped an IED on me?"

She smiled. This, the threat, was better than killing him, better than hurting him. She only wished John had been by her side to witness it.

"You wouldn't blow me up in a hospital. You'd hurt civilians."

"You're right. And I thought of that, too. I'd never hurt civilians—you've done enough of that yourself. So here's the plan. If you run, I'll wait until you're outside, then I'll detonate." She pinched his cheek, then waved the cell phone she'd specially programed. "That's what remote detonators were invented for, silly."

"And if I cry for help and tell the staff you've strapped a bomb to me?"

She shrugged, having already thought of that possibility, too. "Then we'll both be arrested, which is fine because we're both criminals. It won't take the authorities long to figure out that you're an escaped murderer. Any other questions?"

He opened his mouth, but closed it again as a nurse bustled into the room. Alicia collapsed her blade and slid it into her pocket.

"Mrs. Morris, why is he restrained?" the nurse asked in a heavy French accent.

Alicia shook her head and forced a worried, nervous-wife look onto her face. "He was having a nightmare in his sleep, and his arms were flailing everywhere. I was afraid he'd hurt his broken arm or pull out his IV. I didn't know what else to do."

The nurse got down to the task of removing the restraints. "You could have summoned a nurse."

"I'm sorry. This ordeal has me flustered. I thought I'd lost my beloved Michael forever." She smoothed a hand over his stomach and watched the nurse remove the last of the restraints, then Rory's IV.

"Mr. Morris's discharge papers came through." She set a small stack of papers on the bed.

"I don't think I'm well enough to leave," Rory said. "I don't know who this woman is. She's not my wife. I think she's trying to kidnap me."

Bold move. But she was ready for that.

She summoned a sob and held out a photograph on her phone of the two of them embracing in wedding fineries that had only taken a couple minutes to fake on Photoshop. "Oh, Michael, the doctor thought this might happen. He said the best thing for your memory was to be at the condo, surrounded by your family. We can look at more of our wedding pictures tonight and I'll make your favorite dinner. The children have been so worried about you."

"Everything is going to be all right, Mr. Morris. I know you're groggy, but your wife is right. Being with your family is the best thing for you right now." The nurse then proceeded with a tedious accounting of the orders, what he should eat and how much he should sleep, as well as several prescriptions for pain relievers and sleep aids that Alicia had fake-ordered for him.

When the nurse was done, she patted the back of Rory's hand. "You two are free to leave. Let me summon a wheelchair and escort."

Rory must have believed her threats to be real—which they were—because he gave nary a sound nor put nary a toe out of line.

As a polite young man pushed Rory's wheelchair from the elevator into the lobby, Alicia said, "Our car's right out front. Thank you for taking such great care of him. Bless you all for the work you and this hospital do. You gave me my husband back."

At the curb in front of the hospital, she waved, the cell phone detonator in her hand. "I'll be right back with the car. Don't you go wandering off again. That's what landed you in this hospital in the first place."

Despite the obvious threat of the bomb, she half expected Rory to make some kind of move when she turned her back to him. It must have been a testament to how injured he really was because when she pulled her car to the curb, he was still waiting benignly in the chair under the watchful gaze of the hospital attendant.

The logistics of driving him in the car while keeping Rory subdued were tricky, because there was no way she was going to blow them both up, and so she was grateful that she'd taken time to think this part out, too. She got out of the car to help him into the passenger's seat along with the attendant's help, then waved the attendant away and returned to the driver's seat. Before she hit the road, she showed Rory the stun gun she'd been carrying around as back up in her computer bag.

She'd never considered the stun gun as an effective means of neutralizing a hostile until Rory had used it on Diego right before he shot her. But now, she loved its versatility and ability to take down men far bigger than she, and so took it with her everywhere.

"You remember this? You used it to disable Diego. It was an ingenious idea, so I bought the same model. You want me to try it out on you?"

"You're going to pay for this, you bi—"

She depressed the button on her stun gun as she rolled forward, hoping no one saw the spectacle, though she was sure enjoying it. Even if somebody did see, she and Rory would be long gone before anybody could do anything about it.

It bothered her, how much she enjoyed watching Rory writhe in pain. It wasn't a noble way to feel about inflicting pain on someone, but she couldn't help it. She'd grown into a woman in the CIA family. She'd killed for the first time at twenty-two, then participated in her first enhanced interrogation—aka torture for information—at age twenty-four. The muscle memory of the amoral life she led was bound to linger for years to come. Still, it was shocking how much further from humanity she'd fallen since getting shot, since she let Rory and vengeance drag her down.

John had been right when he'd told her that killing for revenge was completely different than killing on the job or in self-defense and that it would destroy her spirit. It definitely would have had he not been there to save her from herself. As it was, it had already destroyed her future and chance for happiness with the man she loved.

She pulled into the alley behind the three-story office building near the beach that she'd scoped out earlier, the one with the palm tree that had crashed through the lobby during the hurricane and now stood vacant. She'd been there earlier and had been impressed to find that the building still had power and a strong Wi-Fi signal—the two requirements she needed to make her plan a success.

"I'm not getting out of this car. You can just kill me here."

Sighing, she got out and popped the trunk, then unfolded the wheelchair she'd stolen. She rolled the wheelchair to the passenger's side and opened his door. "I'm not going to kill you unless you try to escape or hurt me."

"Then what's your plan?"

She zapped him again with the stun gun. He slumped forward into his seat belt. It took a bit of effort to transfer his limp form into the wheelchair, but adrenaline and purpose spurred her to make fast work of the task because nothing would be worse than a bystander catching sight of them, getting suspicious and calling the cops. The sooner they were in the building, the better.

She used a bungee cord to strap his torso to the chair, grabbed her computer bag, stun gun and pistol, then opened the broken glass lobby door and pushed him through.

By the time he'd come to again, she'd settled them on the third level in a corner office with a view of the ocean. She left the explosives wrapped around him. It'd been a tough choice about what to do with his broken arm. In the end, she thought a little extra pain might encourage him to talk and so removed the soft cast from his right arm.

She zapped him one last time, then got busy setting the stage.

Her heart was pounding with trepidation as she set up her laptop's webcam and tapped into the building's Wi-Fi. It felt like a bad dream, what she was doing. It scared her so badly to think about spending the rest of her life behind bars. How had it come to this? How was it that a little girl from Phoenix had grown into a monster—a dangerous criminal with a thirst for vengeance who was incapable of sustaining genuine connections with the people in her life?

It'd been months since she'd talked to her parents, or Ryan and Diego. And the only time she'd truly felt alive and happy had been the two days and night she'd spent in John's arms during the hurricane. Loneliness settled over her like a heavy quilt, dragging her down, suffocating her. She'd thought she wanted to strike out on her own in the underworld of black market ops, and lo and behold, here she was. Alone with nothing but the man who'd tried to kill her and her regrets.

She walked to the edge of the empty windowpanes that had broken during the storm and stared at the ocean. The world was beautiful. It was beautiful and thrilling and complicated—and she'd squandered not one, but two chances to experience it in all its glories.

She stretched her arm, palm out, and let the breeze wash over her skin.

"I love you, John."

Behind her, she heard Rory stir. Showtime.

She shook out her arms, cracked her neck to the side and took a deep breath. No more dark thoughts and feeling sorry for herself. She had a man's will to break and a confession to make. Most importantly, she had a man's innocence to prove to the world. For the first time in a long time, she recognized that she was in complete control of her life and her future.

She triple-checked the broadcast signals, then clicked on the webcam and hit Record. She'd decided against going to a live feed too soon lest ICE or the police find them before she'd extracted a confession out of Rory, but she was definitely going to document every minute of their chess game.

Rory's breathing changed from deep and steady to sharp and shallow. Then he groaned. "Where are we?"

She whirled and faced Rory, who was watching her through half-lidded eyes that seemed dulled with pain. A sheen of sweat covered his skin and made his shirt damp under his arms.

"The last room you'll ever see unless you tell the truth."

He let out a wheezy laugh. "That's the best threat you got?"

"No. I'm just getting warmed up." She grabbed her knife and flicked it open.

Let the justice begin.

John stood on the side of the road, trying not to berate himself too harshly for how little distance he'd put between himself and Alicia before he'd had to stop and make sure she got the plane off the ground okay.

Less than a mile down the road, he leaned against

the motorcycle, waiting and watching the sky to see Harry's plane take off, Alicia as the pilot.

An hour passed, then another. After a while, he stopped berating himself altogether and instead passed the time deliberating about where in the world he should go next. Every so often, he wondered why he couldn't find it in himself to make a decision and drive to the coast to hire a private charter boat to Venezuela or Brazil. And he definitely didn't understand why he couldn't make himself stop caring about Alicia's fate.

As numb as he was, given all the wrongs that had been done to him, he couldn't help but remember the raw quality in Alicia's voice when she'd demanded to know why he hadn't fought for her after the shooting. Why, when she'd needed him most, he'd been so caught up in his own righteous indignation and insecurities that he'd let her drive him away for good with a handful of harsh words.

This made two times now that he'd thrown up his hands and left her without even being willing to engage in a fight about the problems they had. Two times he'd let pride take the lead. Yes, righteousness was on his side both times. He'd been manipulated, framed and treated like a tool. So, then, why did walking away again feel like the worst choice he'd ever made?

He knew the answer to that. Because walking away without giving Alicia a chance to defend herself or her actions was dishonorable. It went against his core beliefs of loyalty and integrity. The devil on his shoulder said so what? What good was honor and integrity in this world? Those tenets had ruined his career and his relationships with his best friend and his woman.

True. But since when did he embrace the idea that

righteousness trumped honor? He knew better than that. Even if it was only him and his Maker who knew the truth about John's honor, that was enough. When everything else about his life was ruined or lost, nobody could take that away from him except himself.

With a curse under his breath, he straddled the bike and returned to the airport. The guy at the front desk told him Alicia had already left, not in the plane, but in a taxi. He drove to the hangar, anyway, and found the plane still there. Alicia and her computer bag were gone. The sound of rustling papers blowing in the wind caught his attention. In the corner of the hangar, a phone book sat open.

Intrigued, he walked to it. It was open to the *G*s, which didn't mean much, considering the way the wind was whipping them around. He lifted the phone receiver and hit the redial button.

A woman answered, her greeting in French telling him it was a hospital. Odd. But what if…

On a whim, he said, "Yes, hello. I'm looking for a man who was injured during the hurricane while at sea. An American about six foot one, hazel eyes, balding. He had a wounded left leg and a tattoo of a skull on his right forearm."

"Ah. Monsieur Morris. Good news. He was discharged. His wife took him home about twenty minutes ago."

Morris? Either that was a fake name Rory gave or John was way off on this hunch, though the skull tattoo made that unlikely. "Monsieur Morris's wife, was she blonde and thin? Beautiful?"

"*Oui.* Are the Morrises friends of yours?"

He forced himself to speak, though his mind was racing. "Yes. Thank you."

He hung up. Good God. Alicia had done it. She found Rory. Now what did John do? She could be anywhere. She could have already killed him. Maybe he should leave her to it. Maybe his instinct to walk away and wash his hands of his past had been spot-on.

He found the police scanner in the motorcycle's under-seat storage and turned it on.

Post-hurricane salvage was going slowly. There were three missing persons still on the island with many more on Dominica, the island that had been hardest hit.

He was still processing that Alicia had found Rory when a dispatcher came over the police scanner requesting a patrol car to an office building on Rue Jean Jaures in Sainte-Luce because the third-floor office's alarm had been tripped. The woman who called in also reported seeing a woman roll a man in a wheelchair into the building. The police confirmed with the dispatcher that they'd send someone to check it out.

The police would be the least of Alicia's problems, though. Because Logan's team had to have heard that report, too. Alicia had ten, maybe fifteen minutes tops, before she either got herself killed or arrested.

John had asked himself a lot of questions in the past two hours, but they all fled his mind as a new one emerged: Could he walk away and let the woman he loved get captured?

Hell, no.

Because that wasn't the kind of man he was. He was the man who risked everything for the people he loved. He was steadfast and loyal and trusting—and nothing or no one could change that part of him. He wouldn't let it. Stripped of everything else, all he had in this world was his integrity and love for the people who were important to him.

That's when John decided that no matter what had happened, no matter what Alicia was guilty of doing to him, he would not stand by and watch her die. This wasn't about being a patsy or taking the fall for others, as so often seemed his lot in life. This was about love and honor.

It was time to risk everything for Alicia. Again. And for as many times as it took in his lifetime to keep her safe and free.

He swung onto the motorcycle and cranked the engine over.

The way he saw it, he only had a matter of minutes to save her before the cavalry showed up, guns blazing, prepared to neutralize their targets using whatever means necessary.

He rocketed out of the airport and onto the highway, swerving around cars, racing against the clock, against Logan McCaffrey, the U.S. Navy and all the other forces trying to shut Alicia down. It didn't matter to him any longer what happened to Rory. He had only one mission in life from here on out and that was holding fast to the people and values that defined him, starting with his Phoenix.

He performed a drive by of the whitewashed office building that was unremarkable in every way, save for the tree that had crashed through the glass-walled lobby. The parking lot and surrounding streets were quiet. He parked the bike several blocks away, then doubled back on foot, weaving through alleyways with the police scanner in hand, listening for any updates.

A block away from the office building, he froze, then dived into the open gate of a residence's backyard, out of view of an assembling crowd of federal agents decked out in SWAT gear. He didn't chance looking again, but flattened against the wall and listened.

Someone mentioned Alicia by name. How they were so sure it was her remained unclear, but it didn't take him long to figure out that they knew Rory was with her. They thought John was, too. And they were prepared to extract them all from the office using any means necessary. A man with a voice remarkably similar to Logan's even threw out the idea of razing the building. Another, who seemed eerily gleeful about the operation, suggested that if either Rory, John or Alicia shot first, they'd have the legal right to do just that. And that if either Alicia or Rory aimed a gun in their direction, they had permission to shoot to kill.

He sensed movement behind him and pivoted, pulling his gun.

Behind the three assault rifles pointed at him stood Diego, Ryan and a petite, blonde woman John didn't recognize but who seemed to know her way around an M5. All of them were decked out in gaudy tourist garb.

"Don't make a move, or I swear to God, John, I'm going to unload this weapon on you—and I'm not crazy about getting shrapnel on this shirt Vanessa bought me, even though it's the ugliest damn thing I've ever seen." Diego. The leader of their black ops crew and an all-around wiseass. He looked the same as he ever did—a lean, mean Puerto Rican from New Jersey who was ready for battle. To his credit, the button-down black Hawaiian shirt with red hibiscus flowers on it was truly obnoxious.

John lowered his gun. "What the hell are you doing here and why are you guys ready to shoot me?"

"We're here because Ryan and Avery heard word on the wire that Alicia got herself in a real mess," Diego said, holding his aim at John. "We came to see what we could do."

Relief flooded him. He had no idea who this Avery lady was, but as long as they could help him save Alicia, that hardly mattered. He nodded and holstered his gun.

"I don't think I've ever been so happy to see you guys. Alicia's got herself in so much trouble, I'm not sure I can save her this time. But I have to try. Which doesn't explain why you're all still aiming guns at my chest. Unless…" His shoulders dropped, along with what felt like a hunk of lead in his stomach. "You all still believe I'm guilty."

Of course they did. He raised his eyes to the sky and cursed. Unbelievable.

"Hey, now. How do we know you're not here because you're trying to help Rory escape?" Ryan said. "How do we know you're not the one who broke him out of prison in the first place?"

Ryan stood a few inches taller than Diego and possessed a quiet strength that John had always admired. He'd expected Ryan to be the first on their black ops team to realize John was innocent and forgive him, but he'd been as consumed with hate and bitterness toward John for his alleged crimes as Diego and Alicia, the group's original three musketeers.

He briefly considered getting into it with Diego and Ryan about his innocence, even though he knew, unequivocally, that there was no way he'd ever regain their respect. "There was a time I would've tried to prove to you that I'm innocent, but now? Now, I don't give a give a damn what you think of me. All that matters is getting to Alicia in time, so can you stop giving me the evil eye and help me figure out a plan?"

Diego narrowed his gaze at John. "What's going on with you and Alicia? What's this really about?"

So, then, they'd never known. Only Rory had figured out that he and Alicia were having an affair.

"I love her, okay? I've loved her since the minute I first laid eyes on her, and not even your guns or the fact that you have me outnumbered are going to stop me from breaking into that office and helping her escape ICE authorities—who, by the way, are right around the corner planning to neutralize her using whatever means necessary, even a kill shot. So if you want to fight me, that's fine. I'll brawl with you, but we're going to have to make it quick because I have a woman to save. My woman."

He could see the shock in their eyes. Whatever. He didn't have time for shock. Debating about the best way to sneak around the agents in the alley and get into the building, he turned away from his former comrades.

A hand on his shoulder stopped him. Eyes wide, Diego walked around to face him, lowering his gun. "*Your woman?* Alicia? She's like our little sister."

"Not to me. You never knew about us because we didn't want you to. We thought you'd say it was unprofessional, but yeah, me and Alicia." He looked past Diego to Ryan and the woman he assumed was Avery.

"I love her and I'm going after her in about ten seconds, so either start shooting at me or get out of my way."

The woman nodded and lowered her rifle. "My name is Avery Meadows. I believe you, John. What can we do to help? I brought all my best gadgets." She flipped open the side of her bright pink jacket with *Martinique* splashed across the chest in rhinestones to reveal rows of canisters, rope and other odds and ends. "I think a diversion might be in order to get our ICE friends out of our way."

Ryan's eyes shifted her way. "Jumping to conclusions a little, aren't you, babe?"

Babe? Really? Then again, she was sporting a huge diamond ring and Alicia had mentioned that Ryan was engaged, so Avery must be his fiancée. Diego wore a wedding band and had mentioned Vanessa's name, so did that mean Vanessa hadn't died in the RioBank explosion—and that she and Diego had gotten married? John shook his head. God, how long had he been out of the loop? All of a sudden, his years in black ops felt like lifetimes ago.

"I believe you, too," Diego said. "And I think Avery's onto something with that diversion idea. Let's get—"

They heard then saw a black helicopter, hovering over the office building's parking lot.

"That didn't take long," Ryan said.

What sounded like a semitruck rumbled nearby. John looked over the fence and saw two armored trucks stop in front of the back entrance of the building near a rusty red compact car.

John pushed back against a wave of panic. "They're surrounding her."

"You know what that means?" Ryan said.

Diego rubbed his hands together. "It's time to make some noise."

Chapter 16

Alicia stood before Rory and clamped an arm around his broken wrist.

Rory groaned and shifted in his restraints. "Christ, that smarts." He chuckled through his nose. "I guess you don't care that much if the break doesn't heal properly?"

"Not so much. Karma can be a real bitch that way."

His brows flicked up. "So this is where I'm going to die, huh?"

"That's up to you."

"Sure, it is. I feel good to have made it this far. At least there's a window with a view up here. I didn't have that at the prison."

She couldn't let a statement like that go unanswered. She walked to the window and lowered the blinds. "I'll open them again after you tell me what I want to hear."

He gave a wry snort through his nose. "The computer's a nice touch. What's your plan with it? To film how you're planning to torture me so you can relive it over and over again?"

She pressed a finger into the scab of the gunshot wound on his leg until he closed his eyes and groaned. "It's time for you to come clean about John."

"Clean how?" His voice was weak and raspy, but she could tell he wasn't going to make this part easy on her. "He helped me try to kill you."

"No, he didn't," she said with absolute confidence. "That was all you."

"Where is he now?"

"Gone."

He reopened his eyes, looking intrigued. "Gone like dead or gone like gone?"

Her throat tightened. Gone like out of her life forever, but she refused to let Rory see her pain.

"Gone like it's just you and me here, and I've been thirsty for revenge against you for a long time."

"I'm honestly shocked that he didn't follow you here. He never was very good at being on his own and in charge. He'd rather be a lackey."

She harnessed the rage that Rory's words filled her with, wound back and slapped him hard across the cheek. "You don't get to talk about him like that."

John was no follower. He'd saved her life and her spirit. He'd taken her by the hand and pulled her up from the dark place she'd let herself languish in for far too long. He led her back to life with his love and his steadfastness. Her eyes stung with unshed tears that she willed away.

She turned her back to Rory and faced her computer. Pain wasn't going to work as a coercion technique, not that she'd had much faith that it would with an elite soldier like Rory. Which was why she'd devised a backup plan to break his will in a whole different way.

She detached the laptop from the power cord and walked it to Rory. "Before you and John joined our black ops crew, I ran my own background check on both of you. Sure, the tech team at the Department of Homeland Security had, but I wanted to know for myself who these men were whose hands Diego, Ryan and I were putting our lives in."

She clicked to a photograph she'd hidden on her laptop since that background check, a photo she looked at nearly every night before bed and in her darkest moments. It was of John and Rory in their early twenties, linked arm in arm in their Green Beret uniforms. The sight of John, all confidence and smiles in his uniform with his army-issued rifle and gear, made her heart squeeze painfully. He was so handsome, so admirable a man. Even back then, just from his pictures and service record, she'd been in awe. She'd had a crush on him before he'd walked through the door of the tactical planning room where he and Rory had first met the black ops crew.

"We're going to get nostalgic? That's your tactic? Too bad for you I don't give a crap about any of that."

She smiled, no longer caring if Rory saw her emotions. "When I first saw this photograph, I thought, there's no way John Witter is a sniper. Even then, I could see the huge heart he had."

"Then you were already delusional about him because he's one of the most lethal operatives I've ever worked with."

"I know that now. The more I learned about him, the longer you two were with our unit, the more complicated and wonderful I realized he was."

"You're killing me with all this lovey-dovey talk. Get to the point."

"This is the point. He doesn't deserve what I put him through and he definitely doesn't deserve what you put him through. I think, in your own sociopathic way, you love John as much as I do, different, but just as much."

He laughed as if she were crazy, but she knew she'd hit a nerve.

"You said on the roof that the point of killing me was so John would join you, so I know you care about him. You owe it to him to come clean about his innocence. For everything you two had. You went to war together." She clicked on another photo of them, Rory in a hospital bed with a bandage on his forehead and John standing next to the bed. "You saved each other's lives."

He flinched at that. Emotion glimmered in his eyes for a brief second. For the first time, Alicia allowed herself to hope this would work.

"You're going to kill me, anyway, so why would I talk?"

"Why wouldn't you? Why not do one last act of good for the man who was the most loyal person in your life." She clicked on another photo, this one of the two of them deployed in their fatigues, squatting down, a mangy, three-legged dog between them and run-down desert dwellings behind them. The dog was licking Rory's chin.

Rory's torso seemed to deflate along with his bravado. Alicia stayed quiet, giving him time to remember.

"I loved that dog," he said quietly. "We named her Lucky because she came wandering out of this building where we were setting charges to blow it up. We took her back to base."

"What happened to her?"

"No idea. That was when we got tapped to join ICE. We left her in Afghanistan. I hope she's still kicking it on base." He sighed. It was a bone-weary sigh that ended with a wince of pain. "All right. You win. I'll tell you what you want to know, but you have to do me a favor in return."

She heard a helicopter, loud and close, and chanced a look through the blinds. Her stomach twisted. American forces were gathering outside. She had no idea how they'd found her, but it didn't matter. She only had minutes to get Rory on tape, then herself, before the situation was taken out of her hands.

"They're coming," Rory said.

"I know. What's the favor you want?" She braced herself for him to demand his release when he was done.

"Before they get here, I want you to kill me. Or give me your gun and let me do the honor. I'm not going back to prison."

She met his gaze. Conviction poured from his expression. For the first time since he'd shot her, she could see the warrior he once was. The sliver of goodness and honor left in him.

"Are you sure, because until the hurricane, you wanted to live so desperately that you killed civilians and risked a hurricane trying to escape." She couldn't believe she was trying to talk him out of it, but she didn't take this lightly. Not now that they were here together and he was totally helpless and at her mercy.

"You're not going to let me go, and ICE is going to put me right back in that hellhole. I'm done with this life. I thought I had this all figured out. I thought I knew what I wanted."

She directed the laptop at him. It was still recording, though he didn't seem to realize it. She pressed a button and turned the broadcast live, feeding straight into ICE headquarters.

"I screwed up," Rory said. "It was supposed to be golden. Me and John taking the world by storm, making money and living the good life we deserved. I thought getting you out of the picture would be the jolt he needed to come around to my way of thinking, you know? But I underestimated how shooting you would affect him. I knew you two were hot for each other, but I didn't know he loved you like that.

"It was a stupid oversight that cost me everything because he chose you over me. I didn't see that coming. He testified against me—his blood brother—so I did the only thing I could think of. I lied about his involvement because I wanted to hurt him the way he'd hurt me."

He stopped and looked her way, unshed tears and a lifetime of pain in his eyes. "Is that enough?" he croaked.

She cleared her throat. "Yes." Then she turned the laptop toward herself, took a deep breath and looked into the camera. "Rory isn't the only one guilty. I framed John Witter in the prison break of Rory Alderman by planting a false trail of evidence that led to him because I thought he was guilty of conspiracy and treason. But I was wrong.

"John Witter is innocent of all the charges that Rory Alderman, Diego Santero, Ryan Reitano and I accused him of. Even before learning the truth about John's innocence, I had decided to abort my plan to frame him, but in my haste to break Rory out of prison and kill him, I didn't do a good job of erasing the false trail I'd planted. I will spend the rest of my life tortured by my regret over the ways I ruined John's life."

She paused as a wave of sorrow passed through her. After another deep breath, she continued, letting a first tear slip over her cheek. "I broke Rory Alderman out of prison so I could kill him in retaliation for his attempt to murder me. John Witter stopped me from killing Rory. All he wanted was to recapture Rory and convince him to tell the truth about his innocence. I hope this broadcast isn't too little too late to help clear his name.

"As far as other crimes he committed during this past week, I have this to say—John Witter engaged Special Agent Logan McCaffrey in combat on the island of St. Croix because he thought I was in danger. Logan McCaffrey and his team had gone undercover and had taken me into custody. John saw the bruises and wounds I'd sustained when McCaffrey took me into custody and thought I'd been kidnapped."

She had no proof of that, but if it helped John's cause, then a little white lie was forgivable. "John was trying to protect me. And if you want to know why he'd do something like that, since it might jeopardize his future standing in the eye of the law, the truth is that he's the best man I know, with more integrity than every other person in ICE combined."

The irony of all that had happened struck her then. She'd so deeply feared losing her power and sense of self to men, when the whole time since the day she was released from the hospital, she'd been destroying those parts of herself all on her own.

Noises sounded outside, men shouting, thumps and thuds like doors were being broken down and soldiers or agents were flooding into the building. She could sense the presence of the law surrounding them. In a matter of seconds, she was going to be taken into custody and go to prison for the rest of her life.

She closed her laptop, then picked up her gun.

"Are you ready?" she asked Rory.

His expression was stoic. He closed his eyes. "Yes."

Emotion tightened her chest and made her sinuses sting as she steadied her gun against Rory's temple. What a waste she'd made of her second chance at life.

Boots sounded in the hallway, then through the open office door, along with the sense of tension and energy of troops moving in to surround a hostile. She took a last look through the closed blinds at the hint of ocean beyond and turned toward the sound, ready to face her fate.

Gun at the ready, John led the way up the stairs into the building where Alicia and Rory were, with Diego in the back. Avery's diversion tactic had bought them a small window of time to sneak undetected through the front of building, skirting the felled tree.

They conducted a fast search of the ground floor, then the second floor. As soon as they crested the stairs on the third level, they heard Rory's voice and, all at once, without a word from anyone, they stopped to listen.

Rory was confessing.

John tipped his ear toward the door, his mind going a mile a minute. While they listened, Rory confessed to shooting Alicia as a way to convince John to join him as a team of mercenaries, and then, after their arrests, that he'd lied about John's involvement because he hated John for testifying against him, for choosing allegiance to Alicia instead of his blood brother. He was coming clean about everything. How had Alicia managed to convince him to do that?

He replayed Rory's words in his head as Diego, Ryan and Avery stared at him, their faces looking as shocked as John felt.

I thought getting you out of the picture would be the jolt he needed to come around to my way of thinking, you know? But I underestimated how shooting you would affect him.

He'd fantasized about this moment, when the people who'd spurned him heard the truth. He'd fantasized about the feelings of vindication—the high it would give him to prove to them all how wrong they'd been about him. But standing there on the wrong side of the door from Alicia, regret and shock playing on the features of his former teammates, while U.S. authorities were closing in to neutralize the woman he loved, he couldn't have cared less about vindication.

All that mattered was getting her out of harm's way.

Then she started talking. *I framed John Witter in the prison break of Rory Alderman by planting a false trail of evidence that led to him because I thought he was guilty of conspiracy and treason. But I was wrong.*

Love and sorrow burned hot inside him. He was going to get her out of the building, away from the Feds, then spend the rest of his life making up to her that he'd walked away without giving her a chance to explain herself.

"Let's get in there," John said. He cleared his throat against the lump that had settled in it. "I have the love of my life to save."

Diego swallowed hard. "After you."

Rory sat in the center of the room, bound to a wheelchair and looking so beat up it was a wonder he was still conscious. His right arm hung limply at his side at an odd angle. Alicia stood over him.

She turned to face John and the rest of the crew as though facing a firing squad. With solemn dignity. When she registered who it was, though, she stumbled back, eyes widening. "John? You shouldn't be here. You have to save yourself."

"I'm getting you out of here."

She looked past him, to the rest of the crew. "Diego, Ryan, Avery—what are you doing here?"

"We heard you could use some friends," Ryan said. "You've always been there for us, so it was our turn to pay it back."

Tears sprang to her eyes. "I'm in a bit of a jam." She sounded so fragile. John couldn't wait to hold her in his arms. "How did you get here so fast?"

"We can explain all that later. Right now, we have to move," Ryan said.

Behind her, Rory wheezed. "This is a hell of a thing,

isn't it?" His head lolled to the side, but his eyes were sharp. "Here we all are, together again. The old crew."

Rory was right. They hadn't been in the same room together since the morning of the RioBank operation. John looked around, filled with a rush of bittersweet memories. So much had changed since that morning. Every one of their lives altered in irreversible ways.

Alicia was a wanted criminal, Rory a traitor of his nation and murderer on his last breath. Diego was no longer a black ops soldier, but clearly a devoted husband, and Ryan was engaged to an operative John had never heard of and living in France. None of them were the people they were two years ago, for better or worse. But they were all here for Alicia, and for that, John would forever be grateful.

"Did any of you miss me?" Rory said in a sniveling, wheezing voice.

Diego prowled across the room to Rory and socked him hard in the stomach. Rory doubled over.

"Shut up. I'd kill you right now except you're not worth getting blood on this shirt that my wife gave me. Plus, if I killed you, then you wouldn't be able to testify in court that you were lying about John's involvement." He shoved him hard in the chest. "And you know how I know you're gonna do that?"

"Why don't you go ahead and enlighten me?"

"Because if you don't, I'm going to be the one to break you out of prison again so I can end your miserable life."

Boots sounded in the hallway. "Who's that gonna be?" Diego said to John.

Avery walked to Alicia and stood like a bodyguard in front of her, gun out and ready.

John picked up his rifle from where it hung by a strap across his shoulders and walked to the doorway, prepared for battle. At first sight of who it was, he huffed, then glanced at Diego. "You're not going to believe it if I tell you."

"Try me."

"Get ready, because you're about to meet our replacements."

Chapter 17

"A new ICE black ops unit?" Ryan asked. "I must have missed that memo."

Diego snorted and shook his head. "Replacements? Gimme a break. Nobody could replace us."

"I think it's time we remind them of that," Ryan said.

Diego gripped his rifle hard and stood shoulder to shoulder with John and Ryan to form a protective wall in front of Alicia and Avery. "Just a heads-up, I'm naming you all as witnesses when I explain to Vanessa how this shirt got wrecked."

In the doorway, Logan appeared in full SWAT gear, surrounded by his two remaining crewmates.

"Logan McCaffrey?" Diego said, sounding shocked. "You're my replacement? Were the stiffs smoking crack when they gave you the job?"

"Diego Santero. Wish I could say this is a surprise, seeing you all here, but I figured John and Alicia would summon the rest of their band of misfits sooner or later."

Diego tipped his head toward Ryan. "This guy's a comedian."

"I prefer to think of us as ne'er-do-wells," Ryan deadpanned.

"When did they let you out in the field?" Diego asked.

"When they needed someone to clean up the mess you left behind. They tasked me with keeping tabs on rogue agents—Alicia and John, in particular. We're here to bring them in, and if you know what's good for you and your wife, you're not going to stand in my way."

Diego looked at Ryan again. "He just threatened my wife, didn't he?"

Ryan, ever the master of understatement, shook his head in Logan's direction. "Not cool."

John was done standing there watching Diego and Logan posture. "I've delivered Rory to you, Logan. And I've somehow managed to refrain from killing you any number of times in the last week, so it's time to take Rory and your life as the gifts they are before things get messy."

"Things are already messy. There are fifty troops and agents outside this building, ready to raze it if necessary. You have no bargaining chip left. Game over."

"Yeah, well, I have one more bargaining chip for you right here and it's pretty damn convincing." Diego rushed Logan fists first. Behind him, a brawl broke out.

John lunged, ready to dive into the middle of the

fray, but a hand clamped onto his arm and the next thing he knew, Avery was pulling him back from the fight.

She pushed a compact, loaded grappling hook launcher into his hands along with a pulley. "I think the easiest way for you and Alicia to escape is from the office across the hall. There's a building next door to the west that would be your best bet to escape through, but you two need to leave right now. I'll cover you."

He gaped at her, marveling at the disparity in her sweet, kind face and kick-ass, black ops mentality. "Who are you, really?"

"Just the secretary." Before he could question her cryptic reply, she added, "I have a surprise for everyone in a few more seconds." She opened her hand to reveal a remote detonator. "When I push this button, you two get going, got it?"

Ryan had the man on Logan's crew in a headlock while he delivered blow after blow to his gut. He paused and made shifty eyes at John and Avery, but didn't interfere.

"One more thing," Avery said. "Our jet is at an airstrip four miles due north of here. If you and Alicia don't have other plans already, you should come to France with me and Ryan. It's a great place to start over. We'll keep you out of the way of the law and we could always use a few more people on our crew."

They had a jet and a crew?

"Here we go." She held up the detonator.

John grabbed Alicia's arm. "Are you ready to blow this place with me?"

Alicia smiled at John. "Ready."

"What about our agreement?" Rory said behind her.

Alicia turned her head to look his way, then shrugged one shoulder and faked an impertinent hair toss. "All's fair in black ops, as they say. Have fun rotting in prison, you bastard."

With a grin of anticipation like she couldn't wait to blow something up again, Avery depressed the detonator button.

An explosion rocked the building. Everyone in the room except for Avery, John and Alicia hit the deck as ceiling tiles started to fall and sprinklers kicked on, spraying foam fire retardant down on everyone.

Alicia grabbed her computer, then she took John's hand. Together, they leaped over Logan and Diego, who were on the ground, though still locked together with their hands around each other's throats. The air in the hall was thick with smoke and fire retardant. They slogged through it as fast as they could and pushed into the office across the hall. In less than a minute, they'd set the grappling hook line and pulley. Together, they stood in the broken out office window, holding fast to each other and the pulley. Without a moment to spare, they pushed off the window and into the air in a final leap of faith for their future.

Chapter 18

When John pulled into the private airstrip parking lot in the old car he and Alicia had stolen, there was only one plane that seemed large enough for a transatlantic flight like Ryan and Avery's private jet would have to be capable of. It sat at the edge of the runway, its stairs extended as though Ryan and Avery had beaten them there and were waiting.

John threw the car in Park. There was no other way onto the airfield than through the office, so he took Alicia's hand and tried to act as if they belonged there.

A huge, burly, tattooed man with a beard sat in a chair in the lobby reading a magazine as an airport employee barely afforded John and Alicia a glance.

When he saw them, the bearded man stood. "Are you John and Alicia?" That he knew their names threw John off as much as his French accent.

"Yes," Alicia answered with a note of suspicion.

"Avery said you'd be here. My name's Russeaux, their pilot. Come on out. Avery called ahead. They're on their way."

They followed Russeaux through the office and onto the runway. John had so many thoughts running through his head and was still so jumpy that another obstacle to their happiness was going to pop out at them any minute, he couldn't find any words, but just held Alicia's hand and followed the bear of a man.

"Russeaux?" Alicia said at the base of the jet's stairs. "We need a moment. We'll be right in." At Russeaux's nod, she pulled John to the runway behind the plane.

"Alicia, this island is crawling with Feds and soldiers. We need to get out of sight—now."

She took his hand, urging him to slow down. "I think we're safe here and this can't wait. I need to tell you that I'm sorry for everything I put you through. Being shot, it did something to me, but—"

"I know it did."

"Let me get it all out, okay? Before we meet up with the others."

He looked her way, at the hope and determination in her eyes, helpless to deny her this. He had no idea where they went from here, but he loved her and they were safe. For now, that was enough. "Talk to me."

She took his hand. "I'm so sorry I ever doubted you."

"I forgave you a while ago for that. I'm sorry I walked away from you—twice."

"Forgiven. I would have walked away from me, too. I never was really good at trusting, anyway. My whole life, I tried, but I couldn't let go of control like a normal person could. For the rest of my life, I'll regret that I didn't trust you when you told me you were innocent."

It was a balm to his battered heart to hear. "Phoenix, you joined the CIA when you were eighteen. You've never been a normal person and I wouldn't want you to be. Be proud of all the good you've done and the sacrifices you've made for your country. I'm proud of you. So very proud."

Her eyes turned glassy. "I almost framed you for a double murder."

"But you didn't."

A tear jogged loose from her eye and the hint of a melancholy smile danced on her lips. "I didn't. I never thought I deserved to be with someone as good and bighearted as you." Her hand worked its way into his hair and pulled his face near hers, foreheads touching, noses brushing. "But you taught me that love isn't about getting what you deserve. It's about listening to your heart. So I'm going to listen to mine. I want you and I want us. Of all the things I've ever fought for, this is what I want most. You, forever. Because I love you more than anything."

She was so beautiful, with her brilliant mind and nerves of steel. She was perfect for him. And part of being perfect for her was accepting her, faults and all. The idea of spending forever with her left him short of breath and dizzy, it made him so happy. He never thought he'd be happy again. He'd set out to capture Rory because he wanted to fight for a second chance at life. How amazing, then, that it was Alicia who was giving that to him.

Emotion crashed over him, so intense he could

barely breathe. In his arms, he held the love of his life. It was exhilarating, as if he was waking up after a long, fitful sleep. It was time to let it all go—the stubborn chip on his shoulder, the need to prove himself, his anger at Rory and their black ops teammates. What mattered most was that he was alive. With the woman he loved. And everything was going to be all right.

"Do you think this plane has Wi-Fi? I need to borrow your computer for a video chat."

She looked at him quizzically. "With whom?"

"Eugene. I owe him something." From his jacket pocket, he pulled out his good-luck charm—Michael Jackson's *Bad* album.

Alicia threw her head back in a belly laugh. "Do you think the plane's big enough for you to do the moonwalk in? That's my favorite of your moves."

He smiled at her, feeling brighter and more alive than he ever had, even during their secret affair. If the hell he'd gone through was necessary to get to this place with her—this bright future—then he would gladly brave it all over again and so much more.

"For you, Phoenix, I'd do anything." He held out his hand and tipped his head toward the stairs. "You ready for this?"

"If you mean your dance routine, then absolutely. And if you're talking about our future together, then I only have one thing to say—bring it, baby."

And just because he could, because he hadn't felt like it in more than a year and half, he pushed off one foot into one of Michael Jackson's signature spins. Alicia clapped and asked for an encore, which was why John Witter—former Green Beret sniper, former black ops agent and a warrior who'd come back from the dead—took the hand of the only woman he'd ever loved and moonwalked all the way to the plane.

* * * * *

COMING NEXT MONTH FROM

H HARLEQUIN®

ROMANTIC suspense

Available August 5, 2014

REQUEST YOUR FREE BOOKS!
2 FREE NOVELS PLUS 2 FREE GIFTS!

ROMANTIC suspense

Sparked by danger, fueled by passion

YES! Please send me 2 FREE Harlequin® Romantic Suspense novels and my 2 FREE gifts (gifts are worth about $10). After receiving them, if I don't wish to receive any more books, I can return the shipping statement marked "cancel." If I don't cancel, I will receive 4 brand-new novels every month and be billed just $4.74 per book in the U.S. or $5.24 per book in Canada. That's a savings of at least 14% off the cover price! It's quite a bargain! Shipping and handling is just 50¢ per book in the U.S. and 75¢ per book in Canada.* I understand that accepting the 2 free books and gifts places me under no obligation to buy anything. I can always return a shipment and cancel at any time. Even if I never buy another book, the two free books and gifts are mine to keep forever.

240/340 HDN F45N

Name	(PLEASE PRINT)

Address	Apt. #

City	State/Prov.	Zip/Postal Code

Signature (if under 18, a parent or guardian must sign)

Mail to the Harlequin® Reader Service:
IN U.S.A.: P.O. Box 1867, Buffalo, NY 14240-1867
IN CANADA: P.O. Box 609, Fort Erie, Ontario L2A 5X3

Want to try two free books from another line?
Call 1-800-873-8635 or visit www.ReaderService.com.

* Terms and prices subject to change without notice. Prices do not include applicable taxes. Sales tax applicable in N.Y. Canadian residents will be charged applicable taxes. Offer not valid in Quebec. This offer is limited to one order per household. Not valid for current subscribers to Harlequin Romantic Suspense books. All orders subject to credit approval. Credit or debit balances in a customer's account(s) may be offset by any other outstanding balance owed by or to the customer. Please allow 4 to 6 weeks for delivery. Offer available while quantities last.

Your Privacy—The Harlequin® Reader Service is committed to protecting your privacy. Our Privacy Policy is available online at www.ReaderService.com or upon request from the Harlequin Reader Service.

We make a portion of our mailing list available to reputable third parties that offer products we believe may interest you. If you prefer that we not exchange your name with third parties, or if you wish to clarify or modify your communication preferences, please visit us at www.ReaderService.com/consumerschoice or write to us at Harlequin Reader Service Preference Service, P.O. Box 9062, Buffalo, NY 14269. Include your complete name and address.

HRS13R

SPECIAL EXCERPT FROM

H HARLEQUIN®

ROMANTIC suspense

When her family is threatened, detective and single mom
Noelle turns to her new partner, the sexy Duncan Cavanaugh,
never realizing his promise to serve and protect includes her
daughter and her heart.

Read on for a sneak peek of

CAVANAUGH STRONG

by *USA TODAY* bestselling author
Marie Ferrarella, coming August 2014 from
Harlequin® Romantic Suspense.

"Hey, Cavanaugh, this should be very interesting. You're
partnered with The Black Widow," the slightly overweight
Holloway gleefully told him.

The unflattering nickname sounded like something an
irreverent journalist would slap on an elusive perpetrator, not
a label the police would put on one of their own.

"What are you talking about?" Duncan demanded, confused.

Holloway looked at him, obviously enjoying the fact that
for once he was the one in the know while Duncan was still
in the dark.

Grinning broadly, the detective laughed. "You really don't
know, man?"

Holloway leaned in, though he still failed to lower his voice.
"Well, rumor has it she's been engaged twice."

"Twice," Duncan echoed while looking at the woman who at that moment was meeting with the head of the vice department, Lieutenant Stewart Jamieson, before being brought out to meet the rest of them.

"She broke it off?" Duncan guessed.

Holloway shook his head, looking like the proverbial cat that had gotten into the cream. "Nope, she didn't have to. They both died. She didn't even get to walk up to the altar once." Pausing dramatically, Holloway gave it to the count of two before adding, "The first one left her pregnant."

Because he belonged to an extended family that could have easily acquired its own zip code, Duncan's interest went up a notch. "She has kids?"

"Kid," Holloway corrected, holding up his forefinger. "One."

"A daughter. Her name's Melinda. She's almost six. Anything else you want to know?" a melodious low voice coming from directly behind him said, completing the information.

Duncan turned his chair around a hundred and eighty degrees to face her. Up close the energy almost crackled between them. He would have to be dead not to notice.

Don't miss CAVANAUGH STRONG by
USA TODAY **bestselling author Marie Ferrarella,**
available August 2014 from
Harlequin® Romantic Suspense.

HARLEQUIN®

ROMANTIC suspense

A SAFE REFUGE SHATTERED

When former special ops soldier Dave Logston nearly
hit a beautiful motorcylist in the thick Oregon fog of
Devil's Shroud, he never expected to be thrown back
into a world of espionage, deceit and danger.
But secret agent Nicole Steele—aka Tazer—was
desperate for an out-of-the-way place to hide,
and Dave's run-down yacht was the perfect spot.
Though none too pleased at their forced proximity,
the emotionally wounded warrior was powerless to
deny her request...and his rising desire for her.

Nicole was determined to decrypt the stolen database
that would reveal the identity of her boss's abductors.
But soon she learned the threat wasn't just to
Stealth Operations, but to national security.
Would her unexpected bond with Dave survive once
the enemy's identity was finally uncovered?

Look for *DEADLY ALLURE*
by Elle James in August 2014.

Available wherever books and ebooks are sold.

Heart-racing romance, high-stakes suspense!

www.Harlequin.com

HRS27882